ARCANE

CW00502451

LETHAL CONTENTS

JAMI GRAY

Copyright © August 2021 by Jami Gray
All rights reserved.
Lethal Contents - Arcane Transporter
Celtic Moon Press
ISBN: 978-1-948884-45-7 (ebook)
ISBN: 978-4-948884-46-4 (print)

Cover Art: Deranged Doctor Design
www.derangeddoctordesign.com

WHAT READERS SAY...

About Arcane Transporter:
"Taking a refreshing approach to fantasy magic, this fast-paced, economical thriller is told from a highly likable perspective." —Red Adept Editing

About PSY-IV Teams:
"This story is an emotional roller coaster, from betrayal, anger, fear, love..." —InD'tale Magazine

About the Kyn Kronicles:
"...a fantastic paranormal action novel is quite possibly the best book I've read this year. I could not put it down, and had to exercise serious self-control to keep from staying up all night to finish it." —The Romance Reviews

About Fate's Vultures:
"...if you like your characters with a bit more bite, with secrets, with hidden agendas, and all those sorts of things, and your worlds are a far more deadlier place, then this is for you." —Archaeolibrarian

ALSO BY JAMI GRAY

ARCANE TRANSPORTER

Ignition Point - novella

Grave Cargo

Risky Goods

Lethal Contents

THE KYN KRONICLES

Shadow's Edge

Shadow's Soul

Shadow's Moon

Shadow's Curse

Shadow's Dream

PSY-IV TEAMS

Hunted by the Past

Touched by Fate

Marked by Obsession

Fractured by Deceit

Linked by Deception

FATE'S VULTURES

Lying in Ruins

Beg for Mercy

Caught in the Aftermath

Fear the Reaper

BOX SETS

ACKNOWLEDGMENTS

Writing this series has been a blast, mainly because of how much you, my wonderful readers, have enjoyed it. Thank you so much for being willing to take this ride. While this may be Rory and Zev's last lap, I can't promise they won't be back because this world has been way too much fun to play in.

As always, my heartfelt 'thank you' goes out to my unwavering support team of ink slingers - DeAnna, Camille, and Dave. To my personal pit crew - Ben, Bren, Ian, Ang, Kim, and Joanna. To the awesome mechanics extraordinaire - Angela and Lynn at Red Adept Editing and Tanja and Kim at Deranged Doctors, and my newest additions - Audibly Addicted and the sublime voices of Stella Hunter and Connor Crais for bringing my stories to life.

As always, couldn't have done it without any of you!

—Jami

My mantra has always been to have zero regrets in life. Everything I do at one speed, I go all-out.

—*Apolo Ohno*

CHAPTER ONE

I CRASHED through the door of my condo and tossed my keys across the breakfast bar's granite top.

"Dear God, you reek!" Lena, my roommate and best friend, stood in the kitchen and watched my explosive entrance with a jaundiced eye and wrinkled nose.

"I know." I toed off my shoes then yanked my disgustingly smelly and permanently stained shirt over my head. "Next time I do a delivery job for the Magical Menagerie Company, I'm adding a codicil for anything with more than two legs." I wadded up the ruined shirt and tossed it to her. "Trash that, will you?"

"Eww, Rory, what the hell?"

Lena's disgusted tone floated behind me as I rushed to my room, hands at my waist as I unbuttoned my pants en route to the shower. "Did you know," I yelled back, "that *sapo fuerzos* get pissy when being transported?" In fact, the nearly indestructible supernatural Chilean creature that looked like a tubby horny toad stuffed in a turtle shell didn't just get mad about car rides. It got downright nasty. I kicked off my pants and hit the bathroom in my bra, undies, and socks. I flipped on the shower.

"*Sapo fuerzo?*" Lena asked from inside my bedroom. "Isn't that 'forced toad' in Spanish?" She stopped where the bedroom met the bathroom.

"'Strong toad,'" I corrected absently, scratching the dried layer of slimy residue that covered my arms. Thin gray flakes drifted to the tile floor. "Some collector down in South America was donating the thing to the Magical Menagerie for their amphibian collection. I should've known something was up when they didn't hesitate to agree to my delivery fee." A typically reasonable fee that doubled for last-minute arrangements. After this fun-filled adventure, I might have to consider tripling it.

"So all of this"—she held out my ruined shirt like it might suddenly come to life— "happened between the airport and the Menagerie?"

"Yeah." I flipped on the shower.

"And your baby?"

My baby, a restored 1968 Mustang Fastback, was safe from the horror of supernatural frog-turtle spit. "Thankfully, they provided a cargo van for transport. Otherwise, I would be employing your services to help translate the true meaning of 'full disclosure' to the Magical Menagerie coordinator." I took in her outfit, from the spike heels to her leather shorts and cute blousy halter top, clearly a date-night ensemble, and shot a look at my still-open bedroom door. "Please tell me Evan did not just witness my impromptu strip show." Mortification added a panicked edge to my question.

Lena's lips quirked. "Nope, you're safe, but I'm expecting him any minute." She arched an eyebrow. "Speaking of, don't you and Zev have a date tonight?"

"Yes." Which was why I was rushing around like a lunatic. "He'll be here at seven."

Her nose wrinkled. "You're cutting it awfully close."

"I know, so get, would you?" I shooed her off.

"I'm going, I'm going." She turned, still holding the shirt out in front of her. "I'm so burning this."

"Please do," I shot back as I followed her out of the bathroom and through my bedroom as I hit my dresser for clean underthings.

She stepped into the hall and turned back, eyebrow raised. "Should I expect you home tonight?"

If I had my druthers, my answer would be a resounding no, but if the last couple of weeks had taught me anything, it was not to get my expectations up. Since that particular answer would cut into my shower time, I deflected. "Shouldn't that be my question?"

"You're sounding a tad bit frustrated, friend," she teased.

Probably because I was, in more ways than one. "Whatever. Go, burn that mess, leave me to my shower, and have fun with Evan." Then, before she in true bestie form could give me any more grief, I shut the door in her face and hustled to the bathroom.

◆

It took me a solid thirty minutes to get rid of the remnants of the supernatural frog-turtle's temper tantrum. There were a few drawbacks to being an Arcane Transporter, especially as an independent contractor intent on carving out a sterling reputation. One of the biggest obstacles was crafting concise contracts that covered unforeseen circumstances, like additional fees for handling packages that included unexpected biohazards, magical or mundane. That was something that would have been outlined in comprehensive detail, if I was still under the Arcane Guild's aegis. Since that was no longer the case, I didn't have the luxury of an in-house legal counsel, so my contracts tended to evolve based on hard-learned lessons as I navigated the twists and turns of being an independent Transporter for the magically elite.

Still, even dealing with today's nauseating results couldn't outweigh the benefits of being my own boss, like the hefty profit margins earned with last-minute delivery jobs or the nice, fat paychecks from being the personal-driver-slash-part-time-bodyguard for Sabella Rossi, the matriarch of the oldest, most influential Arcane Family, the Giordanos. Of course, my paycheck from her held more zeros because, unlike some of my more recent undertakings, the frog-turtle barf wouldn't kill me, but Sabella's assignments just might.

It wasn't all ooze, doom, and gloom. At least when I worked with Sabella, I got the additional benefit of spending time with Zev Aslanov. Tall, dark, brooding, and yeah, definitely sexy, he also happened to be the Arbiter to one of the local powerhouses, the Cordova Family. Someone, somewhere was laughing their ass off over that little detail, because his job alone should've kept him out of my league. He swam with the sharks of the Arcane world, while I was just another minnow. Yet in some weird twist of fate, all these months later, I found myself merrily gliding through the murky depths as I dated him.

That was not the ending I'd expected all those months ago when I still answered to the Western Division of the Arcane Guild and agreed to an under-the-table delivery job for a private party. Unfortunately, I was unaware of one very important fact—the package was Zev's ten-year-old kidnapped nephew. Once that nugget of information became apparent, I made some adjustments to the intended delivery plan but not before Zev arrived and rerouted the entire job. Initially, we both played things close to our vests, but eventually, we got the situation sorted and Jeremy safely returned to his uncle Emilio, who was head of the Cordova family—and Zev's best friend and boss.

Unsurprisingly, that lovely fiasco had piqued Zev's curiosity about me, so when we once again crossed paths in my attempt to save Lena's life, we'd made a lasting impression on each other. I'd held high hopes that he would follow through on our shared attraction, but he left me hanging for weeks. That should've been the end of it, but then two weeks ago, our roads collided again. This time, after we survived an encounter with a couple of mad scientists and their scary-ass magic-altering serum, he finally asked me out on an actual date, and still riding the high of being alive, I accepted.

Little did I know that dating a mage of Zev's caliber brought its own set of challenges. Such as, if a guy was basically a fixer for a magical family, his idea of fun might not match the expectations of the everyday Joe or Jane. For our first date, he arranged for dinner at a lovely historical landmark. I'm sure he hadn't intended to end the evening by providing impromptu therapy for a crazy pissed ghost, but by the time we got rid of our unwanted visitor and sent him on his way, not only was the romantic mood broken, but then Zev got called in to deal with a Family issue. *Cock block numero uno.*

Date number two looked promising. He took me to spell-tag arena, where we spent a fun couple of hours throwing non-lethal spells at each other while weaving through an urban-style course. Afterward, we hit a park for a picnic dinner. Things were heading toward a highly desirable finish line when Sabella called and requested my services. Thanks to my contract, I was unable to refuse, and it was my turn to cut our date frustratingly short. *Cock block numero dos.*

Tonight, we were on attempt *numero tres*, and I was hoping the old adage of "third time is the charm" would hold true. I didn't know what the Cordovas were up to, but I had checked and knew Sabella was planning on spending a quiet night at home, and Lena had plans with Evan, so that meant that on my side, no one should be interrupting us. As far as I was concerned, it was clear roads ahead.

As for Zev, he hadn't shared much about tonight's plans, just enough for me to ride the thin line between nerves and excitement. I managed to pry out of him that his suggestion to "dress up" meant going above and beyond my typical business casual. With that goal in mind, I dusted off the one little black dress I owned. It wasn't really black, more like indigo, but the light material was perfect for summer nights in Phoenix. The straps of the form-fitting halter top tied at my neck but left my arms and back bare. Thankfully, Lena was a clotheshorse, so I was able to utilize her closet and find a gorgeous featherlight shawl. Heels weren't my favorite, but this particular outfit required them, so I would endure the pain for my legs to look good. I wouldn't put them on until I absolutely had to.

I was bent over, head down, running the charmed dryer brush through my dark hair, praying the waves wouldn't frizz, when a shiver coasted down my spine. I snapped upright so fast that little white dots peppered the edges of my vision. I blinked them clear and snapped, "What the hell, Zev? Are you trying to give me a heart attack?"

"Just enjoying the view, babe."

His shoulder-length black hair was pulled back at his neck, and he wore a button-down collared shirt in an alluring cross between silver and ice blue paired with tailored black slacks. He was the epitome of temptation as he lounged in the doorway, arms crossed, and his gaze aimed at... I followed it through the mirror to find it on my ass. Heat hit my cheeks and started a low burn farther down. Those sinfully dark eyes slowly swept upward, accompanied by a wickedly sexy grin framed by his neat Vandyke covering his angled jaw. By the time his gaze met mine in the mirror, I was torn between throwing the brush at him and jumping him just to break the rising sexual tension. Watching him watch me, I knew which option I wanted to take. "How did you get in?"

"Lena, and she said for you not to wait up." He pushed off the doorjamb and stepped in close. "I like the dress." He glided a finger under a silver hoop and followed the material up until it disappeared under my hair.

Goose bumps broke over my skin, and a series of mini explosions detonated in my veins, leaving my balance shaky. I flattened my free hand against his chest, the solid warmth of him seeping into my palm. "Thanks." It came out husky, but at least it came out. My gaze drifted to his shirt and the way it emphasized his broad chest, up to his throat bared by his open collar, then farther up to those full lips, where it lingered as my very aroused imagination got creative. "You clean up nice too."

Those lips quirked, then they were covering mine. Not greedy and voracious, like the churning hunger and near-screaming sexual tension demanded, but determined and coaxing. I didn't need much encouragement to happily partic-ipate. I let go of my brush, barely registering the clatter as it hit the floor. I used both hands, one at his chest and the other cupping his jaw, to urge him closer. Not that it was needed. He curled his arm around my waist and brought me in tight until there was nothing but the feel of him pressed against me, his tongue tangling with mine in a wild, luscious dance, and a craving that was spinning out of control, sucking us both under the rising tide of hunger.

Heart racing, body yearning, I held on, indulging in his taste and touch, more than willing to follow his lead, at least for now. He steered us out of the bathroom and into my bedroom. Each step was another move in an erotic tango as his mouth laid a trail of openmouthed kisses along my neck.

He found every sensitive, erogenous zone between my ear and shoulder until I was nearly shaking apart. His hands were sure and steady as they swept over my curves and gripped my hips as he guided me backward. I felt the edge of the mattress hit the back of my legs, and I gripped his shoulders, dragging him with me as I fell. I took his weight, my body cradling his as I nibbled along his jaw and the soft brush of his beard until my lips hit hot skin.

He arced his neck, giving me more room, and the temptation was too much. I gave in and left my mark on his vulnerable skin. His fingers, busy at the tie at my neck, faltered. His hips flexed, pressing him deep and causing a momentary distraction. I whimpered, grinding down against what he was offering.

His answering groan resonated in his chest, sparking an ache that arched from my breasts and spiraled down to my center, lighting up every nerve in between. "Babe... Rory..."

"Right here, Zev," I promised as I made quick work of his buttons so I could spread the shirt wide and run my hands and tongue over his exposed skin. *Oh, this is so much better.*

His shoulders shifted and his muscles tightened as he braced his weight on one arm and caught my wandering hands to press them against his taut stomach. Reluctantly, I raised my gaze to find his face dark with voracious hunger. His chest rose and fell as he drew in rough breaths, and his eyes were bright with lust and something I wasn't ready to acknowledge. He licked his lips, and his voice came out rough. "Hang on."

Caught up in the carnal demands rushing through me, I flexed my blunt nails against his stomach in protest. "I'm trying."

He grinned and squeezed my caught hands. "This wasn't what I had planned."

"Okay." I drew the word out, adding a hint of inquiry while I was at it. "But I kind of like where this is going."

His head lowered, and he nuzzled my neck. "I've got reservations."

"For?" It came out breathless as I lifted my jaw to give him more room. *Please don't stop.*

"Eight." He traced the taut tendon with his tongue, and his mouth found a sensitive spot.

I shivered then craned my neck to check the clock on my nightstand and forced my brain to focus. It was just after seven. I turned back, tugged my hands free, and wrapped them around his neck. His head lifted just enough that I could whisper against his lips, "They'll hold it." *Maybe, probably.* Not that I cared right now.

His lips curved under mine. "I promise you'll like what I had planned." He nipped my lower lip, then he cupped my breast and brushed his thumb over one aching peak in a tantalizing caress.

"I like this plan." Deciding to shift gears and speed things along, I stroked one hand down his chest, with a few minor detours, and slid my fingers just under the waist of his slacks. In a deliberate tease, I swept my fingers back and forth over the heated, sensitive skin, smiling in wicked delight when I felt proof that he liked the current state of affairs too. "Let me drive to wherever we're going, and I promise we'll make it."

Laughter and desire flared bright in his eyes as he settled deeper into me, clearly considering my proposal. I hitched a leg over his hip, both to hold him in place and to lure him into accepting my offer. He lowered his head and brushed my lips with his, sharing both a tease and a promise. "I knew you were trouble."

"Only the best kind," I whispered back just before his mouth took mine and we altered our course.

CHAPTER TWO

THE FINAL CURTAIN fell over the stage as Zev and I stood, clapping enthusiastically with the rest of the audience as the cast of Danse des Éléments took their bows. The highly acclaimed performances of the air and fire mages made the production the hottest show in town—no pun intended. Unlike a typical theater production, this one needed more space for the circus-like antics of the high-flying air mages and the dramatic conjuring of the fire mages, which meant the event was housed in the stadium of Talking Stick Arena. Zev used his personal connection to the Cordovas to score primo seats on the floor near the stage, which transformed an exciting viewing experience into a memorable one.

Although Zev didn't take me up on my offer to drive, we missed only the first few minutes of the opening act. But considering why we were late, I had zero regrets. I was looking forward to an encore performance with him after dinner, this time a little slower and a lot longer. I wanted a chance to explore the wild ride promised by the deepening attraction between us, especially after the unexpected twists and turns of the last few months. While I was apprehensive about how fast we were going, the emotions racing through me bypassed anything I'd felt before and overrode it. There was no way to tell where the road ahead would lead us, but I was willing to ride it out anyway.

As the crowd began to exit the arena, I stood at Zev's side, feeling as if I was floating along, tethered only by his arm around my waist. We waited for those in the nearby seats to slip out of the row first, neither of us in a rush. I rested my head against his shoulder. "That was awesome. Thank you for bringing me."

He turned away from watching the crowd and looked at me. His slow grin eased the normally stern lines of his face. "I'm glad you enjoyed it."

I could feel my face stretch as my mouth curved into a big smile. "So far, I've enjoyed everything."

His dark chuckle meant he didn't miss my insinuation. He dipped his head down and brushed a butterfly kiss over my grin. When he pulled back, his voice was deep with a promise of its own. "It's not over yet."

I leaned deeper into him, winding my arm around his waist to squeeze in close, and kept my voice equally quiet. "Yay!"

The last person exited the row, and we finally made our way out. We stepped into the arena's lobby, made our way to the wide-open doors, and walked into the heated night, hand in hand. Confident that Zev would steer me clear of others and flying high on my own bubble of happiness, I let my gaze drift over the unfamiliar faces and indulged in some people watching.

Restaurants and bars lined the open courtyard as we made our way to the parking garage. Laughter and music floated from the open patios and swirled around us. I couldn't help noting how many gazes—the majority of them female but a handful of them male—came our way and lingered. I wasn't surprised. It was a typical reaction when-ever Zev appeared, and it was more than him being shit hot. It was a combination of his looks and the aura of intriguing danger that clung to him like a second skin and acted like catnip to all those who appreciated such things. It also meant that I couldn't quite keep my grin from turning smug when some of those glances landed on me with green-eyed intent.

Zev let go of my hand and curled his arm around my waist. He palmed my hip, nudging me out of the way of a slightly inebriated, giggling twentysomething guy who was wobbling into my path. His friends were equally impaired, so when they reached for him, they ended up pushing him closer instead of dragging him clear. Zev and I glided out of the way as their mumbled sorrys trailed us.

"Hungry?" Zev asked without letting me go.

It was late, but my answer was easy. "Yes, I'm starving." Between the puking frog-turtle adventure and our energetic preshow activities, I had missed dinner, and lunch was a distant memory. I took in the available offerings surrounding us. "Did you want to get something here?"

He softly squeezed my hip. "No, I've got another idea if you can hold out for another fifteen minutes."

"I think I can manage," I said just as a stone rolled under my heel. I caught my balance against Zev, one hand braced on his stomach, the other clinging to his arm.

He curled me in close along his front and slowed to a stop. "You good?"

Tucked against him, dressed to the nines, my body humming in pleasure at being in his arms, I grinned up at him. "Heels and I have a love-hate relationship."

"Let me guess," he teased. "You love to hate them?"

I laughed at his accurate assumption. "Got it in one, Mr. Aslanov." When his arm relaxed and dropped away, I wove my fingers through his, matching his stride as we continued to the parking garage. "I hope that doesn't disappoint you."

"Ms. Costas, the last thing you could do tonight is disappoint me." He lifted our clasped hands and brushed his lips over the backs of my knuckles.

Anticipation zipped through my veins. I kept up the light-hearted double entendres. "Good to know. I'd so hate not to meet your expectations."

"Definitely not a concern, babe." His voice deepened and took on a rough edge. "But if you're worried, I'd be more than happy to discuss those expectations in further detail. Perhaps after dinner?"

Oh yeah. I can't wait. I swallowed hard, and my voice came out husky. "I'd like that."

A hungry heat that had nothing to do with food and everything to do with his promise settled in low and left various body parts aching. I licked suddenly dry lips and snuck a glance at Zev from under my lashes. His dark eyes were alight with carnal anticipation as he watched my mouth. Red rode under his olive skin, and his eyes flashed with lust as his fingers tightened on mine. Nice to know we were on the same page. We picked up the pace on our casual stroll.

At the parking garage, Zev ushered me into the elevator and hit the button. As the doors closed, the validation sigil above the door flared a soft green in confirmation that we had a paid parking spot. My skin ruffled with the flex of active magic. Normally, such low-level magic didn't bother me, but lately, I'd noticed an uptick in my sensitivity to active magic. Still, acclimated by years of similar reactions, I found that one easy to ignore.

We rode the elevator to the fourth floor, our bodies brushing as we stood side by side. The heated air trapped inside grew heavy with unspoken needs and keen expectations, but neither of us spoke. The ride was blessedly short, and the soft ding sounded overly loud in the hushed quiet. The doors opened, and we headed toward the back row, where the overhead lights did little to chase away the shadows. Absently, I noted that no others were heading toward their cars and figured we'd timed our departure to miss the initial exiting rush.

Since we'd arrived late, our options were limited, and we ended up near the top of the garage. We found a spot for Zev's SUV in a corner near a stairwell entrance. The isolated parking slot paired with the broken security ward on the emergency door made Zev grumble. I countered that a public garage was not exactly a hotbed of crime, even pointing out the low-slung pristine beauty—obviously someone's pride and joy—parked a few spots down, saying that if they felt confident in leaving their classic Corvette, Zev's SUV should be safe.

As we headed toward the back corner, I noted the sports car was still there, but the spot next to our SUV was empty. Even though we were alone, Zev stayed at my side, his hand resting on the small of my back, our hips brushing as we walked. As we got closer, he disarmed the SUV's electronic alarm, the taillights blinking in tandem with the sharp electronic beeps. He followed that up with a soft utterance that released the magical ward on the SUV. As the ward powered down, echoes of power ruffled against my skin like the brush of ghostly feathers.

Distracted by the man at my side and the night's potential, I failed to pay attention to more-subtle signs whispering around us. Like the strangely still air that muffled the sounds of my heels against concrete, the unnaturally deep shadows collected around the SUV, or the rising itch of discomfort spreading along my neck. It wasn't until Zev stopped me at the passenger side door and reached around me for the handle that my magic switched from irritating to near painful with desperate warning. Finally cluing in, I grabbed his wrist as his hand closed on the metal handle, knowing I was too late. "Wait!"

Power seared in a blinding flash. It left me momentarily stunned as a magical cage dropped, enclosing us, the SUV, and the shadowed parking spot in a chain of interlocking sigils and ruins. Triggered by the spelled trap, my Prism magic swept in like thunder after a lightning strike, wrapping around Zev and me in a shimmering diamond-hard shield, but it was a second too slow. A violent, purple, multi-tailed whip coiled around Zev, slamming him face-first into the side of the SUV with such strength the metal groaned under the impact. An invisible punch dropped me with bruising force to the hard concrete and left me sprawled on my ass.

As a Prism, I had magic that could not only withstand most magical attacks but also turn them back on the caster. If I had enough warning, I could stretch my shield to include another. This surprise-attack tactic nixed most of those advantages. My power slid over my skin with a click that reverberated deep inside me, but it couldn't lock down on Zev. Thick ropes of deep purple veined with silver trapped him against the side of the SUV and kept my power from reaching him. I could hear the car's metal creak in protest as Zev's body was shoved deeper against the passenger door. I couldn't see his face since it was turned away, but the muscles in his back strained as he struggled against the magical bindings.

I rolled to my side and got to my knees. Trusting my magic to withstand the brunt of the attacking spell, I grabbed the writhing, snakelike lines of power wrapped around Zev's legs and yanked them back. My innate ability buffered the worst of the magical burn, but heat and power seared my palms with shocking intensity. It was like wrestling a handful of vicious electric eels. If it was this bad for me, I couldn't imagine what Zev was dealing with.

The rough concrete ripped into my knees and scraped my bare legs, but it was a minor discomfort swept under the teeth-gritting pain eating through my hands. I tightened my grip and with a guttural grunt ripped the ropes of magic from Zev's legs. As the power tore free, it set off a silent explosion that knocked me back a-freakin'-gain.

Blinded by an array of dancing spots, I fumbled around until my throbbing hand hit the hard rubber of the SUV's tire. Using it to get to my feet—and vowing I was never wearing heels again—I yelled, "Zev!"

A noise somewhere between a grunt and a growl was my only response. I blinked my vision clear and got an impression of Zev, outlined in blue, before my head was viciously yanked back. My hands flew up to keep from having my hair ripped out by the roots, and I felt warm flesh under my fingers. I curved my nails into claws and dug in even as I stumbled. One heel tore free, eroding my already shaky balance. I fell into the body of the asshole behind me using my hair as a damn handle. I risked dropping one hand so I could shove my elbow into him. A pained yelp proved I had gotten lucky with my strike. The hand in my hair loosened enough so I could twist around. I got an impression of a square jaw, a dark brow over mean eyes, and buzzed hair. Even more revealing was the belt wrapped around his waist, a familiar item worn by casting mages.

I gave up on saving my scalp and went on the attack. With a snarl, I swiped out, aiming for maximum damage. Flesh tore under my nails. A large fist knocked my hand away before wrapping around my throat. Furious and beyond pissed, I locked one hand on his thick wrist and used my other to rip at his belt, doing my best to destroy as many foci objects as possible to limit his magical reach.

A couple of objects tore free, hit the ground, and broke, adding more magic to the overabundant power clouding the air. The fingers at my throat dug deeper, unaffected by the loss of their magical arsenal, so I switched targets and aimed for his weakest point. Grabbing between his legs, I squeezed for all I was worth. His eyes bulged, his mouth opened, his face paled, and the crushing hold at my neck finally disappeared. I twisted my grip on his dangling bits, doing my best to geld him, even as I slammed my head forward into his nose. His fist managed a glancing blow against my temple. The combined impacts left me stunned.

"Bitch!" It emerged on a gasping rasp as he shoved me away. He covered himself with one hand, and his other grabbed something from his damn belt. He tossed it up and muttered a word.

I stumbled back as his magic wrapped around me, its touch akin to hundreds of heated knives slicing along every inch of my skin.

He bared his teeth and wiped his bleeding nose. "Your turn."

I held his furious gaze as the pressure of his power clawed at me, and I didn't bother to respond to his taunts. Instead, I hit the instinctive switch of my magic and flicked it from defense to offense. The coil and snap of what made me a Prism grasped his spell and turned it back on him with pitiless intent.

His pained expression turned frantic as a reddish net resembling barbed wire wrapped around him like a second skin. Everywhere his reflected spell touched, gouges opened, parting flesh and leaving the edges of skin black and burnt while tiny incandescent embers buried themselves inside the wounds. His mouth opened on an airless scream.

I didn't bother to watch the inevitable outcome. Instead, I kicked off my remaining heel and spun around, determined to get to Zev. Something tight in my chest loosened when I saw he was no longer trapped against the SUV. Instead, he stood in front of me, his shirt torn and singed, facing off with a female mage. With his back to me, I could see the crisscross combination of welts and burns that reached from his shoulders to his waist. Their magic clashed in a storm of blue and purple, leaving the stench of ozone heavy in the air. Interrupting dueling mages was a dangerous proposition, so I left Zev to it, confident he would take care of whatever threat she posed.

Instead, I focused on locating the mage holding the spelled cage in place. The strange warp around the spot where we were cornered indicated that an illusion mage was tucked away nearby, not to mention that no one was coming to investigate the ongoing fight, and we hadn't exactly been quiet. Hell, Zev had already wrapped up a slender male in a fiery blue net of ruins. Translucent scorpion-like creatures crawled along the sapphire-colored sigils holding him in an unforgiving grip, their tails rising and falling like vicious needles in a horrific rain as the man's body writhed in an agonizing dance in midair.

Three combat mages, and one illusion mage, made this a strike team.

My power swept out in ever-widening circles and hit the cage's boundaries. The sigils fueling the spell flared like a brilliant glowing curtain but held strong. I hit it again, determined to break through. The curtain of interlocked ruins flared but appeared undamaged. The magic bounced back with teeth-rattling intensity.

Magic was powered one of two ways in our world— through a mage's will or through a complex casting ritual. Being a Prism was routed in willpower, and I had no problem being a stubborn bitch. I dug deep and slammed my power against the cage, counting on brute strength and sheer stubbornness to break through. The curtain shivered but held. I choked back my rising frustration.

In front of me, the scorpion-infested mage was on the ground, still twitching. Zev exchanged magical strikes with a female mage. Blood poured from her nose, but her focus didn't waver. Silver-tinged purple magic swept back, slamming into Zev, and he hunched at the impact. His hand swept up and to the right, then he whipped it back. The female mage's body arced as if yanked by chain anchored midbody.

I tore my attention away from their battle and concentrated on what I could do. I took a deep breath and focused, going deeper into my magic. As the mundane world slipped away, the world lit with a barrage of magical echoes in a living tapestry of power.

Seeing echoes of magical energy was a recently discovered aspect of my ability. It was a dizzying and confusing sight, but it meant I could track the magic powering the cage. Even better, I could see the cracks from my previous attacks. Targeting a cluster of darker fissures, with grim determination, I slammed my magic against the cage. The cracks widened, and finally, I felt my magic ooze through a fracture and slip past the cage's boundaries like a silent, invisible tendril. It licked at the thick surrounding shadows, searching for the mage holding the cage in place. It touched an unsettling iciness in the far corner half hidden by the stairwell. *There.* I let it drift along until it completely encircled the hidden mage. I had a moment to worry about the repercussions of snapping the magical bindings on the cage, but hearing Zev's pained grunt, I didn't give the first fuck.

I flexed my magic like an invisible hand, testing my grip. When I was sure I could hold the illusion mage, I took a brutal grip and yanked. Power slammed into me, ricocheting through my skull and sending me flying back again. I grunted as I hit the wall, but by some miracle, I managed to maintain my magical hold on the hidden mage.

Dazed, I slid down, blinking as thin, dark cracks ate through the magical lines that created the cage. The black shadows encircling our fight turned smoky gray and began to drift away. My power pulsed, drawing my attention to the corner where the illusion mage, her face a twisted mask of horror, appeared to be staring at nothing. Her hands were up as if to ward off a blow. Red gouges marred her palms and arms, the existing wounds deep enough for me to see them from where I sat. More appeared as I watched, and I had no idea what was causing them. Whatever it was, it was clearly a creation of her imagination, which meant she had to be either a Mirage or a Nightmare. To stop the assault, she would have to break the illusion herself, now that I had reversed her attack. Unfortunately, she was too terrified to do so. Instead, she dropped to her knees, hands covering her head, as thin, terrified wails erupted from her open mouth. I left her to her nightmare.

Three down.

Using the wall as support, I got to my feet, determined to help Zev. My skull ached, inside and out, and a fuzzy gray edged my vision. The world around me spun, and a metallic taste filled my mouth. I leaned against the wall and closed my eyes, shutting out the magical echoes. I needed a moment for things to settle so I didn't, once again, end up on my ass.

A feminine scream of pain and fury snapped my eyes open just as Zev snarled and his magic flared in a blinding flash. Instinctively, I raised an arm to shield my eyes and flinched. When nothing struck me, I dropped my arm and blinked my vision clear. In front of me, Zev had his hands raised in mage pose while his magic curled around him. At his feet was the crumbled form of the last mage, her eyes open and unseeing as blood slowly pooled around her.

Four down.

I shoved off the wall and took a shaky couple of steps forward. "Zev?" When he didn't respond, I tried again. "Zev, are you okay?"

He turned to me with a disturbing stiltedness, his face a teeth-baring mask of menace. For a moment, my heart stopped. This was not the man I had tangled the sheets with. This was the Cordova Family Arbiter. *A mage you don't fuck with unless you have a death wish.* For a breathless moment, he stared at me without recognition, then he grimaced and shook out his hands. The blood-chilling look was replaced by his more familiar hard, grim lines. His dark gaze swept over me. "I'm good. You?"

"I'm fi—"

Phosphorus silver magic slammed into Zev's back and lifted him off the ground. Power crawled over him like deranged lines of electricity, bowing his spine in a painful arc. I didn't need the sputtered splashes of indigo to know Zev was in trouble. The two competing magics snapped and twisted in a dizzying array. But there was a strange anomaly in the attacking spell. The magical whips sank into Zev, igniting a silvery glow that snaked under his skin and crawled up his body.

I didn't stop to think before I lunged forward on a yell and grabbed Zev's hand, holding it tight. I shoved my magic out, battering at the attacking spell, hoping brute force would break its vicious hold. Electrified shocks bit at me, and my muscles felt like they were trying to pull free from my bones. I held on, gritting my teeth through the paralyzing pain, as the ache in my head rose with every heartbeat.

Zev's head turned toward me with agonizing slowness, his dark eyes holding a silvery tint. I managed to tear my gaze free and look behind him. The twitching scorpion-covered mage was lying on the ground, a grimace twisting his face as he stared in our direction. His hand was up and shaking as he aimed his magic at us. Even as I watched, his hand dropped, and he collapsed, the life in his eyes fading.

With the mage's final breath, the attacking spell sputtered out. Zev dropped. Unfortunately, I was under him, and despite my brain's desperate attempt to get my muscles to move, they didn't. Zev's weight slammed into me, his shoulder clipping my chin so hard I tasted blood as I bit my tongue. The impact whipped my head back, and the only thing behind it was hard concrete. I barely registered the dull thunk before everything went black.

CHAPTER THREE

A RHYTHMIC BEEPING propelled me to consciousness, a sense of déjà vu riding shotgun. *I'm in a hospital. Again.* I floated in the undemanding haze and pondered the wisdom of opening my eyes, but my mental gears kept slipping thanks to the dull ache at the back of my skull. At some point, my tattered memories started coming together into flashes of Zev and me enjoying the show—and each other. Those were soon replaced by the more chaotic replay of the attack in the garage that culminated in the full-on Technicolor visual assault of Zev caught in an agonizing grip of a violently charged spell. My brain and body collided with a painful jerk, accompanied by a hiccup in the monitoring beeps.

Where is Zev? Is he okay?

I wanted to open my eyes but couldn't because they were apparently sealed shut. The sound of someone shifting in a nearby chair sliced through my rising panic and held me in place. A soft, nearly imperceptible sigh followed. Determined to clear the cobwebs out of my head, I kept my eyes shut and listened hard, trying to determine who lay in wait. They didn't give me much to work with, staying still and quiet, disappearing under the faint voices and muted sounds of activity mixed with the annoying beeps of monitoring equip-ment. A click and a rush of air were followed by an uptick in the ambient sound, indicating a door opening. It was followed by a brisk feminine "Hello, just checking vitals."

"She's still out."

Not recognizing the man behind the answering voice, I forced my lids to lift. As shoes squeaked against tile, I managed to get my eyes open just enough for light to turn everything into a blur. Something firm and cool tugged at my arm and brushed over my skin.

"Ow," I mouthed, even though it didn't really hurt. I blinked until the blur turned into recognizable shapes and colors, and then stared at an IV in my arm. It took a few seconds for the image to hit my brain and sink in. Once it did, my skin started to crawl because I hated needles, even more so after my last run-in with them. I winced and looked away, the movement a clear indication I was awake.

"Well, hello there." The friendly, determined nurse standing on the side of my bed and blocking my view continued to mess around with the IV bag, which made the line move and in turn increased the uncomfortable sensation of the needle buried in my skin. My stomach curdled as she smiled down at me, blissfully unaware of how close she was to being barfed on. "How are you feeling?"

In my head, I gave an irritated hiss, but it somehow managed to increase the ache in my skull to unavoidable dimensions, which made my answer a groan.

The nurse, obviously fluent in groan, finally stopped messing with the damn IV. The overhead lights dimmed to a more manageable level. "Better?"

My mouth was so dry, it took a few moments to form the word. "Thanks."

Unfazed by my less than impressive response, she

continued her oral exam. "Can you tell me on a scale of one to ten where your pain level is at?"

I gave her inquiry serious consideration and finally settled on "Four?"

Her answering hum was the kind that could mean anything from "Liar, liar" to "That's good." She did another vitals check and said, "You're up for a dose of acetaminophen, so I'll get that to you."

This time, I managed a thumbs-up with the hand not being using as a pincushion.

Correctly reading between the lines of my nonverbal response, she picked up a plastic cup with a straw from the nearby stand and brought it to my mouth. "Here, take it slow."

Grateful, I sucked down a couple of sips of water that eased the soreness in my throat and rehydrated my tongue to working proportions. She set the cup aside then asked a few basic questions. My answers must have passed because she patted my arm and turned away.

Needing an answer to an entirely different question, I reached out and touched her arm, bringing her to a stop. "Wait, the man I was with, Zev Aslanov? Is he here?"

The answer came from behind her. "He's just down the hall."

As the nurse walked away, I finally registered the well-dressed dark-haired man in the visitor's chair—Emilio Cordova, Zev's boss and best friend but, more importantly, the head of the Cordova Family. Normally, his presence engendered deference, but worried about Zev, I blew right past that to borderline panic. Emilio wasn't someone I knew well. I'd been introduced to him only a couple of weeks ago, but I did recognize the small signs of tension bleeding through his polite mask. The deeper lines bracketing his mouth and the tightness around his eyes were enough to send my stomach plummeting with dread. "Is he okay?"

He held my gaze, and in marked contrast to mine, his voice remained calm. "For the most part, yes."

Despite his tone, I wasn't keen on how he'd phrased that. My heart pounded, and the stupid mechanical beeps picked up the beat. "What do you mean, 'for the most part'?"

Emilio leaned forward and gripped the side rails of the bed, causing it to shift the tiniest bit. "Like you, he was brought in unconscious. Unlike you, he's not showing signs of waking."

His bedside manner was less than reassuring and made me flinch. "How long?"

He blinked and sat back, slowly letting go of the bed rail. He frowned and repeated, "How long what?"

Clutching at patience, because it was obvious he was functioning on truckloads of stress and little sleep, I expanded, "How long have I been here?"

"It's closing in on three in the morning," he answered.

I struggled to sit up, and the jerky movements reignited my collection of aches and pains, which erupted with vehement protests. Gritting my teeth, I rode out my body's complaints and lined up the timing. Zev and I had gone out Friday, and the show had ended around ten thirty. "It's Saturday morning, right?"

"Yes," Emilio confirmed, watching me carefully.

"Ms. Costas, you need to take it easy." The reprimand reminded me of the nurse I had all but forgotten. She stood near the door, where she had been making notes on her tablet.

I held her disapproving gaze and shot back, "I want to sit up." *Stubborn, thy name is Rory.*

Before she could whip out the riot act and read it to me, Emilio pressed the button on the side of the bed and raised the back. The nurse went to her table with a put-upon sigh, clearly recognizing this was an argument she was destined to lose.

I ignored her in favor of grilling Emilio, but when I opened my mouth, I caught the unspoken warning in his eyes. *Right, no discussing Family business in front of an audience.* I clumsily switched gears. "Why are you here?"

A flash of humor eased a few lines on his face. "You know, most people would be happy to wake up to someone at their bedside."

He had a point, but the only family I claimed was Lena, who was also the only one I trusted when I wasn't at my best. As much as I appreciated Emilio's presence—because he was right, it did suck to wake up alone—it was also disconcerting. Because he misconstrued my question, I reframed it. "Why aren't you with Zev?"

All traces of humor disappeared, replaced by watchful scrutiny. "Because Sabella asked me to sit with you while she talked to the doctor."

Sabella was here? I blinked as I grappled with the idea that not only was the head of one of Phoenix's most powerful Arcane houses sitting vigil at my bedside, but so was the matriarch of the oldest Arcane Family. Since I wasn't the target of a mage strike team, Zev was, I kept my voice low and warned, "It might be best if you stay with him."

He studied me for a long moment, something I couldn't interpret at work behind his closed expression. "I've got two guards on his door. He'll be safe for the few minutes I'm here."

"Okay," I murmured, unable to push things further, not with the nurse still in attendance. He settled back in his chair, and I started picking at the sheet. Neither of us said anything, and the silence stretched uncomfortably between us.

Eventually, the nurse finished with her notes and came to the foot of my bed. "Okay, Rory. I'll be back in a few minutes with your pills and more water."

"Sounds good, thanks."

She turned and headed toward the door. Just as she was about to pull it open, Sabella Rossi, my employer and possible friend, swept inside. Tall and curvy, she carried her innate power and elegance with ease. Her hair, a mix of sun-touched golds with the occasional strand of bronze, was pulled back in a neat chignon that highlighted her classic features and hazel eyes. There was something ageless about Sabella, but tonight, concern added visible years to her face. When she saw I was awake, relief flooded her features, erasing some of those signs. "You're awake."

I waited as she and the nurse exchanged nods. Once the nurse was gone, Sabella crossed over to the bed. Emilio rose and offered her the lone chair, but she waved him down. Instead, she lowered the railing on my bed and settled on the edge. She grabbed my hand and gave it a gentle squeeze. "Tell me what happened."

I couldn't help looking from her to Emilio and back. There were things I could share with Sabella that I couldn't with Emilio. I wasn't sure I was up to the delicate dance required to navigate the potential pitfalls. Unlike Zev and Sabella, Emilio didn't know I was a Prism. At least, I was hoping that was still the case. He knew me as a Transporter, and Transporters were not known for having serious offensive skills when it came to magical fights. Sharing what had happened without a misstep was going to be tricky. Doing my best to keep it short and simple, I said, "Zev and I were leaving a show and got ambushed in the parking garage. There were four mages, two went after Zev, one went after me, and the fourth maintained the cage."

"Cage?" Emilio asked.

"Four mages?" Sabella asked at the same time, a small frown marring her forehead. "That sounds like a standard strike team."

Nice to know I wasn't the only one jumping to conclusions, but I had a better question. "Who was their target?"

Instead of answering me, she shared a look with Emilio and murmured, "It could be connected."

"But why?" he asked just as quietly.

Clearly, I was missing something. "Connected to what?" When Sabella pulled her hand back, I caught it, my sudden movement sending a spike through my temples. "Connected to what, Sabella?"

She didn't try to escape my hold but kept her attention on Emilio as she continued their cryptic exchange. "My guess, the same reason Theo was killed."

Theo? The only Theo I knew was Theo Mahon, an illusion mage who'd kidnapped Lena and trapped her in a lethal Drainer's Circle, all because he and his now-dead partner had needed her curse-breaking skills to unlock a stolen flash drive from an Acrapous hex. The last I heard, Zev had tracked Theo's ass down and delivered him to the Arcane Council for judgment.

I tugged on Sabella's hand until she looked at me, then I demanded, "Tell me what's going on."

Her hazel eyes took on a gold sheen, and magic whispered over my skin. It wasn't easy holding that burning gaze, but I was determined, which made me reckless. It wasn't smart to make demands of someone of Sabella's caliber. Not only was she a power in our world, but also her benevolence could be as changeable as the winds. Even knowing I was playing with fire, I couldn't back down, not with Zev lying unconscious in a nearby room. I held her gaze and managed a rough "Please." Finally, she dipped her chin in agreement. I took a deep breath and let go of her hand.

Emilio cleared his throat, breaking the lingering tension between Sabella and me, and stood up. "I'll let you two talk." He gave me a nod. "Rory." He didn't wait for a response but turned to Sabella and squeezed her shoulder. "When you're finished here, would you stop by Zev's room?"

She patted his hand. "Of course."

Emilio headed toward the door, but it swished open, admitting my nurse. She gave him a small smile as he waited for her to pass. He left, and the nurse came to the other side of my bed. She held up a bottle of water and a small paper cup. She shook the cup, and the tablet rattled inside. "I come bearing gifts."

"Yay." I held out my hand, grateful for her interruption. The ache in my head was getting harder to ignore.

She poured the tablets into my trembling palm then offered the bottled water. I took it and washed the pills down, praying they would kick in quickly. When she offered to take back the water, I held it tight. "Thanks, but I'll hang on to it, if you don't mind."

"Not at all. Just remember to take it slow." She asked a few more questions, including whether I wanted to visit the bathroom. Since the answer was yes, she stayed at my side as I wobbled across the cold tile, awkwardly trying to keep the stupid gown closed so I wouldn't flash the room.

By the time I made it back to the bed, I felt like I'd run a marathon. Sweat beaded on my forehead, and my muscles shook. I sat on the edge of the bed and took sips of water, letting the cool liquid soothe my upset stomach as my body calmed. When I was sure I wouldn't pass out, I gingerly settled into my half-reclining position. During my bathroom run, Sabella had moved to the chair Emilio had abandoned and waited patiently for the nurse to finish up.

Only after the door closed behind the nurse did I pick up our previous conversation. "Theo? As in Theo Mahon?"

She studied me for so long I wasn't sure she would answer, then she sighed. "Yes, that Theo." Her polished nails absently danced against the chair's arm. "He was found dead in his cell a few days ago."

"Murdered?"

She nodded.

"How?"

"Poisoned."

I blinked. "Didn't the council have him under guard?"

"They did," she confirmed. "In fact, the council had heightened the security around him because he was scheduled to testify this upcoming Wednesday at the Delphi project hearing."

The Delphi project centered around two rogue scientists who, with the permission of their heads of Family, had defied a council edict and moved ahead with the creation of a highly controversial serum that would either increase a mage's power to the next evolutionary level or, worse, strip their power completely. Unbeknownst to their Family heads, the mad-scientist duo had been paid by some shadowy puppet master to test the prototype serum on unknowing human subjects. The results had been terrifyingly lethal. While the money man's identity was still a mystery, the upcoming hearing was to determine the culpability of the Families involved, and I was on the witness list. *But Theo?* "What does Theo have to do with the Trask and Clarke Families?"

Stephen Trask and Leander Clarke represented the two Families involved and sat at the helm of competing research companies, Origin and LanTech. Both had disregarded the Arcane Council's edict to halt the serum's research and creation. If that wasn't bad enough, they'd also made critical errors in judgment when they sent out rival mercenary teams to kidnap Emilio Cordova's ten-year-old nephew, Jeremy, who inherited a warded flash drive containing pivotal research that both Origin and LanTech needed to move the Delphi project forward.

"The information that Theo was trying to barter with when he took your friend contained copies of Lara's research," Sabella explained.

I struggled to put the pieces together. That wasn't easy to do with the mother of all headaches chiming in. Jeremy's mother, Dr. Lara Kaspar, was the lead researcher at Origin, and before her death, she had been selling her research to LanTech. Hence Stephen and Leander's poorly thought-out kidnapping attempt. That plan had been foiled by yours truly when I realized the package for my off-the-books delivery job was a kid. It was also my initial introduction to Zev, who'd helped permanently eliminate the teams threatening Jeremy, but that hadn't been enough for Emilio. He made his displeasure known by bankrupting Leander's research arm, LanTech, and financially crippling Stephen's lab, Origin.

Both Stephen and Leander viewed the Delphi project as their last attempt to salvage their Families' fortunes, hence their willingness to ignore the council's decree. Their futures looked decidedly bleak, yet another brutal lesson of what losing entailed when one played in the arena of the Arcane Families.

A memory nudged me, and a piece clicked into place. "That's why Zev told Lena the stolen drive belonged to the Cordova Family." When he'd made the comment in passing, I had wondered what he meant, but at the time, I was just happy that Lena had survived. "But I thought Theo never got around to breaking the hex on that drive."

"He didn't," she confirmed.

"So how did he know the information on it was connected to the Delphi project?"

Sabella's mouth twisted with distaste. "I'm not sure he

did, but he does know the name of the individual he was going to sell the information to."

"Who?"

"He didn't say."

Something in her voice had me asking, "But?"

"But"—she lowered her voice—"Theo had finalized a deal to share the name at trial in return for leniency."

"Would the council show mercy like that?" As far as I knew, the last thing the ruling body of the Arcane world could be considered was lenient.

Her gaze met mine, and the concern I saw there left me uneasy. "They would if that name revealed a high-level traitor."

Her grim pronouncement sent ice coursing through my veins. I swallowed hard as an ugly suspicion began to form. "How high?"

She didn't look away as she answered, "Very high."

I studied the lines of stress and worry that had been growing in number during the last week or so and added that to her hushed conversations and last-minute schedule changes. Sabella had her own ties to the council, and it wasn't out of the realm of possibility that she could call a few members friends. For her to discover that one of those friends might not be who she thought they were would be more than painful, it would be disastrous. Hoping I was wrong, I asked, "High, like council-level high?"

"I would hope not, but unfortunately, there are others who also sit on the council who have concerns." She paused then added quietly, "Concerns I share."

Her implication felt like a sucker punch. "Oh, shit."

Her lips curved, but her gaze remained dark and worried. "'Oh, shit' is right."

CHAPTER FOUR

AFTER DROPPING HER BOMBSHELL, Sabella refused to go into details, saying only that we could discuss it when Zev and I were out of the hospital. It was probably for the best, because exhaustion and the pain pills were dragging me under. I tried to insist Sabella go home and get some sleep, but she had years more practice at being stubborn than I did. So I finally gave up and let my eyes close. The next thing I knew, it was morning and the nurse was back, checking my vitals. Thankfully, my headache was down to a dull throb that was easily ignored.

When Lena showed up with nonhospital coffee, breakfast sandwiches, and more importantly, clothes, I asked Sabella to check on Zev since the nurse wouldn't share any information with me, as I wasn't immediate family. While she was busy with that, I changed into the comfortable yoga pants and oversized T-shirt that Lena had brought. When Sabella returned, she delivered the depressing news that there was no change in Zev's condition.

I sat on the bed and, over breakfast, filled both Sabella

and Lena in on the details of the attack. Since both knew I was a Prism, there was no delicate dance around the facts.

"Four combat-trained mages," Lena said as she sat facing me, wiping her fingers on a napkin. "Whoever sent them wasn't messing around. Any idea who sent them?"

Out of the corner of my eye, I caught Sabella's small, warning headshake. *Right, message received.* No sharing with Lena about the whole possible-high-level-traitor thing. I managed a shrug. "Not a clue, but I think it's safe to assume they knew going up against the Cordova Arbiter required more than normal firepower."

"Guess it was a good thing you were with him, then." Lena wadded up her napkin, twisted at the waist, and tossed the paper ball into the garbage bin on the other side of the bed. "I'm sure you threw them for a loop."

I managed a half-hearted smile because she wasn't wrong. "Yeah, I don't think they expected me to be much more than a momentary hiccup."

The thing about Prisms was that they possessed a rare ability. So rare, they'd all but faded into the annals of history as urban myths. Once upon a time, the powerful, which generally meant the Arcane Families, coveted Prisms because they held what was perceived as immunity against magical attacks. I could personally attest that it wasn't immunity so much as a shield that could take a hell of a beating before breaking. Of course, I was still trying to understand what being a Prism really meant since information on my magical ability was difficult to come by. To date, my main source of information was a journal given to me by Sabella, a gift to encourage me to take her on as my main client. It had obviously worked.

Worry about Zev wiped away my half-formed grin, and I tugged restlessly at my T-shirt hem. "I might have helped even the odds, but that last attack was a doozy."

Sabella shifted in the chair, brushing nonexistent crumbs from her tailored slacks. "Tell me again about that spell."

I brought my memories front and center, grateful that the coffee and food had eased the dull ache that I woke up with because my brain felt sharper. "Zev had just taken down the last mage, a woman, and ..." My voice trailed off as I recalled his strange reaction when he turned toward me. His stilted movements as if he was fighting something unseen—magic or emotion, I wasn't sure which—and the momentary lack of recognition that was there and gone. I chalked it up to his being caught up in the heat of the battle, but what if—

"Rory."

Lena's hand touched my knee, breaking the fragile thread on my thoughts. I blinked and shook my head. "Sorry."

"You okay?" Concern colored her voice and face.

"Yeah, I just... got lost for a second." I relaxed my hand that had unconsciously fisted in my lap. "Zev had turned away and was facing me when he was hit in the back with a spell. The magic crawled around him like electrified chains. Zev tried fighting back, but it was like the spell short-circuited his magic."

Sabella frowned. "Are you sure?"

I managed a jerky nod. "When I went to help him, it felt like tangling with a Taser on steroids."

Lena shared a look with Sabella, speculation rife in her voice. "Combat-trained electro mage, then?"

"Most likely," the older woman agreed. "There are a couple of names I can think of that might, for the right price, consider taking on Zev. Neither one are female."

"It wasn't the woman. She was already dead."

Both women turned to me.

I managed an awkward shrug. "It wasn't her. It was the first mage Zev took down. A guy, maybe late twenties. At that point, he wasn't in the best shape, but whatever spell he used looked pretty damn painful. It literally crawled under Zev's skin. Any idea which kind of electro-based spell would do that?" Because then maybe we might know why Zev wasn't waking up.

Lena shook her head. "No clue, but"—her gaze sharpened —"I know someone we can ask."

A spark of anticipation bloomed as I followed her thoughts. "Evan." The top electro mage in the Arcane Guild and Lena's snuggle bunny.

"Evan," Lena confirmed. She pulled out her phone, and her fingers flew over the screen. "I'll see if he can come over and chat with us." She flicked a look up, and it bounced between Sabella and me. "Maybe, if we're lucky, he can track down those names of yours, Ms. Rossi."

"And if we're lucky, who contacted them," I added, because no one was safe from Evan when he started hunting in the electronic world.

Sabella open her mouth but was interrupted by a brisk knock on my door. Whoever it was didn't wait for an answer but pushed the door open. The harried face of my nurse came into view, her hand wrapped around the door's edge, keeping it close to her as her body blocked the figures behind her. "Ms. Costas, the police are here and asking to see you."

The word "police" sent a skitter of unease through me, and my gaze jerked to Sabella, the only one in the room powerful enough to keep the hounds at bay. She wasn't paying attention to me. Instead, with her familiar haughty mask firmly in place, her attention was centered on the nurse. "Is that so?"

The nurse gave a nod.

Sabella sighed, stood, and pulled out her phone. As she typed a text, she moved to the foot of my bed. Whatever message she sent didn't take long, because she looked at the nurse and made a flicking motion with her hand. "Let them in, dear." She slid her phone into her pocket. "I'll deal with them."

I swallowed hard as the nurse stepped back and opened the door wide for my latest visitors. Lena didn't get up from her seat on my bed but twisted around to watch as a woman came through first. Behind her was an older man who waited for the nurse to step past before coming in the room and letting the door shut behind him. Both were in plain clothes with badges and weapons in discreet positions at their waists, a clear indication they were detectives.

Magic brushed against my senses and ignited an itch. Either one or both of them was wielding a low level of power. *Interesting.* The woman's expression was set to friendly but professional, but her brown eyes held a glint of hardness as her gaze swept over us, paused on me, then stopped on Sabella. "Ms. Rossi, good morning."

Sabella inclined her head. "Good morning, Detective Rendón."

Detective Rendón's partner stepped forward and extended his hand. "Ms. Rossi, Detective Hall. Nice to meet you." His smile deepened the brackets already etched around his mouth and joined the sun-worn lines around his eyes. Unlike Rendón, Hall exuded a genuine amicability that spoke more to his personality than his professionalism.

"And you, Detective Hall." Sabella shook his hand and resumed her position, which meant her back was to me. "I appreciate you postponing the interview until this morning, but I will ask a few more minutes of your patience until Ms. Ortiz joins us."

Lena turned to face me and, with her back to the detectives, mouthed a silent, "Ms. Ortiz?"

Since I didn't know who that was, I gave her wide eyes, hoping Lena's body blocked the detective's line of sight to me.

"Of course," Rendón murmured as her polite mask gained a wry tint. "I was unaware Ms. Costas was considered part of the Cordova Family."

Sabella ignored the detective's insinuation and asked a question of her own. "Have there been any developments?"

The two detectives shared a look that gave nothing away, and Hall answered, "We're still early in the investigation yet." His gaze came back to me. "Anything Ms. Costas can share would be helpful at this point."

The door swung open, and a dark-haired, curvy woman strode in, dressed in an understated but classy skirt and shirt paired with stiletto heels. "And Ms. Costas will be happy to share what she can, Detectives."

"Mari, I'm so glad you could join us," Sabella said.

"You know I'm happy to help wherever Emilio needs me, Sabella." Mari strode across the room, her heels making sharp snaps against the linoleum as she joined the growing crowd at the foot of my bed. Her gaze landed on me, and she smiled. "Ms. Costas, I'm Maribel Ortiz, legal counsel for the Cordova Family. Mr. Cordova wanted to ensure you were properly represented during this investigation. I would be happy to either offer my services or, if you're more comfortable with someone else, a recommendation."

I swallowed my rising nerves, grateful she was there despite wondering what a favor like this was going to cost me. "I'd be happy for your assistance, Ms. Ortiz."

Approval warmed her smile. "Mari, please." She moved to my side and faced the detectives. "As Ms. Costas is still recovering from her concussion, I would request we keep this as brief as possible."

"We're here simply to get an account of what happened, ma'am," Detective Rendón said with a hint of impatience. "I'm not sure your presence is required."

I disagreed, especially since I knew there were things

Sabella didn't want shared, and based on Mari's presence, neither did Emilio. Unfortunately, I hadn't had a chance to verify what was off-limits to the police, and when it came to the Arcane Families, there was always something off-limits. So I would have to trust my gut and Mari and pray I picked correctly.

Mari's smile grew teeth. "The Cordova Family is highly concerned about the brutality of the unprovoked attack on Ms. Costas and Mr. Aslanov. They would like ensure the investigation remains focused on uncovering who is behind this threat and eliminating a repeat of last night's incident."

Oh boy. Based on the quickly masked flash of anger from Rendón and the cooling of Hall's friendly expression, Emilio's lawyer was not making friends. I didn't dare interrupt and figured my best bet was to wait until I was asked a direct question.

Lena grabbed my hand and squeezed. When she had my attention, she said in a voice that cut through the rising tension, "I'm going to go see if I can wrestle a few more chairs for everyone."

I cleared my throat. "Sounds good, thanks."

She stood, shared a small smile with Mari, then turned and made her excuses as she left. An awkward quiet descended.

Hall broke it. "How is Mr. Aslanov doing?"

I wasn't sure whom he was asking, but Mari answered. "He remains unconscious, and tests are still in progress."

Hearing her say it out loud hit me harder than expected. I lost track of the conversation for a few moments as fear rose and tears pressed against my eyes. I looked to my lap, hoping to hide my reaction, and did my best to choke back the emotion. The longer it took for him to wake, the more worried I was about what that damn spell had entailed. I didn't want to be there answering questions. I wanted to be out trying to find answers or, better yet, by Zev's side.

Lena and a couple of nurses returned with chairs. As the detectives settled in and Mari arranged her chair close to the side of my bed, Lena said, "Rory, I'm going to run those errands we talked about. I'll be back in a little bit, okay?"

I met her gaze, understanding that her errand would include a conversation with Evan. "Sounds good. Thanks."

She left, and once the door shut behind her, the detectives wasted no time getting down to it. Mari agreed to let them record the interview, but I noted that Rendón was also taking notes. Then they walked me through the evening. I skipped the more private parts of my date with Zev and did my best to stick with simple facts. When I was finished, I braced because I knew what was coming next. Questions. Lots and lots of questions.

They started out easy. Yes, our relationship was fairly new, but we had crossed paths previously in a professional capacity. No, I hadn't noticed anyone following us. No, I was not aware of anyone with an agenda against Zev or myself. No, to the best of my knowledge, there were no upset exes on either side. I managed to get through that one without flinching because I could think of one name that might have a beef with Zev and me, but it wasn't one I could share with the detectives without involving another Arcane Family in this mess. There was no chance I was willing to do that.

Then the questions got trickier. Yes, I was a Transporter. No, I did not currently work for the Guild but was an independent contractor and Ms. Rossi was a client. No, I was not currently working for the Cordova Family, but I did enjoy a professional relationship with them. No, I was not willing to divulge details of any recent transactions, as that would be a violation of my contracts.

That one earned an interruption from Mari. "If it is discovered that this attack was tied to any of Ms. Costas's contracts, we'll be happy to share the specific information needed so long as you provide the proper paperwork." This sparked an argument between Mari and the detectives that sounded as if it was based more on routine than necessity. Mari finally quashed it with "Discretion is key to Ms. Costas's business, and it would not look good for the Phoenix Police Department to irreparably damage the reputation of a locally owned and operated business simply for curiosity's sake. Unless you have probable cause, her client list is off the table."

Stymied, the detectives went back over the sequence of events, poking and prodding. As Hall and Rendón took turns with their questions, I noticed a change in Rendón's attitude. The longer we continued, the worse her attitude got. Clearly, the detective had her own ideas about what had gone down.

After an hour, my head was starting to pound and my fists were clenched in my lap, knuckles white, as my frayed patience and temper snapped. "Look, Detectives, I don't know what more you want me to say. I don't know who they were, why they attacked, or who sent them. What I do know is that they ambushed us and had no intention of letting us get out of there breathing. We did what was needed to survive."

"There are four dead mages, Ms. Costas," Rendón pointed out, her voice hard.

"And Zev is in a damn coma," I shot back, sick of the silent weight of her judgment. "If you think I'm going to apologize for what we did, think again."

"This is not the first time you and Mr. Aslanov have been involved in a suspicious death." She leaned forward, a militant light in her eyes. "In fact, you were there when Bryan Croft was killed, were you not?"

At the unexpected question, my jaw locked, and I bit my

tongue so hard it would be sore for days. Yeah, I was there, and even though logically, I understood that the corrupted magic that had twisted Bryan into something unrecognizable was ultimately at fault and not me, I still struggled with guilt for my part in his accidental death.

Mari had no qualms about shutting down this particular line of questioning. "Detective Rendón," she snapped, her voice ice-cold. "That particular case has been closed, has it not?" She didn't wait for the detective to answer. "I believe the Clarke Family absolved all parties of responsibility, as Mr. Croft died while in pursuit of his duties as Arbiter."

Red rose under the detective's olive skin and settled high in her cheeks. Hall shot her a quelling look she completely ignored as she doggedly stayed on track. "It doesn't negate the fact that Ms. Costas was involved."

Sabella broke her silence and firmly slapped Rendón down. "She was involved at the behest of the Arcane Council, Detective, and I believe your department was asked to direct inquiries on that incident to the council's legal representative."

Detective Rendón wasn't the only one caught off guard by that comment. So was I. Funny that the way I remembered my involvement in the Delphi mess was being brought in by Sabella as her proxy. I sure as hell didn't remember getting called in by the council. But there was no way I would risk pointing out that discrepancy, especially not in front of a detective with an obvious ax to grind.

"The council has no juris—" Rendón started only to have Hall talk over her, "We respect the Arcane Council's request and apologize for overstepping." He shot his partner a scathing look. "Some investigations are more difficult than others."

Something in Hall's expression and phrasing made me wonder what connection Detective Rendón had to Bryan

Croft or, more likely, the Clarke Family, because there was definitely something going on to garner that kind of heated reaction. Thankfully, Mari stood up, her face set in implacable lines. "This interview is done. I will not allow you to attack the woman who is clearly a victim in this. Your time is better spent investigating the deceased. If you have more questions for Ms. Costas, you can relay that request, in writing, to my office."

Hall got to his feet while Rendón did the same. "Ms. Ortiz." His voice stayed calm, completely counter to the simmering anger emanating from his partner. "We're not accusing Ms. Costas of any wrongdoing, but with the garage cameras disabled and Mr. Aslanov unable to talk, she is our only witness."

"And despite her recent injuries, she has shared, repeatedly and in detail, what occurred last night," Mari shot back, proving that if I could ever afford legal representation, I wanted it to be her. "There is nothing more she can give you to assist with your investigation at this time. If," she stressed, sinking enough implication into the one word to make her doubt loud and clear, "new developments arise, we'll be receptive to another meeting."

Hall was better than Rendón at hiding his frustration as he turned his attention to me. "Ms. Costas, we appreciate your time and assistance." He held out a business card that Mari intercepted. "If you think of anything, anything at all, please let me know."

I inclined my head and watched as he and Rendón left the room. Once they were gone, Mari sank into her chair and looked at Sabella. "That went as well as expected."

Sabella made a sound, but there was no way to tell if she agreed or disagreed with Mari's assessment. Before Sabella could say anything more, the door opened and we all turned to look at the young man in scrubs who poked his head in.

"Sorry to interrupt, Ms. Rossi, but you wanted to be informed if anything changed with Mr. Aslanov?"

My pulse jumped as Sabella stood up and started toward the door. "Yes?"

"He's awake."

CHAPTER FIVE

THERE WAS no way in hell I was staying in my room after that announcement, so it was a good thing neither Mari nor Sabella tried to stop me from going. The floor was cold against my bare feet as Sabella and I followed Mari down the hall and past the nurses' station to a small alcove with an unremarkable door. Mari stopped in front of the door, but I stumbled to a halt just outside the alcove, breathing through the stinging sensation nipping at my skin. I sucked in a pained breath and the magical pressure. *Ow, ow, ow.*

Sabella touched my elbow and gave me raised brows in silent inquiry. I managed a shrug, but the ward guarding the door was damn powerful, uncomfortably so. It was leaking out into the hall. Mari sketched a rune in the air just above the door. Power flared and followed her movements, leaving a fading afterimage in its wake. I recognized part of the rune for protection, but that was all I could catch before it disappeared, taking the discomforting press of power with it.

Mari opened the door. "Go ahead. I'll need to reset the ward."

We slipped past and into a private suite, where we waited

just inside the empty hall for her to reset the wards. The heightened security indicated Emilio shared Sabella's concern about a possible high-level threat, and I couldn't blame him. Anyone willing to take out an Arbiter and spark a Family feud wouldn't quibble over collateral damage to get their desired results.

Mari reset the ward then led us through an area that wouldn't be out of place in someone's home. It was like an oversized living room, complete with a small wet bar. Between that and the security, it was clear the hospital catered to Family patients and their privacy.

Mari went to a partially open door on the other side, where a murmur of voices spilled out. She rapped her knuckles on the door and peered around the edge. "Emilio?"

The door widened, and Emilio stepped out. I thought with Zev being awake, Emilio would look less stressed. I was wrong. His normally olive skin held an undertone of gray, his dark eyes were bloodshot, and his hair was a jumbled mess. He touched Mari's arm then switched his attention to where Sabella and I stood. His gaze flickered, and my stomach dropped. *Something's wrong.*

At my side, Sabella stiffened, and her question came out short. "What is it?"

Emilio dragged a hand through his hair, which explained his current messy hairstyle, dropped his head, and gripped the base of his neck.

At his reaction, my head grew light, the world tilting for a dizzying second. I grabbed Sabella's arm and held on. Sabella ignored me, her focus on Emilio. "Is Zev all right?" This time, her voice was less sharp but more demanding.

The normally unflappable head of the Cordova Family cleared his throat, straightened, and took a visibly deep breath. "For the most part, yes."

My knees liquefied with relief, but Sabella was unappeased and snapped, "Explain."

"Physically, he's good, and there's no lasting physical damage." Emilio dropped his hand from his neck. "But he's having a few issues with his memories."

No lasting physical damage. Emilio's phrasing bounced through my head, setting off alarm bells. Considering the concussion I endured thanks to cushioning Zev's fall, I couldn't figure out what was causing Emilio's concern. To offer reassurance, I took a gamble and said, "The doctor told me that some memory loss was expected with head injuries. Especially memories of what happened right before the injury occurred."

"It's a little more serious than that." Emilio's face was grim and his voice rough. "Zev's last clear memory is going after Jeremy."

His answer sent me mentally reeling. "What?" The word came out in a squeak. "Wait! You're saying Zev can't remember the last six months?"

Emilio nodded, delivering an emotional blow that kept on giving. My hand spasmed on Sabella's arm. "Is it permanent?" I croaked.

"The doctor's not sure," he said. "It could be temporary and return in the next couple of days as he recovers. The more he's around familiar faces, the better, but..."

"But?" Sabella gently pried my fingers from her arm.

Emilio took Mari's hand in his as a muscle jumped in his jaw. "But there's no way to tell. The doctor speculates that the longer it takes for them to come back, the higher the chance for permanent memory loss."

Stunned by that possibility, I turned away and struggled to accept the ramifications. Best-case scenario, this was a temporary blip and Zev's memories would return, including everything that was us. *Worst case?* I shook my head, ignoring the spike of answering pain at the movement. I couldn't think about the worst case. Not yet. I cleared my suddenly tight throat and angled my head over my shoulder. "Can I—"

"We," Sabella corrected, her gaze holding mine.

I inclined my head and corrected, "We see him? Maybe a couple more familiar faces will help?"

Emilio's expression said he wasn't sold on the idea. And if I was thinking clearly, I couldn't blame him. If familiarity was the trigger for Zev, then Emilio, the man whom he considered a brother and not just an employer, would be the epitome of all that, but I couldn't quash my unreasonable hope that I was important enough to Zev to make an impact. Emilio looked at Mari, who gave a small nod, then turned back to us and said, "Once the doctor's done with his exam, we'll see what he suggests."

Not in any position to make demands, I clung to Emilio's half-hearted reassurance. I stared at Zev's door, every part of me wanting to rush in and see him for myself. I didn't know how long I stood there, lost in a storm of worry and fear, before something tugged at my arm.

Sabella led me over to the couch. "Rory, you need to sit down before you fall down."

I sank down to the edge of the cushion as a curious fog clouded my thoughts. I braced my elbows on my knees, dropped my head into my hands, and closed my burning eyes. A hand rubbed comforting circles on my back, and I concentrated on that movement instead of the dark paths my thoughts wanted to travel.

It wasn't easy, especially since the last image I had of Zev kept cycling through my head. I went over and over what I could have done to get a different result, each time coming up frustratingly empty. Just as my tension hit a screaming level, Sabella called my name. I lifted my head and blinked.

She stood in front of me, a small impatient frown on her face. "Are you coming?"

"Where?"

"To see Zev."

I pushed to my feet, stumbling before regaining my balance. The doctor stood by the door with Emilio and Mari, all three looking in my direction. I followed Sabella, each step twisting the knots in my stomach tighter and tighter. The small group stepped aside, giving Sabella and me room to pass. We went in, but a privacy curtain was half drawn, revealing the foot of a bed where a lightweight duvet lay folded. I paused inside the door as Sabella moved forward, her composure rock solid. I wished I could say the same about mine. Instead, I drew in a deep breath and faked it.

"Zev, nice to see you awake." Sabella's voice was unconcerned, no indication of the worries swirling outside Zev's room.

"Sabella, what are you doing here?" The rough timbre of Zev's voice sent a shiver down my spine, and I curled my toes against the cool linoleum.

"Visiting you," she answered.

"Obviously," he groused. "Look, I'm fine."

"Really?" she chided gently. "Because according to the doctor, you don't remember the last six months."

Since my gaze was aimed at the floor, I caught the movement as Sabella walked over to the privacy curtain. I had just enough time to brace and lock a smile firmly in place before she shoved the curtain back. My gaze zeroed in on Zev, quickly taking in details. The back of the bed was raised so he could sit up. Between his dark eyes, heavy brows, tumbled strands of dark, shoulder-length hair, and his heavy scruff that merged into his neat Vandyke, his wan face was layered in shadows. A sheet was pulled to his waist, and he'd managed to switch the paperlike hospital gown for a T-shirt that stretched over his broad shoulders and covered his chest.

God, he looks good.

Relief rocked my shaky charade of nonchalance, but it was short-lived.

"What the hell are you doing here?" he snapped, anger and suspicion saturating the room.

Although I barely caught my wince at his reaction, there was jack shit I could do about the obvious strain in my voice. "Hello, Zev."

Zev's gaze bounced between Sabella and me, confusion and anger adding a bright hardness that hurt to see. "Sabella, why is *she* here?"

I forced myself forward when all I wanted to do was turn tail and run. "*She* is here because you and I are..." I stumbled a smidge and picked another way to phrase things. "Working together."

"Bullshit," he shot back. "Why in the hell would I work with you?"

Ouch. Refusing to acknowledge the whiplash of hurt, I folded my arms over my chest, cocked a hip, and gave him my best sneer. "Because I saved your ass, gorgeous."

I didn't think it was possible for his face to get darker, but it did. He folded his arms and jutted his chin, never breaking eye contact. "Again, I call bullshit." He looked at Sabella. "You're sure she's not part of the reason I'm here?"

"Why would I want you laid up in a hospital?"

"Same reason you would agree to deliver a kidnapped kid," he shot back with unerring accuracy. "Money."

Oh for the love of... "Since your memory is on the fritz," I snapped, my temper sparked at his reminder of how much of an arrogant jackass he could be, "I'll remind you that I had no idea Jeremy was what they wanted delivered, and the minute

I did, his safety became my priority. A decision I made well before you showed up, Mr. Aslanov."

He winced at my use of his formal name, but it was so fast, I wondered if I'd imagined it. "So you say, but I still don't trust you."

"No," I corrected, praying I wasn't making a huge tactical error as I stubbornly clung to the emotional foundation we'd laid in the last few weeks. "The correct verb there should be 'didn't.' You *didn't* trust me. That is no longer the case."

Zev's eyes widened in disbelief, and his gaze jumped to Sabella, who stood between us at the side of his bed. Reading his expression accurately, the older woman gave him a serene smile. "Despite the fact the two of you have provided quite the entertainment the last few weeks, even I have to admit you work well together."

His skepticism was replaced by confusion, but that didn't stick around long either because his unreadable mask snapped into place. He looked at me, and even though it hurt to do it, like poking at an open wound, I held his gaze, refusing to crumble under the obvious doubt staring back. His lashes drifted down, obscuring a flash of indefinable emotion, before he swept his gaze over me, foot to head, with an unmistakable deliberateness. When he finally reached my eyes, my face was hot with a mix of anger and arousal, a reaction he correctly interrupted based upon the arrogant curl of his lips.

I dropped my arms, wiggling my fingers so I wouldn't give in to the unholy urge to smack the smirk off his face. "You know, I didn't like your attitude when we first met, and I'm not liking it much now."

His grin widened, and he taunted softly, "Liar." Then he blinked as if the word had escaped without his permission, but he was quick to douse his momentary lapse. With a familiar arrogance that had all but disappeared in the last few weeks, he motioned to the door. "If it's so upsetting, there's the door."

This time, I couldn't hide my pained wince at his cold brush-off, but I managed to tuck my tattered pride around me like a regal cloak. I held his gaze for a heartbeat, maybe two. I had no idea what he saw in my eyes, but his own flickered with discomfort, and red seeped under his skin to ride along his cheeks before he got his jerk face back in place. Still, that glimpse of regret eased the worst of the lingering sting from his comment. Deciding two could play this game, I curled my lip in obvious derision and turned to Sabella, deliberately shutting him out. "Since we don't have time to play 'remember when,' I'm happy to work this on my own."

Zev let out an honest-to-goodness growl, clearly not keen on my offer, but I ignored Mr. Grumpy Pants. Sabella ducked her head and fussed with Zev's sheet, her lips quivering in such a way that I was sure she was trying not to laugh. Sure enough, when she lifted her head, amusement danced in her eyes.

So glad one of us is finding this funny.

"I appreciate the offer, Rory," she said. "But if you don't let him work with you, he'll just make a nuisance of himself."

"As if that's new," I muttered, then I heaved an aggrieved sigh. She might be right, but it didn't mean I had to be graceful about it. "Fine, whatever." I refused to look at Zev.

Something he clearly didn't like, because he demanded, "Exactly how far do you expect to get, Ms. Costas? It's my understanding that this attack targeted me due to my involvement in apprehending a rogue mage for the council. Pursuing such connections are out of reach for a Transporter. Not to mention dangerous."

I clasped my hands behind my back, where my white knuckles wouldn't be obvious, and made a conscious decision to keep my shoulders relaxed. "Dangerous? Like identifying your rogue mage and working with you to reverse a Drainer's Circle? Or protecting your ass from a Mirage-level illusion mage on steroids? Or hey, I know? How about being out with a frustratingly obstinate Arbiter only to get jumped by a strike team of mages and watching his back so he was still breathing at the end of it?" My sneer was full-blown, which was better than bursting into pissed-off tears. "Based on your track record, I'm fairly confident you need me more than I need you."

"I'm not sure I agree." He spread his arms wide, mockingly indicating his current situation. "Seems to me you're a magnet for trouble."

The urge to scream made my head feel like it was about to explode. I gritted out, "You're the one who likes trouble."

He arched a brow. "Not sure I like your kind of trouble."

My emotions were all over the place, but guilt nagged at me. I ignored it and let the devil on my shoulder free. "Could've fooled me. You seemed totally down with my trouble last night. In fact, you were jonesing for it."

Shock wiped his smirk away and left something else, something hungry and speculative. "Is that so?"

Feeling mean, I managed a shrug as I turned away. "I don't know. Maybe I'm lying, maybe I'm not, but you'll just have to wonder, won't you?"

Unable to take any more, I looked at Sabella, who was watching us both with a tiny frown. "If you'll excuse me, I think I'll head back to my room and see about getting out of here." I barely waited for her nod before I turned on my bare heels and stormed out of Zev's room.

Caught up in my misery, I rushed by Emilio and Mari with some muttered comment that I hoped was polite. A hand on my arm stopped my headlong rush to escape. "Rory."

I stopped and turned to find Mari studying me with obvious concern. "Are you okay?"

I managed a jerky nod. "Fine. I'm just going to head back and see about getting out of here." Maybe I would get lucky and Lena would be available as my getaway driver.

Mari's frown deepened. "I don't think it's wise for you to head back to your place." She looked over her shoulder at Emilio. "Until we know who sent that team, it's best to keep her and Zev close."

Oh hell to the no. I wanted as far away from Zev as I could get so I could rebuild my emotional walls. Once they were back in place, I would be able to handle his attitude. I opened my mouth to interject, but Emilio came up and stood behind Mari. "She can stay with us at the house. Sabella as well. At least until we have a better idea of who or what we're facing."

As much as I appreciated the offer, I wasn't comfortable accepting. "I'm not—"

"That would be lovely, Emilio," Sabella said from behind us.

Mari's hand dropped from my arm, and I slowly turned to see my employer standing in Zev's doorway.

I clenched my teeth because yelling at my boss was not wise, but I must have made a noise because her attention swung to me. "If what we suspect is true, it would not be safe for you to go home."

A pulse of trepidation smothered my emotional turmoil. If she was right, I wasn't the only one at risk. "What about Lena? Is she safe?"

Sabella looked at Emilio. "Can you get eyes on her?"

He considered it for a moment then said, "Yes, although it's my understanding she works for the Guild." He looked at me, and when I nodded, he continued. "That could be problematic with their confidentiality clauses for contracted jobs. She may not want eyes on her. Is there anyone she could stay with for the time being?"

I could think of one person, but that would be up to Lena. "I'd need to check with her, see what she'd like to do."

"Why don't you do that and see if she'd be willing to pack a bag for you as well?" Sabella said.

There was no missing the order couched in her suggestion. With no other recourse, I gave in. "Fine."

A few tense lines in her face eased. "Brilliant," she said, her attention shifting to Mari. "Would you mind taking Rory back to her room?"

I huffed out a breath. "I can go by myself, Sabella."

That earned me a sharp "Humor me."

Fine, whatever. I was done. If agreeing got me alone quicker, so be it. I turned to Mari. "Shall we?"

Despite the amused pity dancing in her eyes, she merely nodded and headed toward the exit, leaving me to follow.

CHAPTER SIX

MY BEAUTIFUL BABY, a rebuilt 1968 Mustang Fastback, prowled up the long curving drive to Emilio's Mexican villa that doubled as his not so humble abode. Late-morning sunlight danced along the midnight-blue paint, igniting the tiny starbursts that matched the white racing stripes. I agreed to let Lena drive my car over, and watching my sleek motorized beauty prowl closer, I found my low-level anxiety created by that decision lessened. Evan's familiar modest sedan followed.

I wandered down the stone steps toward the four-car garage, doing my best to ignore the grim-faced security positioned around the house. I waved to the older man sitting in Sabella's sedan on the far side. He touched his forehead with an acknowledging flick. According to Sabella, he was my temporary replacement. The doctor had advised her that I shouldn't drive for another twenty-four hours, so she requested a driver from the Guild.

I recognized the silver strands that belonged to Bernard —"Call me Bernie" when not on the job. A good man, he was a solid Transporter, even if a bit of a fuddy-duddy. Lena pulled in next to Zev's sleek matte black Harley, and then shut down the engine.

I turned as my girl's low rumble fell silent, then I edged around Zev's bike, unable to resist brushing my fingertips over the sun-warmed surface of the fuel tank. Yes, I was petting his bike, but there was something compelling about the blacked-out, liquid-cooled V-Twin-powered beast that made it hard to resist. Of course, the same could be said of its owner, but I wasn't going there. Not today.

I had spent last night locked in my head while I paced the spacious confines of my assigned guest room. I churned over the personal impact of Zev's unexpected memory loss, unable to settle on hurt, understanding, or resentment. Not that there was a right emotion to land on since it wasn't something I could fix, which left me equally parts frustrated and depressed. I couldn't change what had happened, but going forward, I could work with Emilio and Sabella to find out who was behind this mess. That approach was more problematic than it sounded for a couple of reasons.

First, I was still forging a reputation with the movers and shakers of Arcane society. Despite the combined influence of Sabella and, more recently and unexpectedly, Emilio, those doors were slow to open. Having Zev, a known entity, at my side meant that at least when I knocked, someone answered. But if I went out solo and started kicking down doors and asking pesky, intrusive questions, I could do more harm than good. Not just for Zev but for all involved. Not a smart move when Emilio's approval was still shiny and new. Even Sabella's opinion, as weighty as it was, wouldn't' be enough to hold back the resulting flood of irritated Arcane notables.

As much as I didn't want to admit it, I wasn't ready to swim in the shark-infested waters of Arcane society without Zev playing lifeguard. Even if he didn't remember why he would want to haul my ass out of deep waters in the first place.

Then there was the additional teeny tiny factor of what I was, a Prism. That fact was one that I wasn't comfortable sharing, because long ago, Prisms were used as personal magic shields for the rich and powerful, which gave new meaning to "putting your body on the line." Prisms were rare and highly coveted, to the extent that they had been ruthlessly targeted by powerful Arcane Families until they were all but wiped from modern history. An unhelpful result for someone who was an orphaned street kid filled with questions.

The only reason I even knew what to label my unusual ability was a chance meeting I'd had with a schizophrenic street tramp when I was a kid, long before joining the mercenary storehouse of the magically skilled. Even after I'd settled into the Guild, asking questions about what a Prism could do wasn't something I was comfortable doing. It wasn't until I left the Guild and struck out on my own that I finally started getting answers from, of all people, Sabella. She was only one of the few on my very short list of those who knew my secret, a list that included Lena and, more recently, Zev.

I worried that the list would soon contain more names, powerful names that were beginning to suspect what I was, especially after the Delphi project fiasco. Like Emilio and possibly the heads of both the Trask Family and the Clarke Family. Not to mention Zev's ex-girlfriend and current Trask Family Arbiter, Imogen Frost. So my secret was skating perilously close to being outed in a big, life-changing way.

Maybe the threat of exposure wouldn't have left my blood chilled or my mouth drier than the desert if Zev's current situation didn't put him six months behind in the game, but it did. At least until his memories returned—if they returned. It wasn't like I didn't know how to stand on my own. Hell, I'd been doing it my whole life, but without his buffering advice, my confidence in withstanding the brewing storm was shaky.

Despite my concerns, somewhere in the wee hours of the morning, I finally collapsed. Images of becoming chum in shark-infested waters filled my restless dreams, and I catnapped until sunrise. The thud of car doors closing snapped me out of my grim thoughts as Lena and Evan emerged from their respective rides. Realizing I'd stopped by Zev's bike, I moved forward and demanded, "Keys."

Lena tossed them my way without taking her attention from the stone-and-stucco elegance behind me. Not that I could blame her. Emilio's place was damn impressive.

I caught my keys then walked around my baby, unable to resist reassuring myself that she was fine. *No dings, no scratches. All good*.

"Seriously, Rory?" Lena drawled.

Standing at the passenger side of my car, I faced her over the roof. "What?"

Lena shoved her sunglasses into her gold-tinted auburn hair, her lips twitching. "You realize you're weirdly overprotective of this car."

"There's no such thing as being overly protective," I protested as I gave a sympathetic pat to the door, where Lena couldn't see, then popped the trunk.

"Unless you're an obsessive Transporter," Evan chimed in as he came up on Lena's side and curled an arm around her waist. Seeing them together, the stylish redhead and the silver-streaked brown-haired college professor, made the squishy part of me go, "Awww." It was only when I looked closer that I realized the redhead contained a ruthless streak a mile wide and there was nothing mild-mannered about the college professor hiding behind clear-lens glasses and a keyboard.

"You say obsessive, I say conscientious." I went to the

trunk and pulled out the small traveler's suitcase. I set the wheels on the brick pavers and extended the handle. "Thanks for bringing my stuff over."

"As if I would pass up an invite to the Cordova estate." Lena stepped out of Evan's hold and closed in as I grabbed my laptop backpack from the trunk.

My hand was on the trunk, ready to close it, when I realized Lena was waiting for me to look at her. So I did. "What?"

She studied me and obviously didn't miss the signs of my long night. "You okay?"

Not inclined to lie, especially considering how well she knew me, I gave a half-hearted shrug. "I'll survive." I pushed the trunk closed, hitched the backpack over one shoulder, and grabbed my suitcase. "Let's get this dropped off, and I'll take you on a tour."

I led the way inside, listening to Lena and Evan take in the gorgeousness that was Emilio's home. The front door was a wooden art piece of alder set in glass and wrought iron, and it opened into an expansive great room with stunning desert views framed in the floor-to-ceiling windows that spanned both floors. Leather furniture situated around the stone fireplace offered places to sit and chat. Off to the side, a kitchen decorated in more stone—either granite or quartz; I couldn't tell from where we stood—and stainless steel opened into the room. Despite the understated luxury, the interior's vibe was more along the warm and inviting side instead of the slick and too-gorgeous-to-use type.

I dragged my suitcase down the hall to the left, the rattle of wheels over tile following me to my room. I left it at the foot of the bed and shrugged off my backpack. Lena walked across the room to the French doors that led to a private courtyard that connected with the larger back patio. Ignoring her soft "Wow," I looked at Evan. "Thank you."

Behind the clear lenses of his wire-framed glasses that I knew were for show, he raised a brow. "For?"

I looked at Lena, who was still enthralled with the backyard. "For keeping her safe."

"I can do that all by my little ol' lonesome, Rory," my best friend shot back without turning around.

My lips quirked. "I know, but it doesn't hurt to have someone watching your back."

She turned, and her hands went to her hips. "I could say the same for you." I opened my mouth, but she cut me off, proving she really did know how my mind worked. "Zev doesn't count right now, and you know it."

I scowled, unable to argue her point. "Zev was the target, not me."

"And that makes a difference?" she demanded.

I thought so, but obviously she didn't. "Um, yes?"

She gave an exasperated huff and rolled her eyes. "Look, I know you can't tell me everything."

I appreciated the fact that she recognized it was "can't" and not "won't." Granted, it was a slight difference, but it was important, especially since Lena and I were closer than sisters. We had to be since we'd spent years covering each other's asses.

"But," she continued, "don't think I haven't noticed Sabella and Emilio roping you into this thing."

"No one's roping me into anything." I sank to the edge of the bed and ran a hand through my hair, accidentally pulling on strands attached to the still-tender spots on my skull. I winced and dropped my hand to my lap. "I need to be involved in this. Especially since Zev is all..." I waved my hand in the air. "As grateful as I am that he's still breathing, if the goal of this attack was to take him out of the equation, whoever is behind it still succeeded."

Evan cleared his throat and gained our combined attention. "Lena filled me in on the basics. You think one of the attackers was an electro mage?"

I nodded. "Unless there's some spell that can mimic a juiced-up Taser, I think it's a safe assumption."

Evan glanced at Lena, and they shared a long look and matching grim expressions.

Catching the exchange, I demanded, "What?"

Evan shook his head. "There are a couple of spells I can think of, but they would require serious prep work that wouldn't fit a blitz attack." He moved to a chair and sat. "I've got another question for you. The electro mage that attacked Zev, were they casting or combat?"

Since mages had two ways of harnessing their magic—innate strength of will or complexity of ritual—it wasn't an unexpected question. Mainly because a casting mage would demand a higher price tag, a good piece of information to have when dredging through the dark web for a name. "Combat." Then another thought hit me. "And not Guild," I added. Both Lena and Evan still worked for the Guild, so if a similar assignment hit the boards, they would already know.

His lips thinned, not liking the implication. "Which makes me more inclined to agree with Lena. We're probably looking for a mercenary."

Yeah, that felt right to me too. "Any names you can think of that would hire out?"

He pulled off his glasses, closed his eyes, and squeezed the bridge of his nose. "Names that would take on a high-level target like Zev are going to be well hidden."

I didn't like the tone of his voice. "But not to the king of all things electronic, right?"

He opened his eyes and held my gaze. "It's going to take time."

"How much time?"

Instead of answering, he looked at Lena, who came over

and sat next to me. When I did the same, she gave me a small, tight smile and covered my white-knuckled fist in my lap and squeezed. "Longer than we'd like, which means you need to be damn careful, Rory."

That seemed to be my life's theme lately. "I'm trying."

$$\blacklozenge$$

Too keyed up to sit around and brood, I took Lena and Evan on the promised tour of Emilio's house. There wasn't much to tour because I wasn't comfortable enough to go farther than the open, shared spaces—kitchen, living room, formal dining room, another smaller kitchen Lena labeled as a caterer's, and my favorite, the garage. And that was just the bottom floor. Admittedly, I might have drooled over the killer Maybach sitting apart from the other vehicles, but then again, who wouldn't?

As we came inside, we happened upon two men talking in low voices by the open front door. They glanced our way before returning to their conversation. One left and headed outside. The other, after lifting a hand in our direction, disappeared down the far hall. Emilio's security. They were easy enough to recognize because they all carried the low-level buzz of active magic and shared Zev's aura of intimidation. Clearly, Emilio wasn't taking any chances.

Only then did it strike me that there was no in-house staff hanging around. Other than the occasional security, we appeared to be alone. Well, not quite alone since Zev, Emilio, and Sabella were around somewhere. We continued our self-guided tour down one of the other halls and came up on a partially opened door. The sound of raised voices interrupted our hushed conversation. As a group, Lena, Evan, and I came to a stop and fell quiet, unabashedly eavesdropping.

"It's too soon." I recognized Sabella's voice, and she

sounded agitated, which was unusual for her. "The doctor said it could take a couple of days for his memories to return. We should give him that time before we call in a Muse."

"We don't have the luxury to wait and see." The unrelenting response belonged to Emilio. "Besides, I'm not comfortable sending Zev out at a disadvantage."

"Rory won't let anything happen to him." Sabella's comment pulled me up short. Not that I disagreed with her, but her confidence in me was disconcerting and maybe mortifying if Emilio read between the lines.

"I admit your Transporter's luck has been phenomenal. However, I'm not willing to bet Zev's life on the slim chance it will hold." Impatience colored Emilio's voice. "Not to mention she's not combat trained in the slightest."

"Pshaw, that's besides the point."

Because who needs combat training when you can just withstand an attack? I bit my lower lip to stifle the nervous snicker caused by that hysterical thought and shared wide eyes with Lena. Her startled comprehension was followed by a fierce frown, proof she was thinking something similar but, unlike me, not finding it funny. Evan watched us both with a furrowed brow and a gaze sharp with speculation.

"Are you willing to bet it against the agenda of an unknown memory mage?" Sabella's voice carried a chill edge, one not normally heard when she spoke to Emilio, someone that she considered family—or so I'd thought.

There was the sound of movement followed by a heavy silence before Emilio answered. "I understand your concerns, Sabella, but in the end, it's Zev's decision, not ours."

"All I'm asking is that you don't rush—" The insistent beep of an incoming call cut off whatever Sabella was saying. "Apologies, Emilio. I have to take this."

Panicked at being caught eavesdropping, I gazed around the hall and looked for an escape. I rushed to one of the doors we'd passed earlier and tried the knob. It opened, and I peeked around the edge of the door to find an empty workout room. I silently hissed at Lena and Evan and motioned for them to follow. We clustered into the room, and I eased the door almost closed until just a small, narrow slice remained open. We all froze in place, waiting to see what would happen next since we were too far away from the office to hear what was happening. We didn't have to wait long.

Heels clicked on the tile, coming closer and accompanied by Sabella's short, tense "When?" The clicks stopped just outside our hiding spot. "Are you sure?"

I held my breath, my gaze locked on the narrow opening, which Sabella's shadow fell across.

"No, don't do that. It's not safe."

My hands curled into fists at the uneasy note underlying Sabella's voice. It was hard to tell if she was worried, scared, or both. None of that sat easy with me.

"I'll meet you at my place." Then came another pause and a curt "Not necessary, thank you. I'm leaving now."

"Sabella?" Emilio called out.

Sabella's shadow shifted. "I have to go, Emilio. I'm sorry."

"You're not going alone, are you?" He was clearly concerned.

"Bernard's with me," she said. "I'll be fine. I just need to stop at home. I'll be back as soon as I can."

"All right," he said with what sounded like reluctance. "I'll talk to Zev and share your concerns, but..."

"But as you said, in the end, it's his decision." Sabella sounded resigned. "I understand. Just please, suggest he waits."

"I'll do my best."

"That's all I can ask," Sabella said. "I'll be back as soon as I can."

"Be careful," he warned.

"Always."

With that, we listened as the click of her heels faded away and was replaced by a lingering quiet. Lena tugged at my arm and pointed toward a set of double glass doors that led to the back of the house. Evan stood in front of one door, his hand on the knob, the other hovering over the glass pane. The uncomfortable buzz of magic raised the hair on my arms as he took care of whatever alarm monitored the exits. Then he slowly eased the door open and motioned for Lena and me to slip out. In seconds, we were outside and following the terra-cotta pavers around the house to the expansive patio that could easily be its own room.

We collapsed into a group of cedar-framed chairs clus-tered around a table instead of one of the many offerings edging the pool and stunning fire pit. For a few minutes, we stared at each other, not saying anything. I was trying to get my racing heart under control. Maybe it was the same for Lena and Evan, but I wasn't ready to ask.

Despite the smothering heat of the late morning, it was surprisingly comfortable under the combined efforts of the misting system and the lazily swirling fans perched in the rafters. Finally, I blew out a long breath. "Well, damn."

"Yeah, you can say that again," Lena muttered as she laid her head against the back of her chair and settled her sunglasses in place. "I need a drink."

"So do I." Feeling decidedly more steady, I pushed to my feet. "Water or..."

"Water works," she answered.

"Evan?"

"Same." He straightened his long legs and crossed them at the ankles. "Thanks."

I slid open the glass door leading inside to the living room, thankful it wasn't locked, and walked to the kitchen. My mind picked over Emilio and Sabella's conversation as I searched the cabinets for glasses. It was clear they were both worried, and it wasn't just about Zev.

There was one important reason Sabella would be resistant to calling in a memory mage. Zev knew what I was and what I was capable of, and as both Zev and Sabella had warned me, when that information became public, I would find myself in the crosshairs of the Arcane elite. It was why I was so keen on developing alliances like the one with Sabella, the matriarch of the oldest Arcane Family, and by some weird twist of fate, the Cordova Family, a local powerhouse.

Or maybe I'm giving myself too much credit.

My secrets probably paled in comparison with some of the others taking up room in Zev's head. He was an Arbiter, had been for years, and he grew up alongside Emilio, deep within the Cordova Family. Secrets were the lifeblood of his position, so maybe there were other, much more crucial reasons for Sabella to be worried. Other reasons that would explain her behavior. She wasn't the type to rattle easily, and something was definitely rattling her cage. Which made me wonder what was locked in Zev's head.

I finally found the right cupboard and was pulling down glasses when I heard, "Looking for something?"

CHAPTER SEVEN

At Zev's question, I froze, my view blocked by the open cupboard. "Glasses." The word came out steady with barely a squeak to reveal my racing heart. *Go, me!* I pulled down the glasses and closed the door, only then looking at the man behind me.

He shifted his dark eyes from me to the still-open patio door where Lena and Evan sat quietly talking. I used the fridge's in-door ice maker to fill the three glasses and did my best to subtly gauge his appearance. He looked good for someone recovering from a head injury. Yesterday, pale undertones had washed out his normally olive tone, but today, it was back to normal. He stood with his hip against the counter, his long legs encased in well-worn jeans paired with a simple navy-blue T-shirt and rubbed a hand over his shadowed jaw.

Cold water splashed over my fingers, and I bit off a surprised hiss. *Quit ogling the man.* I focused on the task at hand, with the harsh self reminder that this was not my Zev but the initial pain-in-my-ass Zev from months ago. I concentrated on filling the glasses and nearly jumped out of my skin when he brushed against me. Once again, water splashed over my fingers from the nearly full glass in my hand. I set it on the counter then wiped my wet fingers against my jeans. Only then did I risk shooting him a narrow-eyed glare. "Not cool."

"Sorry." He didn't sound sorry but continued to reach around me, opened the cupboard, and grabbed a glass.

I lifted my chin and narrowed my eyes. "If you give me a second, I'll be out of your way."

He looked down at me as he closed the cupboard. "Never said you were in the way."

I deliberately looked at the small space between us, silently indicating his invasion of my personal bubble. "Could've fooled me."

His lips curved up, and he put a few more blessed inches between us. My internal "boo" of disappointment coincided with my breath of relief at gaining a sliver of Zev-free air.

Damn, I'm losing it.

Gathering up my three glasses, I gave him a magnanimous "Thank you" and skirted around him. Escape was within reach when he called my name. I stopped at the threshold of the patio. Lena looked over and raised her eyebrows in silent inquiry. Since my back was to Zev, I was free to roll my eyes to express my aggravation. She sent me an unrepentant grin. Plastering on a patiently polite half smile, I turned. "Yes?"

Zev was at the fridge, his glass under the water dispenser and his attention on me. "You mind if I join you?" He indicated the patio.

I searched his face, looking for a clue about his motivation. Finding none, I said, "No, feel free."

"Thanks." He checked his glass then pulled it away. "I wanted to—"

"Zev." We both turned to see Emilio coming down the hall on the far side of the living room. "You got a second?"

Zev shot me a look, but answered, "Yeah."

Emilio caught sight of me. "Morning, Rory."

"Morning, Emilio." I ruthlessly squashed a squirm of guilt about eavesdropping on his discussion with Sabella but couldn't help wondering what Zev's decision would be.

Emilio looked out the windows and spotted Lena and Evan. He raised a hand, and they waved back. He turned to me. "I'm guessing Lena brought your stuff to you?"

"And my car," I blurted, suddenly feeling awkward.

He frowned. "I understood you couldn't drive. Doctor's orders."

Okay, that sounded a little too close to patronizing for my comfort. My smile tightened as my independent feathers ruffled. "Another twenty-four hours, then I'm good." An awkward silence reigned as both men continued to watch me. I managed a single, careful shrug despite juggling three glasses and tilted my head toward the patio. "I'm just going to..."

"Of course, sorry." Emilio waved me off. "Didn't mean to keep you." He turned to Zev. "I have something I want to discuss with you."

I left them to it and rejoined my friends. Evan was working on his phone, lines of concentration on his face. Hopefully, he was digging through the dark web in search of a mercenary needle in a money-grubbing haystack. I set the glasses on the table with a relieved sigh.

Lena leaned forward and grabbed her glass. "What's wrong?"

Instead of admitting to my endless loop of "Will he, won't he?" on Zev's answer to Emilio's proposal on bringing in a Muse, I kept it simple. "I need to get out of here." I set Evan's glass in front of him and took mine to my seat, which I promptly collapsed into. "I don't think I can handle being stuck here all day."

"You know, people pay a pretty penny to be stuck in what amounts to a private resort," Lena teased as she lifted her glass. "There's this thing called relaxation. You should try it."

"There's nothing relaxing about staying here," I muttered as I stretched out my legs, slumped farther into my chair, and stared unseeingly at the pool. I drank my water and thought through my options. I had questions, lots of them. First and foremost, what the hell was going on with the council and the circumstances surrounding Theo's death? Names would be great, like the names of who Sabella suspected was behind this and why. If the gods of fate really liked me, I would love a few minutes with whoever was sharing their concerns with Sabella because their insight might trigger a lead on who was targeting Zev.

I was fairly sure Emilio would be privy to that information, especially after his earlier comments in the office, but there was no way to ask. Not only would he have no reason to share, but my asking would also just raise uncomfortable questions. At least with Sabella, I stood a chance at getting answers, but she wasn't there. She was off to some mysterious meeting that I was doing my damnedest not to worry about. A rational little voice reminded me she had survived the wilds of Arcane shenanigans for over half a century and would be fine on her own for the afternoon.

So if I couldn't pester Emilio or Sabella for information, where else could I poke around?

Scene of the crime.

I shoved myself upright then planted my feet flat on the ground. My sudden reaction caught Lena and Evan's attention. I ignored Evan in favor of my best friend and premier partner in crime. "You busy this afternoon?"

"It's Sunday, so no." She considered me for a long moment. "Do I dare ask why?"

I shot a look over my shoulder at the empty living room then leaned in and dropped my voice. "I want to go back to the parking garage."

Lena pushed her sunglasses up into her hair, her gold-flecked green eyes sharp. "Again, why?"

I hesitated, mainly because Evan was sitting there. "Maybe if I go back, I'll remember something important." That sounded lame, but trying to explain my actual intentions without cluing in Evan was beyond me at the moment.

"Like what?" Lena pressed.

I shrugged. "I don't know. Something, anything. I can't just sit here and twiddle my thumbs."

Long, painted nails drummed against the table as she studied me. "You're not telling me something."

Evan looked up from his phone, clearly joining the conversation even though he didn't say anything.

Their combined scrutiny was making me antsy. "There are many things I'm not telling you and not because I don't want to. I can't."

Lena made a noncommittal sound, but Evan called me out. "She wants to go back and see if there's a magical echo of the attack."

My jaw dropped, and I sputtered. "I... you..." I finally settled on "How long?"

"How long have I known what you are?"

I managed a jerky nod.

"A few weeks." He gave me a small smile. "But I started putting the pieces together after you dragged my ass out of that dual-level trap."

"Dammit." It came out soft but not soft enough because he chuckled. I gave him a half-hearted grin. "I wondered if you'd start digging after that."

"You should've known I would." He set his phone facedown on the table, braced his elbows, and laced his fingers together in a true professor pose as he studied me. "When you reversed the magic through the sub-rosa runes, it should've fried your ass, leaving you in worse shape than me. Especially as you aren't an electro mage and it was configured with a magical infinity loop. Instead, you snapped the spell and hauled me out of there, singed but alive. Made me wonder if there was more to you than met the eye."

Unable to hold his gaze, I scratched a nail against a bump of dirt on the table. "How far did you get?"

He waited until my gaze went back to his, and this time, I couldn't miss the sympathy in his eyes. "Far enough." He templed his index fingers. "You know I can bury the clues deeper if you want."

It was tempting, very tempting to take him up on his offer, but...

Lena gave a derisive snort. "Don't bother. It'll just be a waste of your time."

She wasn't wrong, but it didn't stop me from shooting her a dirty look before I turned back to Evan. "I appreciate the offer, but smart-ass over there is right. I'm running on borrowed time." It was a sad truth considering how hard it was to hide the fact that I was a Prism when I kept ending up in situations where that was the only thing I had to save my ass. I thought of Zev and Evan. *Or the asses of others.*

Evan broke the quiet. "Then I hope you have some sort of fallback plan in place."

"I'm working on it." Which wasn't a total lie. When I left the Arcane Guild and set myself up as an independent contractor to the Arcane elite, I hoped that by the time my secret was out, I would have cultivated the necessary alliances to cover my ass. Should've known that was harder than it sounded. Silly me.

Zev had about lost his mind once he realized what my

plan entailed. He was quick to point out that contracts were not alliances and there was a world of differences between the two. His exact words? *"Contracts will turn on your ass once the check is cashed and the job is done. Hell, some won't even wait that long."*

At the time, the surety in his voice had smothered my desire to argue. Especially after gaining unwanted attention from both the Clarke and Trask Families thanks to my recent role in the Delphi project fiasco. So that sterling reputation I was trying to build held a few tarnished spots. It also meant I was racing against the clock toward a finish line I wasn't ready to cross. My pit crew was frighteningly small, and if I had a blowout, I wasn't sure the combined efforts of Lena, Evan, and Sabella would be enough to keep me in the race.

"I think you need to work faster." Evan's comment yanked me out of my dismal thoughts.

In a bad Scottish accent, I shot back, "I'm givin' her all she's got, Captain."

He shook his head as Lena snorted in amusement. A figure moved out from around the house and gained our attention. *Security.* We watched in silence as he walked along the perimeter, well out of earshot, but none of us wanted to test that theory.

When he disappeared, Lena got us back on topic. "You are not going to the parking garage again."

"Why not?" I replied.

"Because," Lena said even as Evan's phone vibrated on the table. "You're staying here under guard because Emilio and Sabella don't think you're safe."

"Or they want to keep an eye on you," Evan muttered as he picked up his phone.

Since I couldn't argue Evan's point, I ignored him and stuck with Lena. "Which is why I'm asking you to come with me."

"No, you're asking me to let you be bait." She wagged an admonishing finger. "Don't deny it. I know you, babe. Besides, it's been two days since the attack. Not only has the scene been processed by the Arcane Criminal Response Team and the Phoenix police, but there's no guarantee any magical echoes survived the processing."

I ground my teeth in frustration, unwilling to concede her very valid point. The ability to "see" magical echoes was a recent discovery and a skill I was still developing. As a highly skilled Key, Lena knew all about reading magical traces, as it was essential in breaking curses, so as much as I didn't want to, I would have to bow to her expertise. If she believed there would be nothing to follow, then a trip to the garage was pointless.

She continued to hold my gaze, but her voice softened. "Give me another option."

I looked away, aimed a glower out across the yard, and considered my alternatives. "I can't just sit around. It's not who I am."

"Not to mention you're avoiding Zev," Lena drawled.

I switched my glare to her and didn't bother lying. "So? It's hard to be around him right now."

Sympathy softened her features. "I get it, but if we're lucky, Emilio will get that Muse in and bring your Zev back."

Unable to shake off Sabella's concerns about the solution, I bit my lip, torn. "I'm not sure it'll be that easy."

"Maybe, maybe not, but if you want your man back, I'd say it's worth a shot. Wouldn't you?"

Oh, I wanted *my* Zev back, but not if it would harm him. I mean, we managed to find our way to each other before, so we could do it again. *Right?*

Before I could slide down that rabbit hole, Evan asked, "Want my suggestion?"

"Does it involve hacking ACRT or the police system so

we can access the reports?" I was borderline joking but quickly realized that might just be plausible.

"No, something that won't get me in trouble." He lifted his phone. "I'm going to go do lunch with a buddy."

"Okay?" I drew the word out.

"Buddy?" Lena asked, her attention on the phone in Evan's hand.

"It's just Max," Evan reassured her, clearly picking up on the hint of green in Lena's question.

The frown forming on her forehead cleared. "From your D and D nights?"

"One and the same," he confirmed. "He happens to work for ACRT in their IT division, as a database administrator."

Cautious excitement stirred. "And how do you plan on getting this buddy of yours to agree to share internal reports without losing their job?"

"Leave that to me." Evan sent one last text and pocketed his phone.

As far as reassurances went, it was questionable, but since he didn't appear concerned about the possible ramifications and I had enough on my plate, I did just that. "Okay."

"And while he's doing that, I'll swing over to the Guild," Lena offered. "And see if anyone's been hit up for a big-money side job."

"Whoever they were, they weren't Guild," I reminded my friend.

"I know." She sounded exasperated. "But a job like that, requiring the skills to target someone like Zev, they might approach a Guild Blade."

Blades were assassins and one of the Guild's two shadow groups that worked outside of the public light. Their names were not made public, not even to other Guild members, but I could think of one who shared a personal connection with Lena. "Are you sure he'll talk to you?"

Evan froze in his chair, his head whipping toward Lena, his eyes narrowed. "You are not talking to Cas."

The fact that Evan knew exactly who the Blade was surprised me. It also indicated he and Lena were a lot deeper into the relationship game than I'd suspected.

But Evan had also made a massive blunder, and true to the red in her hair, Lena's temper erupted. "Excuse me?"

Before things got hot, I redirected the blast. "I wouldn't think Cas would take a job like that."

"He wouldn't." Lena sounded sure. Probably because, as she had once explained, he had a personal code, and one of his rules was similar to mine—you had to be able to live with whatever job you took. "But he might have heard about it or have an idea of who *would* take it." She shot a look at Evan. "Either way, it gives us another angle to work with. Right?" The last was a dare to Evan.

Temper flashed in Evan's eyes, but he reluctantly agreed. "Right." He pushed up from his chair, clearly done with the conversation but not done making his point, because he stalked around the table toward Lena. She watched him advance, her jaw angled in a silent dare. Which worked, because Evan caught her chin, tilted her head back, and kissed her—hot and hard. When he was done, her face was flushed but not because of her temper. "I'll drop you off and then pick you up after lunch."

"Fine." Her voice was husky, and I hid my grin.

"Fine," he echoed, then he stepped back so she could stand.

I collected our glasses and followed my friends inside. After leaving the glasses in the sink, I followed Evan and Lena to the door. "You two enjoy your lunch. I'll just..." I trailed off and waved my hand. I had no idea what I would do, but this place was big enough that I could avoid Zev. Maybe.

Lena stopped at the bottom of the steps, her hand in Evan's, and turned to me. "We'll call you, okay?"

I nodded and managed to keep my smile in place as they got into Evan's sedan and drove away. Heaving a sigh, I turned back to the house. I had another floor to explore.

CHAPTER EIGHT

THERE WERE FEW SURPRISES UPSTAIRS, but strolling the halls gave me a chance to tuck away my frustration at being sidelined. Three halls branched off a main gathering area mimicking the floor below. The first hall was lined with closed doors, most likely private bedrooms or unused guest rooms. As tempting as it was to peek inside to verify my assumptions, I didn't. Mainly because I'd gained a shadow when I returned from seeing Lena and Evan off. Leaner and lighter than Zev, the shadow clearly belonged to Emilio's security. He was good at being unobtrusive, but the itch of his magic against my skin acted like a warning sensor.

In the second hall, I found a couple of offices with the sterile feel of a hotel business center, and a game room complete with a beauty of a pool table. If I hadn't been so antsy, I might have picked up a stick and indulged, but with my concentration shot, I continued my self-directed tour.

In the last hall, I found a library tucked behind a set of stained glass doors. I left one of the doors partially opened as I slipped inside. Wide wooden shutters guarded the windows on the far wall and kept the sunlight at bay. Hints of lemon oil and sandalwood drifted on the air, easing my edginess to something less twitchy. A book lover's buffet filled the custom wall shelves. Unable to resist, I peered at the titles and found a little bit of everything available.

I picked my way through the shelves. I would pull out a book, flip through it, put it back, and move on to the next eye-catching title. As the minutes passed, the annoying prickle from my silent watcher faded. I looked up from a dog-eared thriller and, with a small smirk, stared at the empty doorway. *Guess someone got bored.* I put the book back and continued perusing while the last tendrils of tension drifted away.

When I came across a thick leather-bound tome on Arcane Families, curiosity got the better of me. I pulled it free and took it over to the couch. Bracing the thick tome on the arm of the couch, I toed off my shoes, curled up into the corner cushion, and proceeded to get lost in the maze of connections that made up the Arcane Families.

For some reason, I had assumed the book would simply contain a directory filled with outdated dynastic lines that ended a generation or so earlier. Yet when I started with the most obvious family first, the Cordovas, I found that wasn't the case. It gave a historical overview of the Cordovas' rise to power in the Southwest, with references cited for more detailed information. After flipping the page, I found a lengthy list of business ventures and charitable organizations directly connected to the family. After that came the genealogical tree, the branches thick and heavy with names, titles, and dates. When it transitioned to the current genera-tion, not only did it have Emilio's name noted—with his date of birth and current position—but his nephew, Jeremy, was also included. The label of "presumptive heir" was handwrit-ten, along with the date of Jeremy's mother's recent death, but his father's date of death was in typeface. *The poor kid had a hell of a year.*

I found Zev's name easily enough since he was the Cordovas' Arbiter. Absently, I noted his date of birth and realized he'd celebrated his thirtieth birthday a couple of months back, which made him just shy of three years older than me. But it was the familial line connecting him to Emilio that shocked me. Maybe it shouldn't have since Jeremy had referred to Zev as "uncle" when I first met the two, but when I had asked Zev about the family connection, he denied it, saying he was more of an honorary uncle than a blood-tied one. But if I was translating the genealogical chart correctly, Zev was Emilio's first cousin on his mother's side.

I stared at the page, trying to figure out why Zev would lie about his heritage, my finger absently tracing the lines. *Solid line from Jeremy to his father, Alan. Solid double line from Alan to Emilio.* My finger stilled on the dotted line connecting Zev to his parents. *Dotted line?*

On a hunch, I scanned the page for a key that would indicate what the different line types meant. There wasn't one, so I flipped to the back and found an appendix, complete with the all-important key. A dotted line indicated adoption.

My mind churned over this newly discovered fact, uncertain what to make of it, if anything, but my heart squeezed a little at the tiny insight into Zev's life. Watching Emilio and Zev, I didn't doubt the strong connection there, one closer to that of brothers than cousins, but Zev had always stood a little apart. I thought it was because of his position, but what if there was something more to that? Not that I was one to talk. Orphaned young and splitting my time between shelters and group homes by the time I was seven or eight, I didn't have much in the way of family memories to pull from, but the inherent loneliness that came from not having roots, that I got. Did Zev ever feel the same?

I continued to flip through the pages, stopping at names I recognized. There were a few more handwritten notations on various pages, but most of the information appeared to be fairly recent. It made me wonder if such a book was something all families kept. If so, did they submit annual updates to some central entity? When I got to the entry on the Clarkes, Lena's name at the bottom of the page, complete with an asterisk, yanked my wandering mind back on track. I didn't know why it caught me off guard. I knew the story and could guess what the asterisk meant, but I still turned to the key for the notation. There it was: *Line Excised.*

The entry for Lena's mother noted she was the bastard daughter of one of Leander Clarke's brothers. That wasn't to say that Leander—the head of the failed LanTech, a company specializing in magic-infused technology and part of the Delphi project debacle—would ever acknowledge the connection, but there was no denying DNA. But that wasn't Lena's mom's only sin. When she'd had the audacity to get involved with a First Nation Shaman, she was all but blacklisted from the Clarke Family Christmas card list. As their only child, Lena became a negotiating tool in her parents' constant conflicts. To get away from that hot mess, when she was thirteen, she voided all claims to the Clarke Family or the First Nation Tribes and joined the Arcane Guild. Essentially, she made herself an orphan. It was a drastic but, as she explained, necessary step, especially when her mother was disowned a couple of years later. It wasn't my place to argue, and after my own recent experiences with various families, including the Clarkes, I totally understood her decision.

All those notations made me curious enough to look up Sabella's family. Not the Rossis, which she had married into, but the one she was born into, the Giordanos. No way could there be a record of notable Families without including one of the original Arcane Families. Sure enough, the Giordano

Family was there, taking up their fair share of pages. Unsurprisingly, I discovered that the family originated in Italy, where Sabella still kept a home.

I skimmed the overview, absently noting that the list of attached businesses and charities was much longer than the lists of the Cordovas or the Clarkes. I flipped to the genealogical chart and went straight to Sabella. Three solid lines led to her grown children who were scattered across the globe, something she freely shared during her amusing stories of her offspring's adventures. Her late husband was also listed, and I noted that he had died roughly twenty years ago. From the way she spoke of him with such love and lingering sorrow, I had expected the loss to be more recent. That it wasn't spoke volumes about the depth of their relationship. I rubbed at the ache in my chest that the realization brought.

Sabella's date of birth put her closer to seventy than the sixty I had assumed even though she could easily be mistaken for a timeless fiftysomething. My eye caught a double line with a slash through it, connecting Sabella to another name, Juliana. *A sibling?* Studying the names, I realized the two women shared the same date of birth. "No way," I muttered, shocked. Just to be certain, I went to the key to check. Sure enough, that slashed double line indicated twins. "Holy cow," I breathed. As much as she spoke about her family, it was strange that Sabella had never mentioned a twin sister.

After flipping back to the family tree, I looked closer and discovered something disturbing. Juliana and her husband shared the same death date and were survived by their only daughter, Alessandra. Using Alessandra's date of birth, the only information listed for her, I did the math. She would have barely been out of her teens when her parents died, and if she was still around, she would be in her late forties with fifty closing in fast. I ran my finger over the name, something skittering on the edges of my mind. Before I could pin it down, a knock on the doorframe sent the thought tumbling away. I lifted my head and blinked back to the here and now to find Zev standing in the doorway.

When I didn't say anything and just continued to stare at him, he cocked his head. "Am I interrupting?"

I dropped my attention to the pages in my lap, heat rushing under my cheeks as I gave a short headshake. "Nope, sorry." I closed the book and then lifted my gaze. "I was just killing time." When I noted Zev's frown, my preoccupation disappeared. "What happened?"

"Nothing." He came in, and instead of taking one of the chairs facing the couch, he wandered the room.

Watching him, I murmured a disbelieving "Right."

He stopped near the shelves and turned to face me.

I wasn't surprised when his frown deepened to a scowl and he folded his arms over his chest. It was a familiar pose and one he liked to use, especially when I called him on his shit. Like now. I held his stormy gaze. "Normally, I wouldn't bother, but considering your current circumstances, this once, I'll remind you that look doesn't work on me."

His jaw flexed, then he looked away, one of his hands going to the back of his neck, where it stayed as his scowl eased and frustration replaced it. "I don't even know why I'm here."

I waited until he looked at me before answering, "Do you want me to leave?" Not that I wanted to. Not only had I been there first, but it was hard to ignore his agitation. Obviously, his conversation with Emilio had not gone well.

"No." He dropped his hand, and it curled into a fist at his side. "Stay, please. I need to talk to you."

"Okay." I drew the word out, uncertain of what was coming.

"I owe you an apology."

I blinked. *Not what I expected.* "For?"

"We can start with my comments at the hospital."

I bit back my initial snippy reaction, because although he was clearly uncomfortable, he sounded genuine. A tiny flicker of hope sparked. "Did you... Are your memories—"

He shook his head. "No, it's still a blank."

"Oh." I tried to hide my disappointment, but his sympathetic grimace indicated I failed. It was my turn to look away. I played with the book in my lap, not wanting to watch as sympathy morphed to pity. I wasn't sure my heart could take it.

"Rory."

I refused to look at him.

He left the shelves and took one of the nearby chairs. He leaned forward, his arms on his knees, his attention on me. "Emilio caught me up on what's been happening."

I glanced up. "That's good."

He dipped his chin but didn't break eye contact. "Yeah, seems things have kind of hit the fan in the last few months."

I couldn't help my lip twitching at his massive understatement. "That's one way to put it."

His gaze drifted to my mouth and came back up. "He wants to bring in a Muse, see if we can get my memories back."

My fingers tightened on the book, but otherwise, I refused to react. "Isn't that what you want?"

"Considering there's a very high probability that something locked in my head will help us figure out who attacked us, sure. Not to mention, I don't like working in the dark, and without knowing all the current threats, I can't do my job."

"Family first." It slipped out before I could censor it and carried the bitter edge of an old argument.

Zev didn't miss it. "Yeah, that's kind of my job description."

"I know what your job is, Zev." Boy howdy did I know. "I know exactly how the game is played."

"Do you?" he shot back. His eyes narrowed, and he cocked his head as if listening to someone or something. "This feels familiar."

My choked laugh was strained. "Because it is." Before he could push us deeper into treacherous waters, I waved my hand as if wiping away our conversation. "It's my turn to apologize. I took us off track. Let's go back to my question."

He arched an eyebrow with enviable ease. "Which one?"

My smile was real, mainly because I appreciated his willingness to let the painful conversation go. "Do you want a Muse poking in your head? Is it safe?" When he opened his mouth to answer, I held up a hand. "For you, Zev? Is it safe for you?" His dark gaze searched my face, but I had no idea what he was looking for, and I wanted to ensure he understood what I was asking, because I couldn't forget Sabella's unease about bringing in a Muse. "I get that you agree with Emilio and want to protect the Family, but I'm more concerned with you and your well-being. Is there a risk to using a Muse?"

"Any time magic is involved, so is risk." His answer sounded memorized, as if he was giving it only half of his attention.

I wasn't in the mood to play word games. "But will you be safe?"

He shook off whatever was bothering him and gave a negligent shrug. "I'm sure I'll be fine. The doctor believes my memories will come back. He's just not sure when. Bringing in a Muse is just nudging the process along."

It sounded like he was quoting Emilio, and I wasn't quite successful at stifling my disbelieving snort.

For the first time, that spark of wicked humor emerged, and he asked, "Are you trying to protect me?"

"Someone needs to." My response revealed too much. Even knowing that, I couldn't stop pushing. Hell, to be honest, I wasn't sure I wanted to. "Let me ask you a different way. If it was just you, no Cordovas, no Emilio, would you take this chance or wait it out?"

I held his gaze as the quiet stretched between us. Finally, he said, "I'd still want to do it."

"Why?" I pushed, looking for something different than a ready-made response.

It took a long moment, but he finally admitted, "Because of this right here."

I frowned, not understanding. "This what?"

His gaze gained a peculiar intensity, and for a moment, I thought he was fighting a grin, but then he said, "Whatever it is that's between you and me."

I blinked. "That... what..." I couldn't get my tongue untangled.

This time, there was no missing his amusement in the brief flash of white in his goatee. "Yeah, that." His grin faded. "I may not remember specifics, but I know myself well enough to recognize there is something between us, something strong enough to override my doubts about you, that drives me to seek you out, wants your opinion, and keeps me hard and aching at night." For a heart-stopping moment, I caught the burn of a slumbering hunger that ignited my own before he banked it. "So yeah, even if the Family had no part in this, I'd still want to take this chance."

I stared at him, and the near-constant ache I'd carried in my chest since I walked into his hospital room and realized he'd lost us eased. My mouth was dry, and I wasn't sure if it was nerves or anticipation or both, but I had to swallow a couple of times to find my voice. "Well, okay, then."

His grin reappeared at my lame response.

Before I could figure out what to say, my phone vibrated.

I dug it out of my pocket with a muttered "Hang on." An unfamiliar number was on the screen. I bit my lip, hesitating. Part of me, the one all about what was currently happening with Zev, wanted to ignore the call, but logic prevailed. "I'm sorry," I said as I accepted the call. "I've got to take this." I set the book aside, brought the phone to my ear, and got up from the couch to walk away from Zev. "Hello?"

A jumble of sounds hit my ear, and it took a few seconds to piece them together. Heavy breathing. Faint shouts. Running feet. Then my name in a harsh voice. "Rory."

"Who is this?"

The answer was a garbled response I couldn't understand, but I could make out faint shouts growing louder, sharper.

"Hello?" I pressed the phone tighter against my ear, hunching my shoulders and sticking a finger in my other ear as if any of that would help me figure out who was on the other end. "Who is this?"

The muffled response cleared enough for me to catch "... waiting for... at Sabella's..."

Comprehension hit on a cold wave. "Bernard! Where are you?" I spun around and met Zev's gaze as I rushed to the door. "Bernard!"

A pained grunt filled the line, followed by the sharp crack of impact, then nothing.

CHAPTER NINE

I was in the back seat of one of Emilio's SUVs, white-knuckling my phone as I hit Redial for the umpteenth time, praying the result would be different. It wasn't. I hung up after the fifth unanswered ring and tried not to dwell on how difficult it was to relinquish the wheel to my security shadow, who was introduced as Locke.

After Bernard's aborted call, I blew by Zev and raced down the stairs, determined to get my keys and haul ass to Sabella's despite the doctor's orders not to drive. It didn't take Zev long to catch up with me and pick another course of action, one where Locke did double duty as driver and potential backup. Once in the SUV, I kept trying to reach Bernard as Zev gave Locke directions to Sabella's. Thankfully, Locke knew what he was doing behind the wheel and managed to avoid getting pulled over even though we were breaking all the speed limits. We managed to turn in to the pricy Eagle's Nest subdivision in record time.

"Rory." Zev's quiet voice from the front passenger seat brought my head up.

I followed his gaze and saw that the electronic gate that

guarded Sabella's long drive was wide open. The dread crawling along my spine deepened. "Shit," I whispered.

Locke didn't even slow as he took the entrance and we raced up the curving drive. The sedan came into view, parked in its familiar place by the front courtyard. I tossed my phone on the seat as the SUV rocked to a stop behind the car, then I threw my door open, ignoring Zev's hissed warning. There was an unnatural stillness in the air and a heavy, disturbing quiet. I left my door open, unwilling to break the strange tension by closing it.

My magic slipped over my skin, and by the time I moved up to the sedan, it was firmly in place. First, I noticed the slashed tires. The second thing I noticed was the clear skid marks where someone had peeled out in a hurry. I looked over the sedan's trunk to find Zev frowning, his attention aimed low. "Slashed?"

He turned his hard gaze to me. "Yeah."

"Same here." Both of us kept our voices quiet.

Locke came up behind me on a wash of power that pressed against my shield. His voice was equally low when he said, "Door."

Zev turned to where Locke indicated, and I did the same. Sabella's front door was wide-open. I rounded the sedan to Zev. Only when I was at his side did I murmur, "That's not good."

"No, it's not," he agreed.

Locke came up on my other side until all three of us were facing Sabella's house. "Rear access?"

"Won't work. Backyard's all but built into the mountainside." Zev's voice was curt. "Give me a second."

A thin aura of blue ignited around him as he brought his magic up. The pressure against my shield rose, and bookended by the two mages, I deepened my hold, thickening the buffer between me and their power. Just enough to regain some breathing room. In my head, a dull, protesting throb awoke.

Zev lifted his face, the blue of his magic turning his eyes blind. A faint shadow danced overhead and quickly gained the shape of a raptor. A pulse of magic echoed along my shield as Zev's magic connected with the bird. Its lazy glide gained focus as it silently tightened its circles above Sabella's house and dropped lower with each pass. Unlike the inky feathers of the first hawk I'd met during my initial encounter with Zev, this one was a mix of browns and whites. Even better, it wasn't trying to gouge my eyes out. I tried not to fidget as the bird continued its back-and-forth sweep, but with each passing second, my tension rose.

Finally, the hawk disappeared behind the house, and a moment later, Zev said, "No movement near the house." His voice came out detached as he continued to stare ahead. It was a little strange to realize he was sharing the hawk's vision. He cocked his head in an eerie avian echo, and a small frown lined his brow. "I think there's blood on the patio."

"Don't take him in too close," Locke warned. "If some-one's inside, they may realize what you're up to."

My patience waned, and I went to take a step forward, but Zev grabbed my arm, holding me in place. "What do you think you're doing?"

As disconcerting as it was, I held the unearthly glow of his gaze and explained, "No movement, skid marks, slashed tires, open door, and no one's attacked us." Not to mention our arrival would have been hard to miss, but I didn't point out the obvious. Instead, I said, "I'm pretty sure they're gone."

"Doesn't mean that they haven't left some nasty surprise behind," Locke said from behind me.

"Well, let's find out." I shook off Zev's hold and headed in.

Using the same magical muscle that let me pick up on Arcane echoes, I eased the hold on my power and let it spread out ahead of me. Arcane abilities fell under two main categories, Elemental and Mystic, with a rarely used third, Divine. Prisms were classified as Mystic, just like Transporters, which was one of the reasons I was able to hide what I was for as long as I had. Right now, I needed that aspect of my Prism ability that recognized any lingering magical signatures. It was the only way to ensure we weren't walking into a trap. Magic was not easily explainable—never had been. It was personal and innate, so instinct tended to be the driving force behind a mage's strength. Instinct and, in my case, determination. Through trial and error, I'd found I could shift my perception until reality receded and magic took its place. Using it was draining and uncomfortable but doable.

Leaving the two men to follow or not, I let my power lead the way. I approached the entrance, trying not to panic when I noticed the long, snaking crack running through the door's glass panes. I stopped at the foot of the steps, closed my eyes, lowered my mental shields enough to see what my magic would reveal, then slowly opened my eyes. The world had stepped back, blurring at the edges, but lines of power hung on the air in a multilayered curtain that made my brain hurt. Even worse were the ragged, torn shreds that indicated a violent breach of Sabella's wards. Breaking such entrenched wards, especially as strong as Sabella's, took seriously powerful magic. I closed my eyes and whispered, "Dammit."

"What?" Zev's voice came from my left.

I swallowed my nerves, opened my eyes, and studied the fading lines. A couple of runes were familiar enough for me to get an idea of what had happened. "It looks like they used a modified breaching spell." Straining my magic, I tried to see if anyone or anything lay in wait. A dull spike of pain arrowed from temple to temple, but I kept going. There was no warning rasp of active magic, but the echoes of what had gone down licked along the edges of my mind. "I think we're clear, but let me take lead."

I didn't wait for their agreement. Didn't dare. If I missed a trap, better I took the brunt of it than them. At least I had a chance at surviving. I stepped over the threshold and into the entryway. Sunlight spilled through the massive glass windows overlooking the backyard. I got a few feet inside before I registered the dark smear near the foot of the stairs to my left. "Zev?" Even I could hear the wobble in my voice.

He stepped around me and crouched next to the spot. When he turned back, his eyes still burned with a blue flame, but his face was carved in stone. "Blood."

I pressed a hand to my stomach, covering the nauseating pit that opened up at Zev's confirmation.

He made a motion, presumably to Locke, because the other man slipped around me and disappeared farther into the house, a wave of earth-tone color trailing him.

I took in the rest of the interior, trying to see beyond the magic. A scuff mark was on the tile near the kitchen, and the drywall on the rounded corner was marred with a deep scratch. Small though they were, it was proof that some kind of altercation had occurred. A fading wash of color wound up the stairs. "We need to go up."

I started up the curving staircase and stayed close to the wall. Keeping open the barrier between the real world and magic shot my sense of balance to hell. I could feel Zev at my back, and for once, his magic wasn't an uncomfortable weight but a reassuring one.

A tiny voice of dread babbled in the corner of my mind and spouted dire predictions of what lay in wait above, but I tuned it out. Instead, I focused on not tripping any left-over spells. At the top of the stairs, I followed the echoes down the left hall. It was clear where shit had gone down because there was an angry knot of dark colors and indecipherable but clearly broken runes splattered around an open door.

The pulsing ache at my temples morphed into a painful vise that wrapped around my brain and squeezed. I grabbed my aching head and stumbled to a stop. Leaning over, I braced my hands on my thighs, closed my eyes to shut out the visual assault, and breathed through the pain.

A warm weight stroked my spine, and Zev asked, "Rory? What's wrong?"

I didn't dare shake my head for fear it would split wide open. Instead, I held up a hand in the universal sign for stop. "Give me a second," I gritted out. I fought my way through the discomfort and managed to raise my mental walls enough to find some steady ground. When I was sure I wouldn't collapse on my ass, I slitted my eyes open. I kept my eyes on my feet but couldn't escape the licks of color swimming on the edges of my awareness.

Sucking in a deep breath, I tugged my Prism magic around my shoulders like a cloak and slowly straightened. This time, the colors were muted, and so was their impact. I could study them without wanting to hurl. "Some serious magic was being thrown around."

"Anything we need to worry about now?"

"I don't think so." It wasn't the most resounding vote of confidence, but it was the best I could do.

Zev stepped around me and moved to the doorway. He stared, and a low, angry rumble sounded, matching the dark look on his face. The blue glow lining his hands deepened to navy as they curled into fists.

That rock in my gut turned into a boulder, but it wasn't enough to stop me from moving up to his side. "Oh my God," I breathed, ice slipping through my veins as I stared at what remained of Sabella's office.

"Are you sure there's no active spells or wards?" Zev's

voice was so close to a growl that I could barely understand him.

Inching inside, I swallowed hard, trying not to think about what could turn thick shelves into kindling or leave such damage in the walls. I did my best to ignore the destruction and sifted through the lingering echoes of magic. I was grateful Zev didn't rush me. Finally, I said, "Nothing active, but"—I pointed at the overturned desk—"something was there, and"—I pointed over toward the mangled built-in bookcase—"there." Then I angled to my left and pointed at where something or someone had hit the wall with enough force to crack the plaster. "And there." Feeling the weight of Zev's gaze, I turned to meet his eyes. "What?" It came out husky, but holding that power-filled gaze was damn difficult.

"You're a Transporter Key."

Déjà-fucking-vu. He'd guessed that once before, but just like then, he missed the mark. It was a legit assumption considering that both curse breaking and transporting were Mystic in nature, but that wasn't my dual-level ability. I sighed and looked away. "No, I'm not, and we're not discussing this right now." I cut off any more speculation on his part. "Focus. We need to figure out what happened and where Sabella is."

Apparently, he agreed with me, because after staring at me for an uncomfortably long moment, he began moving around the space, picking his way through the wreckage. When he stopped, he held a hand above the overturned desk, where a dense tangle of shadowy colors writhed like a nest of slow-moving snakes. "It started here."

He turned his head and looked over his shoulder at me, but his gaze shifted to something behind me. I turned where he was looking and realized the door had been slammed open so forcibly the knob had left a hole in the wall. "How'd they get this far in without her knowing?"

"Cloaking spell." Zev nudged one of the broken shelves aside with his foot and dropped to a crouch. He picked up something and held it so I could see. "They were already here when she walked in."

It looked like a quarter, but when I went to stand beside him, I realized it was a disc of some kind. "What is that?"

"Shielding slug, black market, used to bolster Occlusion Spells."

I took it from him and put it in the palm of my hand. It lay there inert, no echoes of power, just a round object marred with fractures. It wasn't made of metal but looked like some kind of ... "Wood?"

Zev rose. "No, bone."

I bobbled the disc. "Eww."

Zev took it back and dropped it into his pocket. "Probably animal."

Somehow, that didn't sound as reassuring as he clearly meant. "Still, eww."

He shook his head and kept moving around the office before stopping at various spots as if looking for whatever signs made sense to him. "I'm assuming you see magic?"

Watching him work and worried about what we were finding, I wasn't expecting his question so didn't check my response. "More like echoes." Realizing what I'd revealed, I froze and braced for his reaction.

It wasn't what I expected. With his back to me, he paused for a moment then continued his search near the desk and asked, "So what do the echoes in here tell you?"

I watched him like I would a rabid wolf, afraid that if I twitched, he would turn and pounce. "I don't know."

He rounded the desk to the other side and looked at me, a disbelieving look on his face. "Excuse me?"

"I don't know," I repeated, feeling an edge of resentment

at being forced to admit my ignorance. "I'm kind of new to this sort of thing."

"You want to explain that?"

Nope. I shook my head. "I can tell you that a lot of magic went down in the spots I pointed out, but I can't tell who it belongs to or what it was meant to do."

He studied me, his thoughts hidden.

The sound of someone clearing their throat turned us both to the doorway. Locke stood there, face grim, eyes hard, and his attention on Zev. "Got a body."

Zev was around the desk before I could process my initial shock at the pronouncement. "Where?"

Locke moved into the hall as Zev hit the door. "Out back, behind the pool."

Heart in my throat, I rushed after the two men, futilely praying that the body didn't belong to Sabella.

CHAPTER TEN

ZEV and I followed Locke down the stairs, through the open living room and kitchen, and into the backyard. He didn't run, but it was close. Sabella's home blended into the desert mountains, and the rock face played backdrop to her pool. Blooming desert plants and trees turned the backyard into a private oasis with breathtaking natural views. But what caught my eye were the smears of blood trailing along the pool's deck. I dared a glance at the sparkling water but found it undisturbed.

Locke wended his way through a decorative border of oleanders and bougainvillea that filled a narrow space between the pool's lounging area and the low brick half wall guarding the yard's dramatic drop-off into the ravine below and came to a stop. Zev followed and stood at his side. Between the two men and the bushes, there was no space for me to join them, and their backs blocked my view of whatever held their attention on the other side.

"Shit." Zev's curse was grim.

"Zev?" I couldn't hide the sharp anxiety in my voice as I

craned my neck to see around them. It didn't work. "Who is it?"

He looked over this shoulder, but the angle of the sun left most of his expression shadowed. "I think it's the driver."

My initial spurt of relief disappeared under a resentful sorrow. *Bernie.* "Dammit."

"I can go down but not sure I can get him back up alone." Locke directed his comment to Zev.

"We can't leave him there," I shot back.

This time, both men looked at me then at each other. Whatever silent male conversation they held, it didn't last long. Without a word, they hopped the short wall and headed down the hill. I scrambled around the bushes, ignoring the burn of scratches from their pointy bits as I took their place near the half wall. I stared as both men half slid, half walked through the loose gravel covering the steep hillside to the sprawled body resting against a half-buried boulder. A lump settled in my throat and my eyes burned, but I blinked it away, determined to help any way I could.

I watched, breath half held, as the two men made their way along the uncertain terrain. They did their best to come at Bernie's spot from the side to minimize the resulting avalanche of dirt and rock from their passage. Only when they'd both made it to the boulder and the body did I suck in air. The last thing we needed was to be hauling up more than one body. Zev crouched near Bernie while Locke picked his way around the boulder. It took me a second to realize he was checking to make sure nothing nasty had been left behind.

"Anything?" I called out.

Zev looked up at me, one hand shielding his eyes from the sun's glare. He shook his head.

As the two prepared to bring Bernie back, I tore my gaze away and scanned the nearby ground and bushes, not sure what I was looking for but finding it anyway. Broken branches were on nearby bushes, and the ground was littered with torn and crushed blooms of delicate pink oleander flowers. Even more telling were the small dark drops spattered on top of the blooms.

Without moving from my spot, I notice that the sand and gravel on this side of the brick held more footprints than such a narrow space warranted. There were very few clear, discernible tracks, but if we could get a tracking mage there, we might find enough of them to be useful.

I turned to see that Zev and Locke were making slow but steady progress up the incline, despite carrying Bernie's body between them. "Zev, I've got possible tracks up here," I warned. "Should we try to preserve them for a Hound?"

"Already got the scent," Locke answered as they continued to trudge upward.

"Okay dokey," I muttered under my breath, strangely unsurprised that Zev's buddy was a Hound. Probably should've clued in when he was shadowing my ass.

As the men drew close, I carefully picked my way out of the tight space so they could bring Bernie all the way out. A few muffled curses and some grunts, then Bernie's body was set into one of the loungers. We stood around the lounger, Zev on one side, Locke on the other, and me at the foot. There was some damage to Bernie's face, but I couldn't tell if it was from fists or from being thrown over the side of the yard. The severity of it made me think it was a combination of both. "Damn, they did a number on him."

Zev wiped the sweat on his forehead then dropped his hands to his hips. "You knew him?"

"Casually," I admitted. "He's... was a Transporter for the Guild. He's been semiretired for a couple of years. Comes out at the Director's behest." And since Sylvia Ayala, the Western Division Director, was friends with Sabella, this job was definitely at her behest.

Locke crouched by Bernie's body, and the pulse of active magic rubbed against my shield. The extent of my knowledge of Hounds was pretty limited. They were exceptional trackers, and once they had a scent, they always ran their prey to the ground, but right now, I had no idea what Locke was doing.

He lifted Bernie's wrist and turned his hand to show the cut and bruised knuckles. "He got in a few shots." He laid the arm so it rested over Bernie's stomach. Then Locke shifted and tugged up the pants leg closest to him to reveal a still-holstered pistol in an ankle strap. "He didn't get time to draw that, so I'm thinking the initial hit was magical, not physical."

Zev's attention was on Bernie, but he asked me, "Did he have any defensive skills?"

"I don't know." When Zev shot me a look, I explained. "He was halfway out the door as I was coming in. It's not like Guild members sit around comparing magical"—I caught Zev's raised eyebrow and changed my word choice—"muscles. If Bernie had a secondary skill, he didn't share it."

"But the Guild would know?" Locke asked.

"Yeah, they would." I studied Bernie's battered body. "I could ask Evan to dig if it's important."

Zev shared another look with Locke. "You need it, or can you do without?"

"I'm good without. The magical scent trail is a fucking mess, but the physical scent trail is a bit cleaner, easier to separate." He put his hands to his thighs and straightened to his full height. "If I need the information, I'll hit up the Guild." He looked over to the yard's edge. "From what I canvased so far, they had a team inside on the bottom floor, a couple posted outside."

"A third was waiting in Sabella's office," Zev added.

"So we're looking at a what?" Locke absently scratched his shoulder even as he scanned the yard. "A six-person team?"

"At least," Zev agreed.

"Makes sense. I got four separate trails out here, besides the driver." Locke turned to the house and pointed out two of the thick columns. "They stood there for a good thirty minutes, waiting." He continued to stare at the house. "I'm thinking the two inside herded the driver out into an ambush. Take him out, clears the way to get to the main target." Locke's attention went to the dark stains on the deck. "The driver managed to injure two of the four before they took him down. It was a short, brutal fight, and the odds were always against him."

"A six-man team, all waiting under Occlusion spells, means it was well coordinated and they knew she was coming." Zev moved around the lounger and came up to my side.

That phone call.

"What phone call?"

I blinked at Zev's question and realized I had spoken aloud. Heat burned under my face. *Well, shit.* "Back at Emilio's, Sabella got a phone call. Whoever it was wanted to meet. She suggested here."

Zev frowned. "When was this?"

I gave an awkward shrug. "This morning, just before I ran into you in the kitchen."

"Do you know who was on the phone?"

I shook my head, unable to endure his scrutiny while embarrassment at my earlier eavesdropping still burned. "But she sounded as if she knew them enough to be worried about whatever it is they told her."

He stepped in close until my gaze rose to his, then his eyes narrowed. "Where, exactly, did this conversation take place?"

I swallowed hard and lifted my chin. "Outside Emilio's office."

"Evan and Lena hear this call?"

I managed a hesitant nod.

"Emilio?"

I bit my lip and shook my head.

He held my gaze for an uncomfortably long moment, then he rubbed a hand over his close-cropped beard. "Right," he muttered under his breath. He sighed and let it go. He looked at Sabella's house, and his gaze narrowed, his attention caught by something. He moved toward the patio. "Locke?"

"Yeah?"

"Are those security cameras?" Zev pointed toward the beams lining the porch.

Locke followed and moved past Zev until he was directly under the porch's covering. He craned his head. "Yeah, they are."

I went to stand beside Locke and peered up. It took me a bit to see it, and when I did, I turned to Zev. "How in the hell did you see those from there?" The cameras were well hidden, their black eyes camouflaged by the wood grain of the dark beams.

He ignored my question and moved to Locke's side. "We need to find her security room. If we're lucky, we'll have a recording."

"A professional team like this wouldn't be so careless," Locke argued.

"Maybe, maybe not, but let's find out."

Locke loped off into the house, leaving me alone with Zev. "Seriously, Zev, how did you see those?"

He turned his attention to me and raised a mocking eyebrow. "You aren't the only one with secrets." Before I could snipe back, he said, "Upstairs, you said you could see echoes of magic, right?"

I nodded.

"What do you see out here?"

I took a few steps away from him, took a deep breath, and

slid down the barrier enough to peek through. I didn't know how Locke picked up magical scents, but he was spot-on. Even the visible trail was a mess. There were jumbled patches of magic, some of the colors fading as I watched, others a pulsating echo that created a matching ache behind my eyes. The echoes were so tangled I wasn't sure they could be traced before they disappeared altogether. "Locke was right, there was a crap-ton of magic used out here."

"Can you identify anything that links to your driver friend?" Zev's voice came from behind me, so close that I knew if I stepped back, I would bump into him.

I stared at the gut-churning mess and tried to single out something worthwhile to follow. Finally, I found a nearly translucent ribbon of yellowish green that wound a drunken path through the knots. It bounced between the knotted sections like a pinball, and I followed it across the deck. Near the yard's edge, half hidden by a bougainvillea bush and close to where I thought Bernie went over, I found something.

I crouched and nudged aside the branches for a closer look. In the bush's shade lay a discarded snakeskin. Just above that hovered fractured sections of what might have been a circular symbol, its edges losing definition, like wisps of smoke. I held my breath, an instinctive reaction not to speed up the process, and did my best to fill in the blanks. Feeling movement at my back, I held my other hand up, a silent request for Zev to stop moving.

"What?"

"I don't know. It looks like a circle of some kind." A few more sections whispered away, and I realized that one end of the circle appeared thicker than the other. I shifted a few inches, trying for another angle. My change in position allowed sunlight to filter through the bushes and fall over the echo, adding an unexpected depth and new edges to the dwindling wisps. When it hit the discarded snakeskin below, the light refracted into a shower of tiny diamond-like bursts. *That's not normal.*

"Not a circle," I muttered, the thicker end coming together in an image that slid across my brain without me finding its name. I looked up at Zev. "What's the symbol called? The one where the snake eats its own tail?"

He frowned. "Ouroboros?"

"Yeah, that one." Still holding back the bush, I looked around for something to use so I could move the shimmering snakeskin from its protected spot. After finding a stick, I grabbed it and hooked the paper-thin remains so I could pull them free. "Know what kind of magic uses snakeskin and an ouroboros symbol?"

"Not off the top of my head." Zev's answer was short.

I stood up slowly and kept my hand steady so as not to lose the tenuous hold on what I was betting was a foci, an innocuous object used to anchor the magical energy of a spell. "Got anyone who might?"

"Maybe." He stepped back, giving me room. "Give me a second and I'll grab something to put that in."

I stood there, stick extended, gaze caught on the shimmering skin as the occasional breeze tried to tug it free and destroy whatever evidence this was. Zev was back in moments, a small ziplock bag in hand, and once the snakeskin was safely stored inside, he asked, "Anything else out here I need to know about?"

The ache in my head had gained teeth, and I wasn't sure how much longer I could keep the strange double vision going. Still, I looked over the sun-drenched yard and the lingering knots that were slowly, but definitely, fading and knew I couldn't give up. Not yet. I worked my way back toward the house, pausing at each tangle, searching for similarities. I thought I caught glimpses of the ouroboros symbol in a couple of other spots, but they were fractured so bad, it could just be more wishful thinking on my part. By the time I hit the patio door, the world's worst migraine threatened to take over. But I had one more place I wanted to check.

I stumbled over the raised edge between the patio and the house. If it weren't for Zev's quick reaction, I would've ended up on the floor.

He held my arm as I leaned into him until I could find my balance. "You okay?"

"Fine," I lied. When his grip tightened, I added, "It's just a headache." I waved toward the stairs. "I need to check the office again."

Thankfully, he didn't waste time arguing but stayed at my side as we headed to Sabella's office. At the door, I told him, "Stay here." Then I stepped inside and retraced my earlier search.

This time, I started on the far side with the damaged wall and worked my way counterclockwise through the wreckage, leaving the center of the room for last. I was coming up frustratingly empty and had turned away from the upended desk when I saw it. Just inside the office doors on the wall was the shadow of an ouroboros. I walked closer, being careful of where I stepped, while I scanned the area for another snakeskin. I got within touching distance of the wall without finding anything. "Where is it?"

"Where's what?" Zev asked from the doorway.

I motioned to the symbol hanging roughly head height. "There's another ouroboros there but no snakeskin."

He looked at the wall then back at me, his lips tightening, and I remembered that I was the only one seeing the image. Right. I rubbed my temple, trying to ease the persistent ache. He didn't say anything but came over and helped me look for another foci. We picked our way through the jumbled mess but came up empty.

I sat on my heels, wiped the back of my hand over my

damp forehead, and dropped my hand to my lap. "There's nothing here." Exhaustion weighed heavily on my shoulders, and all I wanted to do was curl up in a ball and close my eyes, but none of that would help find Sabella. Lost in a haze of worry and frustration, I was startled to feel a touch on my chin. I blinked, and Zev's face was in front of me.

As he crouched in front of me, his gaze searched mine, a frown carving lines that disappeared into his beard. "You're done."

Not following, I said, "Sorry?"

"You're sheet white and look like you're about to pass out, so shut it down, Rory."

It took a second or two for his order to penetrate my fog. When it did, I dragged my mental walls into place. The threatening migraine decided it was time to move in and set up shop. I winced and shifted my chin free of Zev's hold so I could rub my temples. It didn't do much to hold the pain back, but it did give me a chance to close my burning eyes. "We need to find Sabella."

"We will." Zev sounded a lot more confident than I felt. "Locke's working on tracking what he can, but I need to call Emilio. Tell him what's happened and get a few more hands out here to go through this place." He paused. "You going to be okay here while I do that?"

"Yeah, go." I waved him off. "I just need a minute."

He didn't move, not for a long minute, then finally, I felt the air shift as he stood up and walked away. I listened to the murmur of his voice as he spoke to Emilio, the words indecipherable. I gave it another minute before I carefully opened my eyes. The pain in my skull was still there, but if I kept my movements to a minimum, I should be okay-*ish*.

I slowly got to my feet and wandered over toward the bookshelves. A jumble of books and picture frames lay on the ground, carelessly tossed aside. One of the frames, a heavy, ornate silver type, lay on top, half covered by a book. I pulled it free to find it was a wedding photo of Sabella and her husband. At least I hoped it was her husband. I studied the image of the young, ecstatic couple in their wedding finery against a stunning background of blue sea and green grass. I set it back on one of the intact shelves, carefully positioning it.

Then, unable to stop, I started picking through the mess at my feet and rescuing the remaining intact frames. There were candids of kids on vacation, more of the formal, posed shots of family, snapshots of laughter and fun. Although my chest ached with each recovered photo, my mind stayed blessedly quiet.

I lifted a frame containing a more recent shot of Sabella and a couple of kids around ten or so, most likely her grandkids, all in paint-spattered smocks proudly showing off their paintings, and carefully pulled away the broken pieces of the protective glass. I took my time working the shard free of the frame, not wanting to scratch the photo. I got the last stubborn piece out, and the photo shifted, revealing another tucked behind it.

Curious, I carefully peeled the front photo up to see the one beneath. I got enough space between them to tell that the hidden one was a black-and-white shot. Based on the clothing, it was taken at least twenty years ago, maybe more. The background was a mix of trees and grass and could easily be a park or someone's backyard. It was hard to tell. A young man, on the leaner side, his dark hair cut short and matching the neatly trimmed mustache above his wide smile, was wearing jeans and a button-down shirt. He had his arm around Sabella.

Unable to see the rest and curiosity thoroughly aroused, I tugged on the photo. It held fast, and I had to work at it to make sure not to damage it, but it finally slid free. I set the newer picture and broken frame on the shelf and angled the black-and-white photo to study it.

Sabella stood in the middle, one arm around the young man and the other around an equally dark-haired young woman. The younger woman was on the curvy side with a bit more bohemian vibe, her feet bare, her jeans rolled up, thin braids in her hair. Something about the younger couple nagged at me, and as I stared at the photo, that sense of familiarity grew. Studying the younger woman, I added a few more years, shortened the hair, and replaced the wide smile with a smaller, more cautious one. A weight settled on my chest as recognition slammed home, fracturing my worldview.

Mom. That's my mom with Sabella.

My mom and... still reeling, I looked at the young man, a man I couldn't remember but I was betting was one of the reasons behind my mom's constant sadness.

Sabella and my parents. What the actual fuck?

"Rory?"

The sound of Zev's voice saying my name made me jump. I palmed the photo, pressed it facedown against my thigh, and looked over my shoulder. "Yeah?" It came out rough.

He stepped inside the office, pocketing his phone. "Emilio's sending in a couple more people to help Locke search the house and grounds. You and I are heading back."

I turned away, did my best to tuck the photo in my back pocket without cluing Zev in, and cleared my throat. "And Sabella?" This time, my voice came out closer to normal.

"Emilio's making some calls to see if he can't track down who called her. In the meantime, I asked him to call the Muse in."

I turned to him, taking in the stubborn glint in his eyes and the even more telling way he stood, legs apart, arms over his chest, all of him braced for an argument. I was in no shape to give him one because I was reeling from my own shit. I set aside Sabella's possible betrayal and focused on the here and now as I made my way to him. Even knowing the answer, I still had to ask, "Are you sure that's wise?"

His face was grim. "At this point, I think it's necessary. Otherwise, we'll be stumbling around in the dark."

Head pounding, heart aching, and mind reeling, I finally admitted I was in way over my head. Sabella was gone, Zev was being hunted by unknowns—and maybe me too—and the life I thought I knew was possibly a lie. I needed one thing I could trust. One person in this mess who wouldn't lie to me. I stared at the man who, if his memories were intact, would be that person. Letting a memory mage poke around his head was risky, not just to me but to him, but if he wanted it, I wanted it more. I needed my Zev back. So selfish me, I gave in. "Let's go flip some lights on."

CHAPTER ELEVEN

"LENA'S HEADING OVER," I warned Evan as I read the text on my phone. When all I got was a grunt of acknowledgment, I rolled from my back to my side, a risky proposition considering the love seat's cramped dimensions. "She said she has something she wants you to look at."

Working on a laptop in one of the many rooms of Emilio's house, Evan didn't let his attention waver from his screen. "When?"

Translating the borderline-rude Evan-is-busy-don't-bother-him speak, I said, "Half hour, probably."

That got another grunt, not that I'd expected actual words. Once Evan focused on a job, the rest of the world ceased to exist.

I sat up carefully, testing the lasting effects of a second dose of ibuprofen. When my head didn't split wide open, I gave a cautious, silent cheer and downgraded my earlier monstrous headache to "dull but annoying ache." It probably helped that I'd spent the last few hours lying on the love seat, eyes closed and doing my best not to think at all. And not just because of the pain.

Zev and I had made it back to Emilio's just after lunch. We would've made it back earlier, but Locke put his foot down and refused to give up the SUV's keys when Zev and I insisted we could drive ourselves back. If it hadn't been for the near-blinding headache, I would've just hot-wired the damn vehicle. Instead, Zev and I waited until the backup arrived then hitched a ride with the driver. Locke and his crew would bring the SUV back when they were done. Since I'd dozed on the ride, I really couldn't argue with Locke's assessment, although Zev had pouted all the way to Emilio's.

While we waited at Sabella's, Locke managed to find Sabella's security room. It was no surprise that when Locke tried to view the recordings, they appeared to have been erased. I asked him to pull all the hard drives, then I sent a text to Evan, asking him to meet me at Emilio's after his lunch so I could put his skills to use.

When we got to the house, Zev disappeared with Emilio, leaving me to stumble to my room, down my first ibuprofen, and fall facedown on the bed. That was where I stayed until Evan arrived and woke me up by shaking my shoulder. Unfortunately, my involuntary nap wasn't long enough to make a dint in my headache. However, I did manage to lead him to the first available room with a table and couch so we could set up shop.

Before I collapsed on the love seat, I handed Evan the hard drives and shared what we'd found at Sabella's so he had enough information to start his electronic hunt. I remembered mumbling something about Locke and following up when the team got back, then I was out. I woke a few hours later, head pounding, just not as brutally as before, swallowed another couple of ibuprofen, and resumed my previous position, curled up on the love seat. The soft, rapid sounds of Evan working the keyboard kept me company in my half doze.

That haze had cleared about an hour ago, and while Evan wasn't all that chatty, I did get the update that he was surfing the dark web on the trail of potential hired guns and simultaneously running a search for connections to the ouroboros symbol. There was a bunch of other words that made zero sense to me, but I was sure they were crucial to whatever Evan was doing. I finally dared to ask about the security footage from Sabella's, only to get an abrupt answer.

"Got a program cleaning that shit up but takes time."

I knew better than saying that Sabella might not have time. Not when Evan's hunched shoulders tightened and his half-crazed and bloodshot eyes all but pinwheeled behind his lenses. Said pinwheeling could be symptomatic of either the three empty soda cans surrounding him or stress. Either way, I left him to it.

I concentrated on what little I could do on my end, starting with reaching out to Lena to see what she'd found. That resulted in her telling me she was on her way to share in person, hence my heads-up to Evan.

I got to my feet and wandered over to the window. This room was on the left side of the house and faced the front, where the sinking sun colored everything in red-tinged purple and soft shadows. The shutter's wooden slats were angled to keep the worst of the glare off Evan's screen, but I could see a familiar SUV parked out front. "Locke's back."

"Came back an hour and a half ago," Evan muttered without looking my way.

I turned my back on the sunset, and when he didn't add anything else, I shifted until my shadow fell across his screen. That caught his attention.

He frowned, his fingers paused, and he shot me a disgruntled look. "What?"

"And?"

"And what? He asked about the hard drives, I told him the same thing I told you, and he left."

Instead of snapping out something that would guarantee an argument, since Evan wasn't the only one stressed to the nines, I decided we both needed a break. "Need anything from the kitchen?"

"I'm good."

Taking him at his word, I got out of there. Not that I was planning on putzing around in the kitchen. I had another goal—getting answers from less surly means. I couldn't just go up to Locke and ask because there was no way he would share anything unless Zev or Emilio gave him permission. That meant finding Zev, because Emilio still intimidated the shit out of me. Not to mention I was now a little leery of anyone connected to Sabella. I tried to ignore the part of me wondering whether Emilio knew about my parents and Sabella.

Still not thinking about it.

I shoved aside the million and one questions demanding answers and focused on the immediate problem—finding a lead to Sabella's whereabouts. It was disconcerting how few clues had been left behind. I was halfway down the hall when I heard the melodious descant of bells announcing someone's arrival. I picked up my pace, thinking maybe Lena had made better time than expected. I hit the foyer just as Emilio reached the door. He heard my approach and shot me a questioning look, his hand on the handle.

I slowed, heat seeping under my skin. *Not your house, idiot.* I rushed to explain, "Sorry, I thought it might be Lena."

Amusement eased the lines of stress on Emilio's face. "No apology needed."

He opened the door as Zev stepped out of the hall and joined the welcoming party. He altered course as his gaze swept over me from head to toe. "How are you feeling?"

"Better," I answered.

The door swung open, blocking my view of the arrival. "Mr. Cordova?" a smooth female voice asked from the other side.

"Ms. Quinn? Please, come in." Emilio waved his arm wide in welcome. "Thank you for coming on such short notice."

The woman who stepped inside gave him a serene smile. "Your sense of urgency was contagious." Sable hair in a stylish cut and dark eyes accented angled features that rode the line between foxy and pixie. Freckles dusted the pale skin over the bridge of her nose, but even that bit of whimsy couldn't detract from the overall classy vibe. She and Emilio shook hands, then she turned to Zev and me. "Hello."

Zev dipped his chin in acknowledgment.

Feeling disheveled in comparison, I fought not to fidget and managed a polite finger wave. "Hi."

Emilio closed the door and returned to her side. "Ms. Quinn, this is Zev Aslanov and Rory Costas."

"Shelby, please," she said, including us in that invitation. She took in the surroundings. "You have a lovely home, Mr. Cordova."

"Thank you." Ever the consummate host, he offered, "I'd be happy to show you around afterward."

Warmth thawed Shelby's coolly polite smile. "I might take you up on that." She looked between Zev and Emilio. "In the meantime, it's my understanding that expediency is essential?"

"It is," Zev confirmed.

"Then let's get to it."

"Do you need anything?" Emilio asked.

"A comfortable chair," she answered easily then turned to Zev. "Your preference on where you'd like this to happen." She looked between Emilio and me. "Will anyone else be joining us?"

Emilio frowned. "She's—"

"Staying," Zev cut him off with a sharp look. "This involves her. She stays."

Something told me this was an ongoing argument, but since it appeared Zev was winning, I kept quiet.

A tense moment passed before Emilio gave in. "Fine." He touched Shelby's elbow. "We can use my office. This way." He turned and started down the hall, leaving Zev and me to follow.

I turned to Zev and gave him a quiet "Thanks."

Instead of answering, he gave me a long look, put his hand to the base of my spine, and gently nudged me to move. "Don't thank me yet."

◆

Ensconced in Emilio's office, I sat off to the side, battling a serious case of nerves and doing my best to be invisible. Emilio half sat on the top of his desk, one foot braced on the floor, his arms folded over his chest, and his gazed aimed at the drama playing out in front of him. On the desk and next to his hip was a file.

We positioned two leather club chairs so that Shelby and Zev could sit facing each other over a small side table. Shelby covered the table's top in an intricate chalked circle of runes and sigils, all spiraling out from a silver filigree hourglass filled with shimmering sand. Two candles, one blue, one red, sat at the north and south points, while an unpolished white stone that Shelby called scolecite and an equally unpolished inky-black onyx one sat to the east and west. Both the candles and the stones were etched with symbols.

Zev, being Zev, demanded to know what to expect. Shelby took his request in stride and explained that if Zev's memories were locked behind a spell, she would be able to go in, unravel that spell, and help Zev retrieve the locked memories. "There are a couple of base spells that come to mind. One erases memories permanently."

I didn't like the sound of that, and based on Zev's deepening frown, neither did he.

Undaunted, Shelby continued. "The second most common spell, and the one I think we're dealing with, as you're not a vegetable, simply seals the memories away. Think of it as a never-ending hall of doors. Those doors will be locked tight, maybe in chains, maybe in spelled bindings, but however they're closed, it's simply a matter of unraveling those locks."

She made it sound so easy when I knew that with the money a Muse could command, it was anything but. However, it wasn't my place to push, and Emilio and Zev appeared satisfied with her explanation.

Everyone settled in, and we got down to business.

Shelby appeared relaxed as she sat back in her chair, her complete focus on Zev, but her power pressed against me, the weight of it buffered by my Prism. I wasn't sure what I'd expected, but much like those movie scenes where the therapist hypnotized their patient, once everything was in place, Shelby began easing Zev into a relaxed state, even doing the counting-backward thing. Unlike the movies, it wasn't so much her voice leading Zev into that suggestive state but the power behind it.

At least from my perspective.

When I dared to peek at the play of magic between them, Shelby's grayish-blue power looped around Zev like misty ribbons. When it settled, it shifted from mist into a silvery-gray undulating cloak. By the time she uttered "one," the cloak covered everything but Zev's face.

Whatever magic she was using, it was working. The lines in his face had smoothed away, his grip on the chair's arms had relaxed, and the rigid tension riding his shoulders was gone. The ache in my head that had been easing gave a warning pulse, so I let go of that other sight and paid attention to what came next.

"Zev, can you hear me?" Shelby asked.

"Yes."

"Good." She leaned forward, her attention shifting to the items arranged in front of her. She touched the white stone, and I caught the flash of power she sent into it. That power erupted from the stone and raced through the chalked lines, leaving a soft glow. It curled around the candles and onyx stone without touching them. "I want you to look around and describe what you see."

His eyes moved behind his lids, and a small frown marred his peaceful countenance. "Hard to tell. There's a low-lying fog everywhere."

Shelby's gaze lifted from the table to study Zev's face, and I sucked in a breath. Her eyes were no longer dark but filled with wispy tendrils of white as she stared at something only she could see. It was eerie as hell, almost as if that fog was caught in her eyes. I curled my hands into fists and continued to watch, praying that whatever she was doing would work.

Her unearthly gaze dropped to the table. This time, she touched the onyx, her lips silently moving. Her power moved slower, seeping through the lines, curling around the previous ones until I couldn't tell where one started and the other began. Her attention stayed on the table as she asked, "Can you see now, Zev?"

He shifted, leaning forward. "Yeah. You were right. It's a hall of doors." He cocked his head. "They're locked with chains." His hand lifted as if to pull them away.

Shelby hissed a warning. "Stop, Zev! Don't touch it."

His hand stayed in the air for a moment before he dropped it.

"Zev, I want you to stand there. Don't touch anything and don't move until I give you the all clear. Do you understand?" There was a bite of command in her voice.

"Yes."

I blinked at his unusual docile answer.

"Shelby?" Emilio's voice carried a hint of threat.

The Muse turned to him. "It's what I thought. The amnesia is spell-induced, but they've layered the locks with magical trip spells. Touch the lock and it will erase the memory hidden behind the door."

If possible, Emilio's expression grew grimmer than before, but he didn't appear surprised. "Can you break it?"

Shelby turned back to the table and studied the circle before her. "I can, but once I do, the one who set it will know."

"It won't matter," I said, earning that creepy gaze. "They're dead."

Under normal circumstances, her smile would've received a similar response from me, but she was freaking me out, so it was just disturbing. "Well, that will make this much easier, then."

She went back to her spell and started to chant in a soft, melodic language I didn't recognize. I didn't know what the chant did, but her magic began to rise and fall in sync with her voice. With each undulation, the power increased until a shimmering globe encased the top of the table. The lit flames of the candles froze as if time had stopped, but the power continued to flow through the enclosed sphere so it appeared that everything was caught inside a water globe.

"Zev, do you see the keys?"

Keys? What in the hell is she talking about?

Behind his lids, Zev's eyes moved. "Yeah."

Shelby touched a sigil on the table. "Use those to unlock the chains, but don't open the door until I say so."

Again his hand moved, and we watched him pantomime picking up the keys and unlocking the chains only he and Shelby could see. "Done."

Shelby's fingers traced the symbols on the table, and the frozen flame of the red candle came to life. "Go ahead and open the door but don't go in."

Zev mimed as he was told.

"Good." Shelby's voice was calm. "What's inside the room?"

"Imogen."

Unprepared for the flash of jealousy at the name, I curled my hands into fists and bit my tongue.

"What's she doing?" Shelby asked.

"She's being pissy as usual because she doesn't like my questions."

"What questions?"

"The idiot I dragged in who stole from Trask. Something's not adding up there. I was pushing her for more information on his connection to Origin, specifically Stephen Trask. She keeps trying to insist that Stephen's already discussed this with the Arcane Council, in detail." He frowned. "Problem is, she's lying about something. I just can't figure out what."

Shelby looked at Emilio. He gave a short headshake and rolled his hand in a "move on" motion.

Obviously, this wasn't news to him.

Shelby heeded Emilio's silent prompt. "Zev, let's leave her for a moment and go to the next door. Ready?"

He slowly nodded.

Shelby took him through the sequence again. When he opened the door, his face changed, and heat hit my cheeks. I knew that look. Sure enough, Zev's voice was a low rasp. "Damn, Rory, you look good."

Despite my embarrassment, I managed to meet Shelby's

amused gaze. Without looking away from me, she directed, "Why don't we leave that one for now, Zev?"

One of his hands curled into a fist and his lips thinned with impatience, then Shelby softly prodded, "Zev, let's move on."

He gave a curt nod. Another lock, another door. This one involved Emilio and, specifically, a conversation with Emilio concerning Zev's suspicions about Trask's involvement with Theo Mahon, the Delphi project, and the council's level of involvement with Trask. I wasn't surprised when Emilio had Shelby move on again.

After Zev opened the fourth door, he paused, and I couldn't read the expression on his face, even though something warned that I should.

"Zev?" Shelby prompted when he continued to stare unseeingly into his memory without saying a word.

Zev gave a sharp shake of his head. "Not this one." He pulled back his arm as if closing the door.

"Zev, stop."

The line of Zev's jaw tensed, and his body went rigid. "This is not mine to share. I made a promise. I'm not breaking it."

My heart froze in my chest. *Oh, shit.*

CHAPTER TWELVE

SHELBY SHOT A LOOK AT EMILIO, who was studying Zev, his thoughts hidden behind a frown. His gaze left Zev and came to me. Without looking away, he asked in a low voice, "Zev, is the secret a viable threat?"

The muscle in Zev's jaw jumped, but he finally said, "No."

Emilio's unblinking stare was freaking me the hell out. I prayed my face didn't reflect my rising panic because I knew exactly what Zev was trying so hard not to share. Somehow, by a sheer miracle, I managed to hold Emilio's gaze with breaking down and airing all my dirty little secrets.

Finally, he blinked and looked at Shelby. He did another one of those headshakes, indicating to let it go and move forward.

Heeding the man who signed her paycheck, Shelby returned her attention to Zev. "Okay, Zev. Close that door, and let's move on."

Zev pantomimed closing a door and turning away, leaving my secret behind. Shelby led him down his hall of memories and hit pay dirt when he opened the door on the night we were ambushed. Shelby had him go back through the night in detail. I listened closely, grateful she started with the after-show activities versus the pre-show ones. Unfortunately, I forgot that in Zev's retelling, much more damning information would come to light that would make our naked-time encounter way less interesting.

"We're at the SUV. I reach for the door. Rory tries to stop me, but it's too late. The damn trap is sprung." He winced but kept his attention on whatever was playing out before him. "It slapped Rory back and shoved me face-first into the SUV." His hands curled and uncurled in his lap. "Can't see how many, but they're not messing around. One has to be an electro mage because they used a fucking spiderweb spell to lock me to the car. Hurts like a bitch, but it's not lethal. Guess they want me alive. I'm almost tempted to let them get me, but"—his face darkens—"not keen on leaving Rory at their mercy."

Aww. Hearing his concern brushed a soothing stroke over my battered heart and eased a bit of the ache that had set up shop since he'd lost his memories.

"How sure are you that you're the target?" Emilio interrupted.

"Considering I've got two mages on my ass, pretty damn sure," Zev shot back. Then his head jerked and alarm spread over his face. He struggled in his seat, his movements restricted, as if tied down. "Rory! No, don't... holy shit, woman."

That earned another speculative look from Emilio that I did my best to ignore, even though it was boring holes into my skull.

When Zev suddenly froze, Shelby leaned forward. "Tell me what's happening."

Zev's lips curved up, but it wasn't so much a smile as a

merciless baring of teeth. "She's tearing the spell apart. No! Not that one, don't—" He flinched.

And so did I. I knew exactly what he was seeing. It was the moment when I'd torn the last bit of the spell from his legs and it exploded in my face, sending me back on my ass yet again.

"Dammit all. I don't have time for this," snarled Zev. "Big bastard is dragging Rory back by her hair, which makes at least three mages in play. The cage is a dampener, which means a fourth mage is hiding somewhere close."

While I had no idea what a dampener was, it was clear from the matching grim looks Emilio and Shelby shared that they did. Since no one came to interrupt our fight that night, I could make an educated guess and look it up later.

"Describe them for me," Emilio ordered.

"Only caught the casting belt on big and burly."

Emilio switched his gaze to me and snapped, "Rory?"

My brain scrambled, trying to recapture snapshots of the fight. "Buzzed hair, maybe black or dark brown. Eyes, small and mean, brown, I think. Square jaw, big forehead, bruiser type. Definitely a casting mage. Thick wrist."

Emilio flipped open the file on the desk, pulled out a picture, and held it up. "This one?"

Unprepared for the grisly photo, I flinched. It was a close-up of my attacker, but he was barely recognizable. His face was a bloody, shredded mess. I swallowed hard and nodded.

Emilio set the photo aside and sorted through the file. "Zev, describe the two you're facing."

"Female, electro mage, mid-thirties, trained, but sloppy. She's left-handed and drops her guard just before casting."

How in the hell could he see all that when he's fending off a dual attack? I could barely recall the jackass who'd used my hair as a handle.

Emilio set aside a photo. "The other one?"

"Younger, more street-savvy male, and he's waiting for an opening, so not an elemental mage. Otherwise, I'd have my hands full."

Emilio set aside what I suspected was another gory photo, but my attention was caught by the dark anticipation filling Zev's face.

His hands moved in an unfamiliar pattern. "Let's see how good he is." Then, "Yeah, you saw that, didn't you, you little shit? Come on. Go for it. You know you want to." His body twitched as if reliving the fight, his arms up, hands moving. "Not so much fun now, is it?" His expression changed, and the feral intensity of it set the hairs on my arms on end. He gave a pained grunt, his head whipped around, and he snarled. "Sneaky bitch." His expression shifted again, but when it settled, his smile was far from nice. "Nicely done, Rory."

Probably when I took out the illusion mage. When Emilio looked at me, I said quietly, "There was an illusion mage, half hidden by the stairwell. We both missed her."

Zev's hands wove through the air. His muscles strained, and lethal intensity stained the air, but Shelby leaned forward, a frown marring her brow. "Zev? Don't go in too far."

Obviously, he didn't hear her, because he whipped around and again mimicked a cast, followed by a sharp "no" before he jerked his arms down, held in a familiar mage pose, the same one I recognized from when he'd killed the electro mage.

Sure enough, when he turned his head, he was wearing the same teeth-baring mask of menace from that night. We stared at each other, me unable to look away, him caught in the memory of that night. Then menace bled away, and he shook out his hands. "I'm good. You?"

The seemingly out-of-nowhere question echoed what he'd asked me that night, and knowing what came next, I sucked in a sharp breath as his body bent in a painful arc. His hand gripped the chair's arms until his fingers were bloodless.

"Zev!" Shelby's voice was sharp. "Get out!"

The urgency in her voice had me shoving out of my chair and tumbling to my knees in front of Zev. I covered his hands with mine and gripped tight. My magic, already primed by my own uneasiness, spread and slid up his arms, easing under the cloak of Shelby's spell.

She gripped my shoulder, her fingers digging in painfully. "What are you doing?"

Power rode her touch and coursed through me. Emilio's office wavered, overlaid by a phantom vision of a never-ending hall of doors. I was still on my knees, but I was reaching through a doorway, trying to hold on to Zev. What happened next was pure instinct, and if I'd been asked to explain it, I couldn't.

Shelby's power wound with mine, thickening the magical tether to Zev as she added her strength to mine. My grip tightened, and with a metaphysical yank, I dragged Zev back. It was like hauling his dead weight up a sharp incline while an invisible force refused to let him go. Something shifted in the magic running through me, and suddenly, I found myself back in Emilio's office, ass to the floor at Zev's feet, chills chasing up and down my arms. Only Zev's grip on my wrists kept me from toppling backward. I blinked up at him as he stared at me.

The awareness in his eyes was my first clue that he was no longer under Shelby's spell. Even more telling was a deeper flare of concern as he studied me. "Are you okay?"

Doing a mental check and finding only the lingering headache, I cleared my throat. "I'm good." I tugged against his grip, a silent request that he let go. "Shouldn't that be my question?"

His thumbs brushed against the inside of my wrists before he released me. His gaze rose and focused behind me. "What happened?"

I managed to scoot back until I could see Shelby to my left, Zev to my right, and more worrisome, Emilio staring at me across the table.

"You triggered a secondary spell." Shelby's voice was tight. "You got pulled in before I could stop you." She turned to me. The weird smoke effect lingered in her eyes but was slowly being replaced by her natural warm-brown color. Even more concerning was the understanding forming in them. "Rory was able to hold it back so we could drag you out of it."

"And how exactly did she manage to do that?" Emilio's quiet question was made more menacing than if he had snarled it in my face. Even worse, he slowly straightened from his desk and closed in until I was all but caught between the three.

Scrambling to my feet, I froze like a rabbit surrounded by hungry wolves, my brain scrambling for an escape. Power swept through the room, stealing my breath. My Prism hardened, thickened, holding the worst of it back. I didn't dare move under Emilio's burning gaze, scared it would trigger something I was in no way, shape, or form ready to deal with. Not with the depth of magic hinted in that invisible wave, proving he was no one to fuck with.

Zev's low warning of "Emilio" added another layer of tension to the already unnerving situation. "Let it go."

Strangely, it was Shelby whom Zev should've warned. "You, Ms. Costas," she said as she casually retook her seat, completely ignoring the rising tension, "should not exist."

I didn't break my stare with Emilio, and my response slipped out before I could think twice. "Surprise."

I'd spent years hiding what I was, and in a matter of

months, I'd managed to out myself to Evan, Sabella, Zev, and now Shelby and Emilio. All because I kept getting dragged into Family games. It was enough to make me question my decision to leave the Guild and strike out on my own because this "being independent" thing sucked.

Emilio's dark gaze took on a copper glow, and he traced his finger over his desk in an unrecognizable pattern. His invisible power flexed, and the pressure against my shield turned crushing.

Gritting my teeth, I dug my metaphoric heels in and hunkered down. *Holy hell! He was strong.*

He continued to watch me with unblinking intensity as his finger traced what I was beginning to believe was a carved rune of power.

My head pounded and my muscles strained, but I didn't dare look away from the pissed-off head of the Cordova Family, even as I felt movement around me.

"Emilio!" His name was a sharp rebuke.

Emilio's finger stilled, the press of pressure held steady, and he slowly shifted his gaze to Zev. "What did you bring into my home?"

Freed from Emilio's glare, I realized Zev had put himself between his boss and me. It was a telling move, an important one that I would think about later. *If there is a later,* a grim little voice in my head piped up.

When Zev remained silent, Emilio growled, "What did you bring into my home, Arbiter?"

The air fairly crackled with tension as Zev said nothing and Emilio's glare gained a betrayed depth that sent a startling flash of insight ripping through me.

What the hell am I doing?

My desire to have Zev pick me over his Family was driven by an unwarranted jealousy, namely that he had something I'd always wanted—acceptance. Emilio wasn't pissed because Zev hadn't shared. He was hurt that Zev hadn't trusted him enough to share. If Zev remained silent, it would cost him everything, and whatever was starting between us would choke under his resentment of having made that choice. That wasn't something I was willing to live with, so I brushed my fingers against Zev's hip and gained his attention.

When he looked at me, the war between keeping my secret and upholding his oath to his Family raged in his eyes and hit me like a sucker punch. I couldn't do this to him. I couldn't make him choose. It wouldn't be fair. It was a realization I'd recognized weeks ago but willfully ignored, not wanting to accept the messy consequences of admitting what I was. Just like Zev had warned me, once I entered the game, I had to make my move. *Time to roll the dice.*

I tore my gaze from Zev's and met Emilio's coldly furious one. "I'm a Prism."

The flicker of surprise in his eyes was echoed by a sharp inhale from Shelby. The unceasing push of Emilio's magic took a step back, and the sudden release of pressure left my legs shaky. I swayed where I stood.

Emilio pushed away from the desk and closed in on Zev, leaving only a few inches between them. "You knew."

Other than the tensing of his frame, Zev didn't move as he faced Emilio's accusation. "I did."

The two men engaged in a stare down, one I was loath to interrupt. Finally, Emilio broke the heavy silence. "Are your memories back?"

Zev nodded.

Only then did Emilio aim his gaze at Shelby. "Ms. Quinn, I'm sure I don't need to remind you that all that transpires here is covered by the oath you took for this assignment."

"No, you don't." Shelby's response was solemn, even as she looked from Emilio to me. Whatever she saw on my face had her adding, "Any and all things that occur in this room tonight are sealed under a bond of silence and can only be shared with those in attendance."

Unfortunately, I had to trust that whatever bound her word to Emilio was strong enough to buy her silence. If it wasn't, well, I would have to make some moves a hell of a lot sooner than expected and hope my ties to Sabella were strong enough to withstand the strain.

Apparently satisfied with her response, Emilio turned and walked over to the window, his hands clasped behind his back as he stood in front of the night-drenched glass, staring at something only he could see. "Ms. Quinn, you mentioned a secondary spell?"

"Yes." Shelby rose from her chair, bent over the table, and blew out the candles. A whiff of honeysuckle and roses drifted on the air. "It was set within that specific memory. Most likely to discourage what we were doing tonight, should Zev get that far." She began collecting her items from the table before wrapping them in silk and carefully tucking them inside her oversized purse. "However, Ms. Costas managed to..." She stilled and appeared to consider her words. "Neutralize the spell, so it should no longer be a threat."

"That's good to know," Zev muttered, earning a hard glare from Emilio.

"Then it appears that your job here is complete, Ms. Quinn," Emilio said.

"So it seems," she agreed. She trailed her fingers across the chalk lines on the table, marring them into a thin layer of dust. "A couple of things before I leave." She looked at Zev. "There shouldn't be any lingering effects from the spell. However, should something strike you as off, please have Emilio contact me right away."

She used a bit of silk to wipe the chalk from her fingers then picked up the last candle, wrapped it, and dropped it into her purse. She waved her hand over the table, and the chalk dust rose then drifted away. Resettling the purse strap on her shoulder, she came around the table toward me, hand extended, with a warm smile that didn't match the sharp interest in her eyes. "Ms. Costas, Rory, it was lovely to meet you."

I rose and shook her hand. "You as well, Shelby."

She nodded then offered her hand to Zev. "Zev."

"Shelby," he returned.

She moved to Emilio, hand extended, and murmured, "It's been a pleasure serving the Cordova Family."

He met her halfway, near his desk, and took her hand in his before covering it with his other one. I was startled when a brush of magic swept past me, indicating he was up to something. "We appreciate your service and discretion."

Shelby's smile cooled, but her voice stayed warm. "I honor my covenants, Mr. Cordova."

The brush of magic got stronger, but I didn't dare try to sneak a peek at whatever was going down between the two of them. It didn't last long and, whatever it was, seemed to ease some of Zev's tension, so I made a mental note to ask about it later. I was more concerned with keeping my wits about me, which wasn't easy to do as the ache of rebuffing Emilio's magic dropped to a dull throb.

Emilio let the Muse go and said, "I hope you have a lovely evening." He held Zev's gaze over Shelby's head. "I'll have Zev walk you to your car."

Shelby waved the offer away. "Don't bother. I'll be fine."

Emilio looked at her. "It's not a bother, and I insist."

I swallowed while Shelby gracefully gave in. I wasn't looking forward to being alone with Emilio, but he wasn't giving me much choice. Zev was clearly just as reluctant with Emilio's request, because he motioned Shelby ahead of him with stilted movements. However, neither of us put up an argument with Emilio's decree. Instead, we did as told.

Shelby swept through the office door, and Zev gave me one last, long, unhappy look before he pulled the door closed, leaving me all alone with the rightfully angry head of the Cordova Family.

CHAPTER THIRTEEN

THE OFFICE DOOR closed with an overly loud click, leaving Emilio and me sharing a strained silence.

"How long has he known?"

Emilio's calm question had me studying his expression for some clue as to where this was going, but there wasn't much to find. The sudden shift from his earlier anger to a weirdly polite calm made me leery. Hesitantly, I answered, "Not long."

He dipped his chin, turned away, and paced over to the window. "And Sabella? She's aware?"

My pause was longer. I could almost sense a trap but couldn't see it. "Yes."

That got a sardonic curve of his lips. "Of course." He continued to stare out through the night-drenched glass and took us somewhere unexpected. "I always wondered what kind of woman would get under Zev's skin." He turned only his head and pinned me in place with a hard stare. "You are not what I expected."

I tried not to let his comment rankle me, reminding myself of the merits of being polite. Then I caught Emilio's flash of amusement before he tucked it away. *Screw it.* "Is this where I'm supposed to ask who you expected then feel bad because I don't measure up?"

That earned a derisive snort. "If only it was that easy to discourage you."

"Discourage me from what?"

"Playing whatever game it is that you've dragged Zev into."

My spine snapped straight, and for the first time, I didn't give the first fuck about who Emilio was or what power lay at his command. I was pissed at the unfounded accusation. "That's bullshit and you know it."

"Do I?" Emilio faced me, his arrogance apparent in his haughtily raised eyebrows, jutted jaw, and folded arms. "My nephew is kidnapped and Zev finds him being protected by some no-name Transporter, who may or may not be working for those who took him. After Zev brings Jeremy home, he shares few details about this Transporter person, and months later, when he runs across her again, she's now poking around Family business."

Damn, Zev shared more than I expected.

Emilio's voice hardened. "Then somehow, this mysterious contractor with no Family ties manages to get herself attached to Sabella Rossi, *the* matriarch of the oldest Arcane Family. Even more puzzling, Sabella decides to name this same unknown as her proxy for a private Family investigation surrounding information that would be very delicate and damaging, should it get out to the Arcane world. An investigation during which this contracted Transporter, with no combat training, somehow manages to protect two highly skilled Arbiters from a bespelled, crazed third combat-trained Arbiter."

When laid out like that, things looked sketchy, but it

wasn't my choice to be Sabella's proxy, and there was no way I could stand aside and let Bryan kill Zev and Imogen.

"As much as I appreciate your dubious protection of my Arbiter, as the head of the Family, it is my responsibility to protect those under my care, even those who are least likely to need such protection," Emilio concluded with icy precision. "However, I warn you, I won't stand aside while you and whoever you're working for set Zev up."

His accusation slashed across my fraying hold on my tongue until equal parts defensive anger and frustration won out. "Are you nuts?" Probably not the smartest thing to ask the head of the Cordova Family, but that was the dumbest thing I'd ever heard. "No one is setting Zev up. Not to mention, he doesn't need protection from me." If anything, it was more likely to be the other way around, as the man had a tendency to shove me out of my comfort zone on a regular basis.

"I disagree." Emilio dropped his arms and glided closer before stopping behind the chair Zev had used earlier. He gripped the top edge of the padded back, his fingers digging in until they were bloodless. "Lest you forget, Zev and I grew up together. He's stood at my side through hell and high water, and not once in all that time have I ever had a reason to doubt him."

Behind us, the door opened, but neither of us acknowledged it.

Emilio kept at me. "You show up, charm Sabella into being your champion, and now he's keeping secrets from me." His gaze shifted behind me then came back to rake me from head to toe in a mocking perusal. "I can't say you've been a good influence on him."

His disparaging attitude turned my vision red. "First, no one manipulates Zev," I snapped, ignoring a familiar presence closing in at my back. "Second, it wasn't his secret to share."

Emilio's face darkened. "That's not the point."

Undaunted, I shot back, "Isn't it?"

"No, it's not." He let go of the chair and straightened. His gaze lifted to behind me, where I knew Zev stood as silent witness to our argument. When Emilio's gaze returned, it was flinty. "You have been in and around the Arcane elite for months now, correct?"

"Yes."

"Then I shouldn't have to explain why someone in my position can't afford to be blindsided by their own people." Emilio shifted his attention to include Zev. "When I threw her my support at that meeting, you should've come clean about her, about what she is." He looked at me. "That he didn't worries me."

"It shouldn't," Zev said, finally entering the discussion. "When have I ever put the Family at risk?" He didn't wait for Emilio to answer before tacking on, "She's no threat to you."

"But you are to me," I cut in, unwilling to let it go. "History's proven that people like me aren't safe with people like you."

Emilio cocked his head. "How exactly do you figure that?"

His question pulled me up short. *Is this his idea of some sort of test?* The Families had a dark, convoluted history of hoarding the unusual and rare then grinding them underfoot until they were nothing but dust. "Arcane Families used Prisms as personal shields, throwing them in front of their precious heirs to take the brunt of magical assassination attempts until the Family vendettas all but wiped out the entire designation. Prisms' only path to survival was to hide what they were until they were all but erased from Arcane history. With that kind of history, is it any wonder that I wouldn't admit what I was to you, or any Family?"

Emilio appeared unmoved by my explanation. "If you truly feel that way, then I have to wonder why you choose to share your secret with one of the oldest known powers in our society?"

It wasn't the question I'd expected, but perhaps I should have. Then I wouldn't have felt like I'd just had my feet swept out from underneath me. "Excuse me?"

"What did Sabella promise you?" He pressed. "Protection? Knowledge?" I must have flinched, because something close to pity flashed over his face and softened the hard edge in his voice. "Knowledge, then." He sighed. "Did you ever stop to think why someone in her position would seek you out?"

Behind me, I felt Zev shift. Not much, just enough to earn a frowning glance from Emilio. But since I was reeling from Emilio's well-placed blow, it barely penetrated. "The Guild director—"

Emilio waved that off. "Yes, I know your reputation as a Transporter was gaining traction, but still, you were a relative unknown, no matter who recommended you." Not done rocking my world, he continued, "You strike me as an intelligent young woman, Rory. Tell me you haven't wondered about Sabella's motives? Not even once?"

The photograph of my parents with a smiling Sabella flashed through my mind, and the suspicions haunting me gained ground. But that was between her and me and not something I was ready to share with Emilio. I scrambled for solid ground. "I thought Sabella was your friend."

"She is," he answered, not unkindly. "But she's also the head of the oldest Arcane Family, and she's not known for being benevolent. Clever, manipulative, ruthless, yes. Benevolent, no. Which makes me wonder, why the change when it comes to you?"

His point sank deep, fracturing my confidence in Sabella even more. I didn't like it, but I couldn't deny it. "I don't know, but if we find her, I'll be happy to ask."

Emilio's unhappy look intensified. "A word of advice, you

may want to brace as you may not like her answer." He looked at Zev. "And that goes for you as well."

"I've known Sabella as long as you have, brother," Zev said. "And right now, I'm more concerned with getting her back than I am about her intentions toward Rory. Especially considering your concerns about the council."

"That's a discussion for later," Emilio warned with a pointed look at me.

More than happy to leave the previous discussion behind, I said, "Sabella told me about your concerns."

"My concerns?" Ice dripped from Emilio's voice as he stared at me.

"Yours and hers," I qualified. "How you both believe there's a high-level traitor close to the council. Most likely the same someone who took out Theo Mahon before he could share their name or testify at the hearing on the Delphi project."

Emilio's face hardened, but before he could say anything, there was a knock on the office door. He frowned and looked at Zev.

I shifted enough to catch Zev's shrug.

Emilio moved to the door and pulled it open. A familiar voice asked, "Mr. Cordova, is Rory with you?"

"Yes." He stepped back, taking the door with him. "Come on in."

Lena swept through with Evan on her heels. "We apologize for the late visit, but we found something interesting that might help track Sabella." She pulled up short, the tension in the room finally penetrating her excitement. She looked from me to Zev to Emilio, who was closing the door. "I'm sorry. Is this a bad time?"

Emilio shook his head, his polite mask falling neatly into place. "No, you're fine. Please"—he waved at the chairs —"take a seat and tell us what you found."

Evan waited until Lena took one of the chairs in front of Emilio's desk before taking a seat in the other one, leaving Zev and me standing off to the side. Lena waited until Emilio resumed his seat behind his desk before she started in. "Earlier today, I did some asking around. A high-risk, high-return contract was offered by a private party outside of the Guild. My source didn't pursue the offer but could confirm it was picked up by a small, known team of mercenaries."

"Mercenaries like those that attacked Zev and me?" I asked.

"Maybe," she said. "But the thing is, this job popped up a day or so ago."

"So after the attack in the garage," Zev confirmed.

"Right," Lena said. "Which makes me think this was a backup response should the first one fail."

"Lena brought me everything she could find on the job," Evan said. "From there, I was able to narrow my search parameters on the dark web, and the results started coming in about an hour ago. I won't go into the nitty-gritty, but I used the promised payment for the job as one parameter and found some interesting hits. One of which belonged to the Trask Family. They weren't the only Family shifting finances around, but the amount Trask was moving was closest to the one offered for the job and fit the timing."

Emilio's gaze narrowed, and he leaned forward. Next to me, Zev's presence gained a predatory edge.

Evan, caught up in his recitation, ignored the rising tension. "Unfortunately, it's been routed through what basically amounts to an electronic maze." He shifted in his seat, his face intent, excitement kindling deep in his tired eyes. "At first glance, it appears to be a typical outsourcing contract for company file purge. Not a surprise considering his biotech company, Origin, is on the edge of financial collapse, but the more you scrape away at it, the funkier it looks. The thing is, this maze is seeded with electronic trip wires. One wrong move and what trail exists will be erased, leaving us with nothing." He looked from Emilio to Zev. "My gut says this is connected, but I can't prove Trask is the one who authorized the payment or if someone is simply using his accounts."

"Plausible deniability," Zev murmured, sharing a look with Emilio.

Grim frustration drew deep grooves into Emilio's face. "There are many unacknowledged but accepted reasons for a Family to be doing business via the dark web." He turned to Evan. "We'll need more than a possible financial trail to go after Trask without repercussions."

"Once I get through the maze, I might have something more solid, but…" He shrugged. "No guarantees."

"How long will it take you to get through the maze?" Zev asked.

Evan ran a hand through his messy hair, worry dimming his simmering excitement. "Longer than what Sabella has, most likely."

"Then we need to figure out another way to track Sabella." I turned to Zev. "What about Locke? Was he able to find anything?"

"Who's Locke?" Lena asked.

"My Hound," Emilio answered as he picked up the phone on his desk and hit a button. "My office, please." He set the phone back in the cradle. "His team was still tracking the scene before our meeting with the Muse."

"Oh yeah, the memory-retrieval thing. How did that go?" Lena asked Zev. "You back up to speed yet?"

Zev's lips twitched. "Yeah, it's all good."

"Good." She waggled her eyebrows at me.

I rolled my eyes, because what else could I do?

We all sat in tense silence, waiting for Locke to arrive. It didn't take long. There was a rap on the door, then it opened, and he peered around the edge. "You called?"

Emilio waved him in. "Your search at Sabella's, what did it turn up?"

Locke came and stood next to Zev, one hand rubbing his tight jaw. "Not much. Someone used a nullifying spell. Other than what was at the scene, we've got nothing. Nothing leading to or from the house. They managed to keep it all contained to the property."

Zev turned to Evan. "What about the security videos? Anything there we can use?"

Evan shook his head. "Wiped with a military-grade pixilation program. Piecing it together will take days."

"Military-grade?" Suspicions spun through my mind. When Evan nodded, I looked at Zev. "Origin held military contracts, right? So how hard would it be for them to get their hands on something like that?"

Zev and Emilio shared a look, then Zev said, "Imogen lied when I asked her about Trask's connection to Mahon."

In her chair, Lena's spine snapped straight. "Theo Mahon? The asshole who almost killed me?" She looked from Zev to Emilio and back. "I thought he was being held by the council?"

CHAPTER FOURTEEN

ZEV LOOKED AT EMILIO, who was studying Lena. Picking up the strained undercurrents between the two men, Lena snapped, "What?"

"He was being held by the council," Emilio said without any inflection.

Lena shook her head. "Was? What do you mean was?" She twisted in her chair so she could see Zev. "You told me that he would answer to the council for what he did to me."

"Emilio." Zev's voice was hard, but it carried a warning. "They can't help us if they don't have all the information."

Emilio's eyes flashed, but instead of arguing, he bit out, "Mahon is dead, murdered in his cell."

Evan let out a low, disbelieving whistle, while Lena blinked and slowly sank back in her chair. "Why?"

"He made a deal with the council," Emilio explained. "Leniency in exchange for the identity of who he was going to sell the drive to."

Lena's hands curled into fists, and her green gaze took on hints of gold. "What the hell was on that drive?"

"That, I won't share, Ms. Davis." There was no give in Emilio's voice. "Suffice it to say, the information on the drive is considered valuable enough to kill for." His voice gentled, and he inclined his head. "As you, unfortunately, found out."

Lena studied Emilio for a long moment, and I knew her well enough to recognize she was debating whether to push her luck. Thankfully, she played it smart and let it go. She turned to Zev. "Right, so back to you, big guy. What's Trask's connection to Theo?"

"That's the problem," he said. "We don't know if there is one or if it's just Imogen being Imogen."

Puzzled, Evan asked, "Who's Imogen?"

"Queen bitch and Arbiter for the Trask Family." When all eyes hit me, I realized I had muttered that out loud.

"Ah, yes, the ex," Lena said dryly.

I caught Zev's amusement and gave him an answering shrug. *So I shared.* Lena was my best friend. It was a given I'd bitch about Zev's ex-girlfriend to her. It wasn't like I'd given away any confidential information, just the fact that the icy witch had it in for me and couldn't keep her claws off Zev during our last assignment.

"So what does she have to do with this?" Lena asked Zev.

"After Theo was killed, I asked Imogen questions about his connection to Trask, Arbiter to Arbiter. She said Trask had already discussed the connection with the council but she wasn't privy to the details."

"But," Locke said, gaining everyone's attention, "you think she's lying."

"Yeah," Zev confirmed.

"So," Emilio broke in thoughtfully, "we can call her bluff." When everyone looked at him, he continued, "I can demand a meeting with Trask, ask my own questions, ones he can't dodge without causing an incident."

"Which would give us an excuse to sniff around Trask's place," Locke said with a hint of feral glee.

"Hang on." I didn't want to put a damper on things but asked, "Do you think he'd really be stupid enough to keep Sabella at his house? Doesn't he own a bunch of other properties? If we focus on his house and she's somewhere else—"

"No, he's right," Evan cut in as he pushed up from his chair before he paced the office and thought out loud. "When I was tracking Trask's finances, I did a secondary run on his properties, specifically those he's shut down, looking for an uptick in utility usage or increase in visitors from nearby cameras." He caught my stunned expression and offered a wan smile. "Protocol, Rory. Remember, I do this shit for the Guild all the time." He went back to his pacing and speculation. "I limited the search to the last few days, thinking if they had to prepare someplace to hold her, they'd be in and out." He stopped next to Lena and addressed Emilio. "Nothing popped."

Emilio leaned back in his chair. "So we stick with Trask's main property, because it's easy enough to have a holding room on standby."

The way he said that made me wonder if that was just SOP for Arcane Families. Scary thought.

"We can eliminate the main house," Emilio said and looked at Zev. "Too easy for, say, staff to slip up and reveal she's there. But he'd want to keep her close, which means holding her in one of the outbuildings. Where he can limit who knows about her presence."

"Makes sense," Zev agreed. "He could use his existing security teams without anyone being the wiser. And if he caught someone poking around, he could take care of it without raising eyebrows."

Caught up in the conversation, I asked, "How many structures are you talking about?"

"Five," Locke answered. "There's the main house, a guest-house, two barns, one with actual horses and stables, one for his toys, and a toolshed."

"All spread over a couple of acres, patrolled by his in-house security," Zev added.

Their recitation was impressive if not disconcerting. Even Evan looked impressed. "We could use drones equipped with an infrared camera," he suggested.

Emilio shook his head. "Too obvious. Plus, if his security is anything close to mine, he'll have that covered."

"I've got a better idea," Zev said. "One that won't be as obvious but can cover as much area as a drone."

Deciphering his riddle, I cocked my head and asked, "You want to send in your feathered friends?"

He gave me a pleased grin. "Yep. No one notices if a hawk or two is circling. Easy enough to use them in flyovers early in the morning before the meet. If we're lucky, we can catch a shift change or pinpoint which areas are most heavily guarded and start there."

Ah, the joys of working with an animal mage. "Too bad we can't send in tracking dogs." I was half joking. "It would make this so much easier."

"You know, there's more than one way to track someone," Locke drawled. "Especially if they're a powerful mage, and Sabella is definitely a power."

Lena caught his meaning. "You're talking about crafting a marker spell," she exclaimed as she shot to her feet, excitement lighting her face. "We just need a foci of Sabella's, something she's imbued with her magic." She spun to me. "The scrying stone!"

Emilio rose from his chair, his hands flattening on his desk. "You have a scrying stone?"

My hand went to the chain that held the polished piece of agate Sabella had given me weeks ago during the Delphi project investigation. She wanted a way to ensure we could communicate without worry of the wrong ears listening in. I pulled it out from under my T-shirt. "I'd forgotten about it." I turned to Zev. "I can try using it."

"Don't bother," Lena said as she came over to me. "It won't work like that unless Sabella has the other stone on her. Even if she does, she may not be able to answer."

"Not to mention, we have no idea if her captors are using magic to hold her," Locke added. "If they are and you try to reach out to her, it could trigger any number of spells. Most of which would not end well."

He didn't clarify for whom, but he didn't need to. I wasn't keen on either one of us ending up on the wrong end of a spell.

"But," Lena cut in, "we can use this as a foci for the marker spell." She held out her hand and wiggled her fingers. "Hand it over."

A strange reluctance had me tightening my fist on the stone. It warmed under my touch. "Explain the marker spell for those of us not in the know."

"It's like a customized divining rod," Evan spoke up, proving that the only one in the room not in the know was me. "If you have something that bears a unique magical signature, you can then craft a spell targeting that same signature. The closer you get to that signature, the stronger the pull on the object."

"So anyone can use it to find her?" I reached up, undid the clasp on the chain, and dropped the necklace into Lena's waiting palm.

Lena cupped her hand and shook her head. "We have to use the existing link between you and her as the base of the spell, so it will only work for you. To anyone else, it's just a necklace."

Before I could voice my concerns about playing spy, Evan

pointed out, "If they've got Sabella under some kind of cloaking spell, it won't work either."

"It will if we craft the marker to pick up both magical and physical scents," Locke said.

I shot a puzzled frown at both him and Lena. "Can you do that?"

A reddish-gold glow crawled over Lena's hand to lick at the agate. Standing as close to me as she was, I couldn't escape the scraping sting of her rising magic as she studied the stone. "There's enough here for a Fusor to work with." When she turned her attention to Locke, her eyes held an amber glow. "So long as you know one that can work with incantations."

"Aspen," Zev said.

Locke nodded and rubbed a hand over his jaw. "She's on night shift, and her clearance is high enough we can read her in."

Zev waited for Emilio's agreement before asking, "How long will it take to set up?"

Locke looked at Lena. "You're a Key, right?" After she nodded, he said, "Between the three of us, I'm guessing a few hours, but I'm going to be wiped afterward."

Zev turned to Emilio. "I'm guessing you want a meeting with Trask for the morning?"

"The sooner the better," Emilio confirmed. "I can bring you, but if I insist on bringing a second person, like Locke, Trask may not take the meet."

"We don't need Locke, just someone who can slip under the radar." Zev looked at me. "Like, say, your personal driver, who won't be armed but will have to remain outside with the vehicle."

"A vehicle they'll insist wait near the garage," Emilio finished as he considered me.

My exhaustion notwithstanding, it wasn't hard to see where they were going with this. "How close is this garage to the other outbuildings?"

"Close enough that both the horse barn and the guest-house are within walking distance," Locke answered. "Should you get bored waiting around and decide to do a walkabout."

It was my turn to do a little pacing as I thought it through and did my best to ignore the combined weight of Zev, Locke, and Emilio's focus. "What about his security? According to what you said earlier, won't they be watching?"

"Watching is all they can do," Zev said. "All they'll see is you walking around outside. So long as you aren't sneaking peeks in windows or trying to break in, they'll simply watch."

I worried my lip, not quite as convinced as Zev that this was all Trask's security would do. I turned to my best friend. "How obvious is this marker spell?"

"It's not," Lena promised. "We can set it up so it marks like hot and cold. Hot, it's found the signature. Cold if nothing's there. Keep it tucked under your shirt and you should be good."

I nodded to indicate I heard her. "Right, then. Let's get this done."

We hammered out a few more details, like the range of the marker spell, the trigger word, what Emilio and Zev would use as the excuse for their meeting in the morning, and next steps for Evan's electronic hunt. Emilio, Zev, and Evan tossed around the idea of using surveillance equipment during the meet then decided not to push their luck. Lena and Locke left to track down Aspen and get to work on the spell. Evan pulled up the layout of Trask's place so I could memorize where the buildings were. If things went according to plan, the only building I wouldn't be able to get near without raising eyebrows was the toolshed. I wracked my brain for an approach, but I straightened, arcing to ease the ache in my lower back from bending over Emilio's desk to study the screens. I checked the clock to see it was well after midnight.

Zev followed my gaze. "We've done all we can for now, so let's call it a night."

Evan nodded, closing out his various programs. "I need a couple hours of downtime, then I'll get back to it. My eyes are starting to blur."

"I'll call Trask and set the meet for first thing in the morning," Emilio added, twisting at the waist and grimacing as bones popped.

Once the office was picked up and computers shut down, we all headed out. Evan bid us a quiet good night and headed down the hall. After a sharp look at Zev, Emilio did the same, leaving Zev and me alone.

"Come on," Zev urged with a hand in the small of my back. "You're about to collapse."

We were both quiet as we walked through the empty house to my room. At my door, I opened it, flicked on the light, and turned to find Zev watching me. As much as I wanted to invite him in to simply hold me and chase back the waiting worries about Sabella, I couldn't find the words. Instead, I stared up at him, my throat tight as the crushing wave of apprehension and fear choked me. I braced a hand against the nearby wall, closed my eyes, and breathed my way through the panic.

Zev's warm hands cupped my face. "You okay?"

I shook my head and opened my eyes to find him staring down at me.

Obviously reading my expression, he said softly, "She's going to be okay."

I wrapped my fingers around his wrists, holding on. "You don't know that," I whispered.

"No, but I know her." He brushed his lips across my forehead. "Get some rest. We'll find her tomorrow."

As he walked away, I wished for half of his confidence. Instead, I went inside, closed the door, and prayed for sleep.

CHAPTER FIFTEEN

STEPHEN TRASK'S home was in the exclusive Biltmore Park area of Phoenix, and the expansive lot indicated it was originally an equestrian estate, complete with a horse-training ring set between the two barns. White fences more at home in the rolling hills of horse country followed us as we turned in to one of two of the gated entries. Trask's estate stuck out like a sore thumb. It took up two city blocks, which made me believe this land had once housed two horse properties instead of the in-your-face one it now held. That was a lot of acreage in the middle of the city, even one known for expansive horse properties.

After being waved through the first entry gate, we followed the graveled drive, and I slowed Emilio's Maybach, not wanting to pit the sedan's finish. The drive led us to the main house, which couldn't decide if it was a farmhouse or an oversized cottage. Strangely, despite its architectural split personality, it managed to blur the line between ostentatious and welcoming.

I brought the luxury sedan to a stop at the top of the circular drive, where two people walked out of a front courtyard protected by a stucco hallway and a wrought iron gate. The house was set back far enough that all I could make out about the front doors was that they were big, wooden, and arched. I put my sunglasses on and got out of the car.

Two men came toward us, nearly identical in their dark slacks and light shirts. Definitely not businessmen, not with muscles like that. They were built to intimidate, and their blank expressions were hidden behind dark sunglasses. I went to the rear driver's-side door and opened it for Emilio. He stepped out as the two guards came to a stop on the other side of the car. Zev didn't wait for me to play chauffeur but got out on the other side, facing down the two guards. I trailed Emilio around the Maybach's trunk and stayed a few feet back as he continued to Zev's side.

The guard on the right spoke first. "Mr. Cordova, Mr. Trask welcomes you to his home." He shifted his body sideways, and his companion stepped back, a clear invitation for Zev and Emilio to walk between them. "If you'll follow me, please."

Emilio nodded then waited for the first guard to take the lead. He fell in behind him, ignoring the second guard, who was busy staring at Zev.

Zev stopped in front of the second guard, and they engaged in a stare down. It didn't last long because Emilio stopped, causing his escort to do the same, and called Zev's name. When the first guard saw what was happening, it was his turn to call back. "Andrew," he said in a distinct warning. Andrew looked at the first guard, deliberately ignored Zev, and aimed his dark lenses on me.

Doing my best to look unthreatening, which wasn't difficult, I waited by the car as Zev and Emilio disappeared into the courtyard. Just inside the gate and off to the side of the stone walkway were some neat garden boxes filled with leafy green things. *Strange to have your garden in front of your house, but what do I know?* Green things did not like me.

As the trio made their way to the front door, it swung open, and I heard a female voice greet, "Emilio, Zev, lovely to see you."

Recognizing Imogen's voice, I did my best not to react, but I did round the front end of the car, hopefully getting out of visual range. No telling what would happen if she saw me, but I didn't think it would be anything good.

"Miss." Andrew stepped forward.

I stopped and turned. "Yes?"

"You need to move the car down to the garage."

I looked over the hood of the Maybach and down the drive. "And that would be?"

"Take a left at the bottom of the drive," he instructed without moving from his position. "They'll be waiting for you at the barn."

Right. I went to the driver's side of the sedan, got in, started the car, and headed down the drive. Safe in the confines of the car, I tugged the pendant out from under the curved neck of my blouse, cradled the stone in my palm, and breathed "Find" to activate the marker spell. Heat sparked against my palm then disappeared. I tucked it back under and took the left at the bottom of the drive.

Tension tightened my shoulders, and a thin line of sweat that had nothing to do with the morning's rising heat ran down my spine. My bloodless fingers gripped the leather steering wheel as I rolled down the path, matching reality to the plans I'd studied the night before.

During the early morning hours, Zev had sent out his feathered friends to do a recon. He reported that there was the typical early-morning comings and goings as the landscaping crew stuck to their routine and the main house got set up for the day. While there was no obvious guard presence on the barns and toolshed, both structures saw their share of foot traffic. Nothing too exciting, but he was able to confirm the property was under both heavy video surveillance and constant foot patrols. Using what the birds had picked up, he advised leaving the toolshed for the last because with the amount of equipment moving in and out of the small space, it wasn't likely to double as a cell. While no one went near the guesthouse, it and the horse barn stayed at the top of our list, followed by the toy barn.

The first building that came up was the guesthouse. Unlike the main house, it stuck with the cottage vibe, complete with a front porch, a pair of dark-blue Adirondack chairs, and pretty yellow flowers along the walkway. Because I had to keep my speed down, not only did I note the two security cameras, one on each corner just under the roofline, but I also realized the large front windows were heavily tinted, making it difficult to see inside.

As I rolled past, I held my breath, waiting for the pendant to signal something, anything. I knew it was a long shot, because Lena and Locke had explained that the pendant would work better if I was on foot, but I couldn't help hoping we would catch a break. When nothing happened, I let out a shaky exhale.

Onward.

The two barns loomed ahead, sharing an open space that stretched between them. The training ring was on my left, and a beautiful dark horse pranced along while a trainer stood in the center, pivoting in sync with the horse's movements. Over on the right, near what I labeled the toy barn, a slender figure straightened from the white fence and waved me over. I followed his directions into what was clearly considered visitor parking.

There was a white panel van with a cleaning service logo, a beat-up Chevy with a bed full of yard debris, and a dust-covered Ford F-150 with bales of hay stacked in its bed. Since I didn't want to be in anyone's way, I picked a spot out of the way of the other vehicles and reversed my way in. It might have been paranoia, but I would rather be nose first with a straight shot to the exit than have to deal with reversing in a three-point turn.

Once I was parked, I shut the Maybach down. After tugging off my fingerless driving gloves, I put them in the glove compartment, grabbed my phone from the console, and got out. No way was I going to wait inside the car. With the day's heat gaining strength, I would have to keep the engine running to power the AC. Not that the Maybach couldn't handle such a feat, but it was a waste of gas, and I needed to be outside to do my thing.

Because I knew I would be standing around outside, in the heat, I paired a thin airy rayon blouse with gray linen slacks, all with an eye toward comfort and practicality. Gray would hide the worst of the dust, rayon allowed whatever breeze existed to make it to my skin, and instead of my normal modest-heeled shoes, I wore ankle boots, which were less likely to dump me on my ass if I had to run.

Once I was outside, my sunglasses dimmed the worst of the sun's glare, and I watched an impressive beast being led out of the huge doors of the first barn, where the whinnied noises of equine chatter joined the human voices and occasional laughter drifting on the morning breeze. Spanish wove in rhythmic counterpoint to the industrious melody and came closer with the crunch of gravel. I turned to see a couple of men in gray shirts, faded jeans, and bandanas wrapped around their face to ward off the dust. They were pushing a wheelbarrow full of branches toward the beat-up Chevy. Just behind them, the slender figure that had waved me into the lot hurried over.

As he got closer, I could see he was a young guy, barely out of his teens. His smile was bright and welcoming, the complete opposite of Andrew's poker face. "Hello." His voice cracked on the *o*.

The urge to pat him on the head was difficult to resist, but I managed. "Hello."

"Andrew said you're waiting while Mr. Trask's guests visit?"

"I am."

"You're welcome to wait inside." He motioned toward the second, quieter barn. "There's a small lounge just to the right of the doors. There's a fridge with water and coffee available."

"I appreciate it." I paused and looked toward the training ring again. "Do you mind if I wander around a bit first? I've always loved watching horses." And if I struck out at the horse barn, I could retreat to the toy barn.

"Um." He pivoted on a heel and looked at the training ring as he grabbed the back of his neck, clearly not used to going off script. He swung around and finished with "Sure, I guess. Just be careful and try to stay out of the way."

I flashed a big smile. "Awesome. Thanks."

Permission granted, I walked toward the training ring. Under my blouse, the agate stayed disappointingly quiet. I kept my pace casual but clocked what security I could see. The most obvious were the cameras tucked under the eaves. Considering they weren't camouflaged, I figured Trask had made it a point to let people know he was watching.

I got to the training ring and walked along the white rail fence. As I got closer, I realized the planks that made up the fence weren't wood but heavy-duty vinyl. I picked a spot where foot traffic was nearly nonexistent but where I had a clear view of the comings and goings at the barn, then I leaned against the post to watch. It didn't take long to pick out the shadows patrolling the property. They didn't blend in at all, and it was clear they weren't trying to either. With a property this large, I figured the cameras couldn't catch everything, but whatever they missed, the hard-faced patrols would pick up.

I garnered a couple of glances, but as I stayed put, seemingly absorbed with the happenings inside the ring, where a teenage girl sat straight back as her horse pranced in circles under the gimlet eye of a trainer. Eventually, those curious looks turned away.

I had some time to kill. Zev and Emilio had promised me at least forty minutes but no longer than an hour to conduct their business with Trask. The minutes trickled by, and while horses were nice and all, if I had my druthers, I would stick to the ones under metal hoods.

After fifteen minutes, I pushed off the post and headed toward the stables. *Time to push my luck.* Lena had sworn the pendant's range would cover a twenty-five-foot radius. I was about to test that, because I didn't think I would even make it that far inside the barn before being stopped.

As I got closer, I felt the weight of attention hit and knew I was being watched and not by those working near the stable. I swore I could hear the electronic whirr as the cameras followed me. Sure enough, when I stepped inside the barn, I made it only a couple of feet inside the hay-strewn concrete before one of those security shadows met me. "Ma'am."

Unlike the harmless teen, this guard was all business. Flirting would get me nowhere, but politeness... "Hello."

"Can I help you?"

"I was just checking out the horses." I took off my sunglasses and offered an apologetic smile. "I asked the nice young man if I could walk around for a bit while I wait for Mr. Cordova to finish up his business with Mr. Trask." Against my chest, the pendant remained frustratingly inert.

"I'm sorry, but this area is not open to the public."

"Of course." I replaced my sunglasses, gave him a tight-lipped smile, and turned around. It wasn't hard to feign disappointment. It just wouldn't be for the reason he thought.

Back out in the sun-drenched yard, I considered my options. Both barns faced the training ring, so circling the horse barn was out, but... A sharp neigh erupted behind me. Turning to the shared open space between the two barns, I watched a horse tap-dance sideways while a weathered gray-haired man did his best to get him to stop. The horse kept shying until he backed into the wall.

Inspiration struck.

I might not be able to circle the barn or get inside, but I could walk along the side of it and hopefully pick up any signs of Sabella. According to Lena and Locke, natural materials like wood wouldn't impede the marker spell, so technically, it should be able to go through the wall. Or at least that was my hope.

Decision made, I kept an eye on the nervous horse and his handler and moved down along the side of the barn. About fifteen feet in, I stopped and hoped that to anyone observing, it would appear as if I was utterly fascinated with what was happening. The handler was slowly calming the horse, inching him away from the wall and out into the open space. I matched their moves as I made my way down the side of the building. Finally, the horse stopped dancing and stood there, sides billowing, head held low by the handler, who ran a soothing hand down a front leg while crooning reassurances.

"Miss, you best stay back."

I almost didn't catch the warning, as the older man's croon didn't change. I froze and kept my voice equally low. "I will." I waited the couple of minutes needed for the handler to get the horse from twitchy to calm. Finally, the handler led the horse away, leaving me alone in the empty yard. After blowing out a breath, I continued to walk along the perimeter of the area. The damn necklace didn't even twitch.

Right, so cross off the stables. Moving on.

I crossed the packed dirt, skirting a couple of unpleasant piles left by the horses, and headed for the toy barn. When I stepped inside, no one stopped me.

As in the stables, the floor was concrete, but unlike the stables, it was obvious that this floor was intimately familiar with a broom. The lounge—or more accurately, the waiting room—was to the right and through a glass door. But what held my interest more surely than the horseflesh were the vehicles parked just beyond the entryway. I bypassed the lounge and moved through the short hall and into the garage proper. Professional curiosity had me evaluating Trask's vehicle collection.

I gave him credit. It was impressive, but it was also a clear mix of a rich man's race cars and practicality. No classics, just sleek and shiny modern beauties. I recognized the low curves of a Ford GT in yellow, which wasn't my favorite color, the more sophisticated lines of a silver Audi Spyder, then the rugged lines of a blinged-out black Chevy Silverado. Just beyond those, I caught a couple of ATVs and a pair of Harleys that, compared to Zev's black matte monster, looked like tame puppies.

Two men worked at the back of the space, where a mechanics bench and tool chests lined the far wall. From where I stood, I knew there was something more back there because the garage was a lot deeper than what I was currently looking at, but it wasn't clear what hid in that space. It could be anything from dedicated repair space to storage space.

I glanced at what I suspected were Trask's mechanics, but they weren't paying any attention to me, so I wandered over to the Fort GT parked at an angle on my left. The paint gleamed under the bright lights, and that same sheen was echoed on the tires, which looked almost new.

Such a waste.

It never made sense to me why someone would spend good money on what was clearly a performance car and not utilize that performance.

The GT was a gorgeous piece of machinery, but the true beauty of it was experienced behind the wheel. Its lack of any real use made my palms itch to get in and let it ride. I rubbed my palm against my thigh and went around the far side. I tried to peer through the dark window, but the tint made it difficult to see much detail, so I straightened and started to turn toward the Spyder.

Two things happened at once. The agate pendant, which had swung out as I leaned over, resettled against my chest with a pulse of heat, and a voice said, "I'm sorry. Can I help you with something?"

I covered my start of surprise by pressing my palm over the pendant. The stone's temperature held steady, not enough to burn but enough to let me know it was picking up something. I turned to the man approaching me. "Hi!" My voice came out overly chirpy, mainly because the pendant's unexpected reaction had left my heart racing. "I was... um... just looking."

My clueless moment worked to my advantage because his sharp-eyed speculation softened to exasperated politeness as he wiped his hands on an oil-stained rag. "And you are?"

"Oh, sorry." I managed a small, discomfited laugh and waved my hand. "I'm Mr. Cordova's driver. I was told I could wait in here while he finishes up his meeting." *Okay, so that's stretching the definition of "in here" a bit.* I turned to the GT. "This is gorgeous." No mechanic could resist a compliment.

This one proved no exception. "That, she is," he agreed.

He tucked his rag in a back pocket and held out his hand. "Name is Jon."

I took his hand and shook it. "Rory." Hopefully, even if Trask asked his mechanics about me, my curiosity about the cars would be considered justified instead of suspicious. "Interesting collection."

He grinned, revealing a gap between his front teeth that added character to his lined face. "I wouldn't call it a collection. Mr. Trask, he likes nice things, but he's practical about it."

I raised my brows and looked at the Audi. "I can tell."

Jon followed my gaze. "He picked that one up at Barrett-Jackson last year."

Barrett-Jackson was the annual car show held in Scottsdale and pulled a global audience of car enthusiasts looking to acquire some of the world's most sought-after vehicles. I made a point to go each year just to drool over pretties that were years beyond my checkbook.

I took advantage of the conversational opening and started up a back-and-forth on past showstoppers as Jon stayed at my side while we wandered through the garage. I managed to segue the conversation to maintenance and repairs, during which Jon confirmed that he and Sam, the other mechanic, did all of it in-house.

The deeper we moved into the garage, the warmer the pendant got. Normally, conversing with another gearhead was relatively easy, but distracted by the increasing burn of the pendant against my chest, I could only stay on topic and keep my gaze from drifting to the back area that I was starting to believe held something a lot more interesting than a repair stall. I was grateful that Jon liked to talk since he had no problem sharing story after story, while all that was required of me was the occasional "Really?" or "I can see that" type comment.

By the time we got to the Harleys parked near the mechanics bench and the mysterious back area, the pendant's burn was persistent enough to be uncomfortable. To ease the ache, I kept shifting my shoulders, only to finally clasp my hands behind my back so as not to touch it.

Just as I was about to give in and reach for the pendant, my phone vibrated in my pocket. I murmured an "Excuse me" to Jon, pulled out my phone, and saw Zev's one-word text of "Ready."

"I'm so sorry, Jon, but duty calls." I wiggled my phone. "Thank you so much for letting me take up your time." As much as I didn't want to, I turned toward the exit, leaving the echoes of Sabella's magic behind.

"Don't mention it," he said as he escorted me across the garage and to the exit. "It's nice to meet another car lover."

With each step I took, the pendant cooled. Jon and I exchanged goodbyes at the door. I resettled my sunglasses and headed to the Maybach with one last wave at Trask's mechanic. It sucked to walk away, but my edgy excitement overrode my frustration. All I wanted to do was dash to the Maybach, get Zev and Emilio, then storm through the garage to find Sabella. Instead, I made a conscious effort to keep my expression easy and my pace casual as I got in the sedan, started the engine and AC, pulled out my gloves, slipped them on, and slowly rolled out of the visitors' lot and up the drive.

CHAPTER SIXTEEN

WITH IMPECCABLE TIMING, I pulled up and parked in the same spot where I'd dropped Emilio and Zev off as Trask, Emilio, and Zev appeared around the corner of the courtyard. Trask stepped off to the side, letting Emilio and Zev pass, and I turned to check their progress through the passenger-side window. Emilio was in the lead with Zev following. I couldn't read either man's expression and not just because they both wore sunglasses. Emilio reached for the small gate just as Imogen came around the corner behind Zev, followed by the guard who had initially reprimanded Andrew.

Damn and double damn.

I sat there, caught by indecision, wondering if I should risk revealing my presence to Trask and Imogen, when Zev raised his hand just enough for me to catch the movement but not enough for those behind him to see it. I guessed I wasn't the only one concerned about the two seeing me because he made the universal palm-forward motion for "stay."

So I did, praying the heavy tint on the windows was enough to keep them from recognizing me. I resettled behind the wheel, face forward, and hard as it was, watched through the rearview mirror as Emilio stopped on the passenger side and turned to Trask. I heard his voice but couldn't make out the words, then Zev opened the back passenger door.

"... around eight for a late dinner to discuss the issue further?" Emilio asked.

Stephen frowned. "I'll be there."

"Good." Emilio moved into the open back door. "Until then." Then he settled into the back seat, face blank, as Zev closed the door, rounded the trunk, and got in on the other side.

I waited for both men to fasten their seat belts before I put the car in gear and sedately pulled away. A charged silence filled the car. I couldn't help sneaking one last glance in the rearview.

Imogen stood next to Stephen, watching us leave. I couldn't catch her expression, but my spine still crawled. It wasn't that I was afraid of Imogen but more that I wasn't keen on finding a knife in my back. That was something she wouldn't hesitate to do if she could and not just because she was Zev's ex. Imogen and I would never be more than coldly polite to each other. Not after Sabella had all but forced my involvement on the Delphi investigation to ensure that the three Arbiters worked together instead of for themselves and their Families. Then, after the fiasco with Bryan's death and my apparent nonreaction to being injected with a magically twisted serum, that resentment had shifted into calculated curiosity. Imogen didn't like being kept in the dark by someone she viewed as a nobody, and I wasn't a fan of haughty, insecure blowhards, but we all had our crosses to bear.

I pulled through the last gate and onto the public road, finally able to shake off some of my tension.

Emilio broke the silence. "Did it work?"

To make sure he was talking to me, I flicked a glance in the rearview. He had taken off his sunglasses and was watching me. "It did, yes." I turned my attention back to the road.

"Where at?" That was Zev.

"The toy barn." I didn't wait for a request to elaborate. "The front half is a combination showroom and garage, but there's space back behind the wall of the mechanics bench. There's no way to see what's back there because both mechanics were on site, but one of them confirmed they do all maintenance and repairs in-house."

"What difference does that make?" Emilio asked.

I hit my turn signal for the upcoming freeway exit. I'd been noodling the garage's dimensions in the back of my mind and came up with a couple of ideas, perhaps a bit out there but definitely probable. "If they work on the cars in the barn, it means that back space has to be big enough for at least a repair stall plus tools."

I checked my mirrors and decided the Maybach could outpace the compact coming up on my left. I hit the gas, pulled ahead, and merged with the freeway traffic as I considered how much to share. "Depending on how it's equipped, it means either there's enough space to be used as storage rooms or holding rooms, dealer's choice."

Correctly reading my tone, Zev pushed, "Or?"

"Or"—I chose my words carefully—"if Trask spared no expense on his garage, he could have a repair pit back there instead of a lift."

"What the hell is a repair pit?"

Zev's irritated question sparked a tiny burst of humor, but I made sure to keep it from my voice. "Basically, what it sounds like. A pit in the garage floor where a mechanic can stand to work on the car's undercarriage. It's a hell of a lot cheaper to install and maintain than hydraulic lifts, works with limited roof heights, and it's a lot easier on the mechanic." I aimed a quick glance at the rearview. "It also means there's enough space under the garage to hide any number of things." Saying that, something that had been bugging me clicked. "Huh, that would make sense, then."

After my non sequiter, Zev prompted, "What?"

"I just realized that the spell didn't trigger outside the barn or even just inside, which it should have if they brought Sabella through the garage. It wasn't until I was well inside, near the GT, before it picked up anything. Then it got progressively warmer the closer I moved to the back." I managed to slide the Maybach across the lanes until we found our spot in the carpool lane, where we were less likely to get stuck in traffic and it was easier to note if we picked up any tails.

"Which would make sense if they were holding her in a basement level." Zev easily followed my logic then threw in, "Or if they brought her in a different way, say, like a rear entrance, maybe?"

I wanted to smack my forehead. *Duh.* "There would have to be a rear entrance, because the interior door to the back wasn't big enough for a car to get through."

"Was the spell's reaction strong enough to believe that they're still holding Sabella there?" Emilio asked.

Thinking of what I'd felt in the garage, I gave a hesitant headshake. "I don't know." I rubbed the inert stone and felt the faint ache in my skin at the pressure. Maybe I should've asked Lena and Locke for more details, like how hot the pendant would get if Sabella was physically near. "It got pretty uncomfortable."

"So it could just as easily be picking up a recent echo," Zev said.

"Recent or not, it's enough to warrant investigating." Emilio's voice was grim.

"The sooner the better," Zev agreed.

Emilio was obviously on the same page because he said, "Tonight, then. Can you make it work?"

"I'll need to make a showing at the dinner," Zev said. "But I can slip out later without looking suspicious."

I was curious about this dinner but not enough to interrupt.

"You can't go alone," Emilio all but ordered.

"Wasn't planning on it," Zev said.

"I'm going with you." I couldn't have stopped my mouth if I'd wanted to, and I definitely didn't want to. I had my own reasons for wanting to get Sabella back. I risked another glance in the rearview and met Zev's dark gaze. "Marker spell, remember?"

Humor broke through his harsh mask. "Yeah, I remember."

I let out a silent breath of relief at his easy acceptance. Of course, even if he hadn't included me, I would've tagged along. This way, at least, I wouldn't have to avoid him and whatever lay in wait at Trask's.

"I'll tag Locke as well," he told Emilio. "Between the three of us, we should have it covered. In and out, hopefully, before Trask gets home."

My grip on the steering wheel tightened. The sensitive steering gave a tiny jerk in complaint, and I loosened my hold. *And if we're really lucky, we'll have Sabella with us.*

"I'll do my best to drag out the evening and keep Trask busy." Emilio's voice was wry. "You'll have until midnight or thereabouts."

Zev grunted then added a disgruntled, "Maybe we'll get lucky and he'll drag Imogen along so I don't have to worry about her interfering."

I got a huge kick out of his apparent irritation with the ice mage.

Emilio's amusement seeped into his voice. "Might make it harder to slip out unnoticed if he does."

Zev didn't respond, and for a moment, the earlier silence resettled but without the nervy edge. I did another mirror check, relieved to see that our rearview remained clear. Maybe it was overly paranoid to think Trask would set someone on our tail, but it was definitely in line with his past behavior, so I wasn't taking any chances.

"You were right, by the way."

Emilio's comment came out of left field. I checked the mirror and saw he was talking to Zev. I turned back to the road as our exit was coming up, but curiosity had me listening intently.

"About?" Zev asked.

"Something isn't right in the house of Trask." Emilio's voice was thoughtful. "Did you catch Imogen's reaction when I pressured Trask on his connection to Mahon?"

"Hard to miss," Zev admitted. "If she could've stopped the conversation, she would've."

Emilio made a quiet *humph* as I slowly began crossing lanes to get in position for our exit. "Trask was quick to put her in her place."

"He better watch his back, because she doesn't take kindly to shit like that," Zev pointed out.

"Who would?" Emilio murmured. "I find it interesting she felt comfortable enough to interfere in the first place. It makes me wonder if there's a power struggle going on there."

"I think we can safely assume that's a yes," Zev said.

I hit the turn signal and took the exit then slowed as we came up to the light. While Zev didn't sound overly concerned, he had enough surety in his voice to leave me worried. Didn't we have enough to handle with Trask's apparent kidnapping of Sabella and what I was starting to suspect was his betrayal of the council? Add a discontented

Imogen and an already tense situation could easily graduate to completely fucked, in my opinion. The light turned green, and I made a right.

"I'm sure I don't need to remind you how vital it is that your actions tonight not be discovered?" Emilio's tone was dry, but there was no escaping the seriousness underneath.

"I don't intend to be the match that lights a firestorm of a Family feud, Milo," Zev assured him.

"I'm not just worried about sparking a war between Families, which wouldn't last long anyway," Emilio said with the casual arrogance that came from knowing he was the bigger threat. "I'm more concerned with tipping off our traitor or endangering Sabella, wherever she is."

"If we're lucky, we'll get Sabella back tonight," Zev said. "Then we can find out who set her up and why."

I thought the why was pretty obvious. "Someone doesn't want Sabella to make the council meeting because she knows something she hasn't shared."

"You're probably right." Emilio didn't sound upset by that, merely reflective. "But I am curious who it was she was planning on meeting."

He wasn't the only one. I thought back on my conversation with Sabella in the hospital, just after I woke up, about how she wasn't the only one convinced there was a traitor at work. "What about those on the council who share your concerns? Maybe it's one of them?" I didn't have to look in the mirror to know Emilio was looking at me. I could feel it, and it was disconcerting. Instead of stopping there, I kept talking. "I mean, it's possible it's not just Sabella who's missing, right?"

The press of Emilio's presence eased up, and he finally said, "Right."

A musical chime sounded, and I could hear Emilio and Zev shifting around, likely going for their phones. I didn't bother, because my phone stayed on silent when I was driving. We weren't far from Emilio's house, so hopefully, whatever it was wasn't another emergency.

"It's Mari," Emilio murmured, and rapid ticks followed as he typed a response. He didn't share anything more for long minutes.

We were turning onto Emilio's street when he finally spoke again. "Mari got a call from Phoenix PD."

Zev didn't sound happy when he asked, "What do the police want on a Sunday?"

There was more texting as Emilio carried on two conversations at once. "Seems they found out you were released from the hospital and now are requesting you come down and give your statement."

I turned in to Emilio's drive and caught motion in the rearview mirror. I looked to see Zev dragging his hand through his hair, looking put out. "Today?"

I hit the button to activate the garage door.

Emilio continued to type. "Yes, at two." He finally looked up as we came to a stop to wait for the garage door to roll open. "I've directed Mari to request they come here to take it. That way, she can come over now and run through things with you beforehand."

Pulling the Maybach into its spot, I made a mental note to hide in my room or hole up with Evan.

"Fine." Zev ungraciously gave in.

I shut down the engine. The back doors opened almost simultaneously as Zev and Emilio got out. Pulling off my gloves, I grabbed my phone and exited as well. Closing the door, I looked up, surprised to see both men waiting for me by the back door. I joined them before coming to a stop beside Zev as Emilio opened the door.

He waved me through. "After you."

His politeness was unexpected but not unwelcome. I went

inside, leaving the two men to follow. As we moved through the utility room and into the kitchen, Emilio called my name. I pulled up short and turned. "Yes?"

"You may want to stay out of sight for the next few hours," he suggested carefully.

Not at all offended, as I had no desire to visit with the detectives, I wrinkled my nose. "No problem. I'll go pester Evan and see if there's something I can help him with." An extra set of hands was always welcomed on electronic hunts.

Emilio managed a small smile, then he turned to Zev. "I have a couple of calls to make before Mari arrives, then I'll join you for the upcoming interview."

Zev grimaced. "You don't need to be there. Mari and I can handle this."

"Of that, I have no doubt," Emilio said. "However, Mari commented that one of the detectives is a bit on the aggressive side. I'd like to sit in to ensure they don't push too far."

Detective Rendón's frustrated face flashed in my mind. It sucked, because while I appreciated her frustration at how dodgy Families could be, I was happy that was something that worked in my favor. Hopefully, Rendón wouldn't step too far over the line with Emilio around. If she did, I was sure Hall would drag her back like he did before. Either way, at least I didn't have to be there.

I was busy watching Emilio walk away, so when Zev grabbed my hand, I startled. I gave him a puzzled look as he pulled me down the hall to my room but didn't say anything until we were inside with the door closed. "What are you doing, Zev?"

"We need to talk."

Okay, nothing good ever comes of those four words. "We do?"

"We do." His voice was resolute.

"We could've talked in the kitchen," I muttered, and he led me to the bed. My pulse picked up because, well, bed and

Zev in the same space led to intriguing and distracting thoughts.

"I didn't want to be interrupted."

In true queen-of-split-personalities style, I was caught between an anticipatory "oh yeah" and an ominous "oh, shit." Still, when he tugged on my hand for me to sit on the edge of the bed, I did.

He grabbed one of the chairs, brought it close, and sat down, his knees on either side of my legs, leaving me with no escape option unless I was willing to crawl over him. If he'd cornered me this way days earlier, I might have given the crawling option serious consideration, but now, not so much. Instead, I simply watched him and tried to figure out what was going on.

He didn't make me wait long. "What did you find at Sabella's?"

Surprised by the unexpected question, I jerked back. "What?"

His dark gaze remained steady. "Yesterday, at Sabella's office, you found something and pocketed it." He braced his arms on his knees and leaned in. "What was it?"

Damn. He was scary sharp and frighteningly patient to wait as long as he had to question me on this. Especially considering I wasn't someone he trusted at that point, not with his memories missing. Since they were back, which also meant *we* were back, I didn't want to lie to him, but I wasn't quite ready to deal with the whole "Sabella might know my parents" thing. I tried to evade. "I don't want to talk about it."

"I think you need to." He didn't relent.

I didn't appreciate being cornered and snapped, "Seriously, we have other things we need to foc—"

"Stop. Just stop," he said quietly. "You know, I didn't expect it, but maybe I should have."

Confused by his rapid conversational shifts, I asked, "Expect what?"

"Your defense of me to Emilio."

"He was wrong." Even now, hours later, it still pissed me off that Emilio would think Zev would turn on him. Not even for me would Zev betray his Family.

"He was," Zev agreed, a hint of humor lurking around the edges of his eyes. "But you sticking up for me, especially considering the situation—"

I raised my eyebrows. "You mean, the whole not-trusting-me thing?"

That hint became a full-blown grin. "Oh, I trusted you."

"No, you wanted me," I corrected. "Big difference."

He lost his smile and turned serious. "No, I trusted you, Rory. Even with that spell in place and my memories gone, it was still you I searched out to discuss what to do next. The spell might have locked away the memories, but what's between you and me was still there, anchoring me despite the noise in my head. Why do you think I kept seeking you out?"

I wanted to believe him, but doing so meant acknowledging the hurt he'd caused. "Are you sure about that? Because it seems to me that you had no problem believing the worst of me."

He winced. "When I woke up in the hospital, I was off-balance and pissed as hell, especially since Emilio and the doctor couldn't give me answers other than to give it time. I took it out on you." He searched my face, regret darkening his eyes. "I'm sorry I hurt you."

His heartfelt apology triggered a flood of emotion, and I had to look away, just for a second, so I could hold on to my composure. When I was sure I was steady, I turned back and said, "Thank you for that."

As if that was what he was waiting for, he finally touched me. Taking one of my hands in his, he held it as his thumb brushed back and forth over my fingers. He managed a passable grin. "And for the record, I never once thought you were manipulating me."

Hearing the unspoken word, I prompted, "But?"

His grin faded, and his gaze flickered. "But I do worry about Sabella's interest in you."

"You've never made that a secret," I managed.

"No, I haven't," he agreed. He cocked his head. "Do you remember my warning? About what would happen if you admitted to what you were?"

It was a conversation we'd had during the Delphi investigation. After finding out my secret, Zev had warned me that once that knowledge became public, I would forever be watching my back, never knowing whom I could and couldn't trust, and to navigate those dangerous waters, I would need the courage to forge alliances, not welcome masters. He made it clear that he worried Sabella was more a master than an alliance, especially if she continued to be my only source of information on my ability. He offered to expand those sources with no expectations except to ensure I was strong enough to stand on my own. It had been an eye-opening discussion because it hit me that I was subconsciously looking for a family of my own, and that need left me vulnerable in a world where vulnerabilities could be lethal.

"Yeah, I remember," I admitted.

Proving he didn't give up on anything easily, he asked again, "What did you find at Sabella's?"

I remembered what he'd said when I asked why he would offer to help me, to stand at my side. *"I want you strong enough to survive in my world."* There was a depth to his answer that carried an implied vow that I'd held tight to while his memories were gone. It was a promise that if we trusted each other, we would find our way forward.

It was my turn to trust. I bit my lip, pulled my hand free

of his, and shifted my weight to one hip so I could pull out the folded photo. Strangely, I hadn't felt comfortable leaving it behind, so I carried it with me. After unfolding it, I stared at it for a moment before wordlessly offering it to Zev.

He took it carefully and studied it. Finally, he said, "She looks like you."

"She should," I answered and waited until he looked at me. "She's my mom."

CHAPTER SEVENTEEN

"YOUR MOM?" Zev asked with clear disbelief.

I nodded.

He looked at the old photo. "Well, shit."

I did the same. "Yeah."

He handed the picture to me. "Where did you find it?"

"Stuck behind another photo of her grandkids." I refolded the picture and tucked it in my pocket. "At least, I think it was her grandkids."

Zev gave a small nod but was clearly thinking. "The man, is that your dad?"

"Probably."

His gaze sharpened. "You don't know?"

I gave an uncomfortable shrug. "He was gone before I could remember, but the way they are in that picture, it would be a safe guess."

"So that's why," he said, mostly to himself.

"That's why what?" It wasn't fair to leave me hanging like that, even if I did have a good guess as to the answer.

His flash of sympathy was quickly masked but not fast

enough. "Why you dodged Emilio's question about Sabella's intentions."

Yep, that would be the one. "A little hard to argue when I'm starting to wonder why she wouldn't share this with me."

"Maybe she intended to." He played devil's advocate. "But with all that's gone down, she just hasn't found the right time. There's no way this would be an easy conversation."

I raised my brows in disbelief. "No, it wouldn't, but she's had plenty of opportunities to share before now. That she choose not to makes me wonder why."

"That's fair," he agreed. He sat back in his chair, templed his fingers, and studied me. "So now what?"

"Now," I said, bracing my hands behind me and leaning into them. "Now, we go and find her and bring her back." Even though space was limited, considering how close he was, I straightened my legs and crossed them at the ankles. "Once she answers Emilio's questions, she can answer mine."

His lips quirked as he adjusted his feet, giving me a little more room. "And if she doesn't?"

It was a question that haunted me because ignorance was bliss, and part of me was afraid of what her answers would be. Yet as Zev had pointed out over and over, knowledge was power, especially when navigating the sticky web of the Arcane Families. "Aren't you the one who told me there are other ways to get information?"

He gave a slow nod.

I pulled in a breath and let it out. "Then if she won't share, I'll find others who will." We both understood that if I took that step, I would be striding right into the avarice eyes of the Arcane's elite. Especially if we went poking around in a history involving someone like Sabella. The older the family, the darker the secrets.

"You can start with Emilio."

His unexpected suggestion made me blink. "You think he'd know?"

"I think," he said slowly as he arranged his legs along mine, "if he doesn't recognize either of your parents, which he might not, based on the age of the photo, then he'll know who to approach next."

I gave him a small nod. I was torn between taking the photo to Emilio now, or, even better, Evan but was held back by the part of me that wanted to believe Sabella had a damn good reason for keeping this from me. I sat up, hands fisted in my lap, drew in a breath, and slowly blew it out. When I met his gaze, I said softly, "For now, I just want to find her and get her home."

He reached out, covered my hands with his, and gave them a gentle squeeze. "We will."

"I hope so." As much as I appreciated Zev's confidence, holding someone as powerful as Sabella captive wasn't easy. Even if we got lucky and found her at Trask's, God only knew what state she would be in.

"Come on." He pulled me to my feet, wrapped his arms around my waist, and drew me close. "Let's get you something to eat before you head into the geek cave and I go in to get grilled by the police."

Needing the comfort he offered, I leaned in to his hug and returned it. I tilted my head back and deliberately moved us out of somber and into something less depressing. "Don't worry. They won't dare mess with Mari again. Last time, she all but filleted them, verbally."

He grinned down at me. "Yeah, that's why they pay her the big bucks." He surprised me by taking advantage of our position and pressing a soft kiss against my lips. When he lifted his head, he cupped my jaw and brushed a thumb over my cheekbone. "Whatever happens, Rory, I've got your back."

It was nice to hear and even nicer to believe, something that came much easier than I'd expected. Probably because even under the compulsion of the Muse's spell, he'd managed to keep my secret, and that said something. Something that felt damn good and made it easy to say, "And I've got yours."

◆

It was closing in on ten thirty when Zev, dressed in the same cat burglar black as Locke and me, opened the passenger door of Locke's black Dodge Charger and got in. To ensure no one saw us leaving Emilio's, Locke had parked his car around the block in a neighboring drive. Emilio had confirmed the owner was out of town. As much as I would have preferred driving, there wasn't enough room in my Mustang to comfortably fit three people, much less a possibly incapacitated fourth. And since no one wanted to risk linking Emilio to this misadventure, Zev's SUV was out as well. That left us with Locke's car.

"Have any trouble getting loose?" Locke asked as he put the car in gear and pulled away.

"No." Zev tapped his ear. "Fields, radio check?"

"Loud and clear." Evan's voice came through the small radio tucked in my ear. Throughout the afternoon, he and I had painstakingly chipped away at his list of potential hired guns while one of Evan's customized deep dive programs did a search for the ouroboros signature.

It was brain-liquifying work, shifting through financial transaction records that slithered through the dark web in a convoluted maze. The good news was we had five viable names to share when we got Sabella back, and hopefully, she could confirm the ID. Maybe once the deep dive program finished its task, that list would be even smaller.

"Davis, is Trask still occupied?" Zev asked.

"Emilio and Maribel are keeping him busy," Lena confirmed. She was riding shotgun with Evan as they did overwatch, splitting their electronic surveillance between our activities and Emilio's dinner party.

Once Zev finished his interview with the police, he, Locke, Emilio, and surprisingly, Mari, gathered in the office Evan was using so they could set tonight's plan in motion. It was pretty straightforward. Emilio and Mari would keep Trask at the dinner while Locke, Zev, and I bypassed Trask's security, infiltrated the toy barn, and used the marker spell to find Sabella or, worst-case scenario, find her trail. All without tipping off Trask to our activities.

I wasn't sure if Mari's presence was simply a way for Emilio to cover his ass or what, but as I was learning, when the head of a Family made a decision, arguing tended to be a waste of time. Like Emilio's decision not to inform the council that Sabella was missing.

I was pleasantly surprised to find out he'd taken my comment to heart about the possibility of a council member also being missing in action. He'd directed Mari to reach out to each of the five members with some legal question tied to the upcoming meeting and see who answered. So far, two had returned her calls, and messages were left for the other three. If one of them didn't return her call, then it would be another investigative avenue. Unfortunately, with just over twenty-fours to go until the scheduled meeting, we were all feeling the pressure to get answers, one way or the other.

"Locke." Evan's voice came over the earpieces. "We've got a fender bender coming up at the next major light. I'm going to take you down an alternate route."

"Copy." Locke remained unruffled.

Evan was monitoring the street cameras because none of us wanted to be immortalized on video, but in the case of an accident, even a minor one, if he continued to interfere with the cameras, it would be noted.

Utilizing the innate skills that made me a Transporter, I recalled the map we'd studied when plotting our routes. I leaned in toward the front seat. "Left in a quarter mile, follow the street to the light, and make a right. It should bring us back to Twentieth and below the intersection."

"That'll work," Evan confirmed.

Locke's gaze flew to the rearview mirror, his brows raised.

"Transporter," I answered his silent question. "Eidetic imagery on maps and innate GPS. Works every time."

Locke turned back to the road and followed my directions. Considering how large Trask's estate was, we decided to park in the back lot of a church located across the road and within easy walking distance. Evan would take control of the church's surveillance system, effectively hiding the car, a much easier feat than overriding the street cameras.

"Coming up on the church now," Locke warned Evan.

"Copy." There was a pause, and just as Locke began his turn into the lot, Evan said, "You're green. Park in the back west corner."

Locke parked in the heavy shadows of the unlit spot. I got out and joined the men at the Charger's trunk and braced for our next step, a concealment spell. Unlike the magic of Locke and Zev, who were Hunters, my magic wasn't made for skulking around. So to evade being spotted by both electronic and magical surveillance, I would have to endure being cloaked by their magic.

Zev handed me a wolf tooth. "Ready?"

Gingerly taking the off-white magic-filled piece from him, I sucked in a bracing breath as the slumbering power bit at my fingers, and tucked the foci in my front pocket. Then I tugged my shield into place and nodded. He ran quick, impersonal hands from head to feet, leaving me draped in an uncomfortably prickly spell powered by the tooth. When he stepped back, I made some minor adjustments to my Prism until my discomfort was a nagging itch in the back of my mind. When I was as comfortable as I was going to get, I told the two silently waiting men, "I'm good."

Zev took the lead, leaving Locke and me to follow. He blended so completely into the shadows that he was nearly invisible. The familiar rasp of his power against mine acted like a tether, pulling me along in his wake. Behind me, Locke did the same disappearing act.

Buffered between the two Hunters' concealment spells, I jogged across the church parking lot and toward the main street. We avoided crossing at the light because Evan had warned us that although the Hunters' cloaking spell should keep us all but invisible to a camera, some video equipment tended to pick up a strange ripple effect that trained personnel knew meant active magic was nearby.

To avoid that, Zev took us to a spot between streetlights where the shadows lay the heaviest. This late at night, the road was quiet, which meant we were less likely to play frogger with passing traffic. Once safely across, we slipped through pools of shadows and in between buildings and bush-filled lots until we reached the back line of Trask's property.

Thankfully, Trask's neighbors had decided to use old-growth palo verde trees as privacy fencing instead of the real deal. The dense foliage provided deep shadows that pooled along Trask's property, marked by the white horse fence. The combination of trees and shadows made for a great hiding spot to monitor his security patrols and test whatever magical defense was in place. Locke and Zev had a solid idea of Trask's security force, their numbers and their routine, but it was Evan who confirmed that more than electronics guarded the property. My job was to be the early-warning system for Zev and Locke before we triggered those magical traps.

No pressure or anything. Yeesh.

As we crouched in the shadow of one particularly thick tree, nerves left me hyperaware. Between my Prism and the additional cloaking spell, my magical nose was twitchy, making it difficult to separate the competing magics. Zev tapped my left knee to warn of an approaching sentry. On my right, Locke fairly vibrated with coiled tension.

I closed my eyes, leaving the guard to the two trained men at my side and focused on the press of magic just outside my shield. I thinned the mental wall between me and where magic lived, and when I opened my eyes, Trask's spell-crafted security flared into brilliant life. Unlike the horse fence, this secondary wall of power was twice the height of the actual fence and dense enough to appear solid. I bit my lip as I tried to find some break we could slip through.

The wall shimmered as if brushed by fingers, and I turned to see a guard heading our way. Based on the bulge at his hip, he was armed, but that didn't bother me as much as the power surrounding him. It writhed in an unsettling ugly reddish orange, little flares brushing against the security spell as he moved. As he got closer, the air around him got warmer, which solidified my suspicion he was a pyro mage.

I froze, barely daring to breathe until he disappeared into the night. Only then did I touch Zev's shoulder to gain his attention. When he turned, I shook my head, indicating the lack of an entry point. He motioned to Locke, then we were moving down the fence line in the opposite direction of the guard and farther toward the back end of the property line, where the toy barn was located.

When Locke tapped my shoulder, I stopped, dropped into a crouch, and studied the spell-crafted barrier. It was well worth whatever Trask had paid for it. The lines of power were braided in a tight weave that at first glance would appear impenetrable. But the longer I watched, the more I was able to spot where the weave had loosened, leaving the magic less dense. Evan had given me a fast and dirty lesson on the most common types of spell weaving used in magical security. Unsurprisingly, those patterns mimicked ones used in textile weaves.

I touched my tiny earpiece. "Evan, I'm looking at a plain weave."

"Figured Trask would cheap out." His derisive tone shifted to serious. "You need to find a spot that's both dim and loose. Look close to the ground. They tend to fray near the bottom. See if you can find one big enough for what we discussed."

Evan had gone over the weak points of each weave. The simple pattern of over and under, unique to the plain weave, kept the main magical structure strong but the edges weak. Since there was no way to go over the top, I crab walked my way down the line until I found a section where the eroding soil had left a divot barely screened by the spell. "Found one."

"Good. Remember what to do?"

"Yeah." I turned to Zev and Locke. "How much time until the next patrol?"

"Six, maybe seven minutes," Locke answered without looking at me.

It wasn't much, but I would make it work. Manipulating magic was never easy, especially since the mirroring aspect I needed that night was a recently learned skill. The magic behind being a Prism was instinctive, so honing the ability to deliberately redirect a magical attack to a specific target or targets took concentrated effort. Add the distracting rasp of the cloaking spell and the thickened encasement of my Prism and the difficulty level rose. But thanks to Zev's insistence on practicing over and over during the last couple of weeks, tonight's spell should require only a few minor shifts in intent and focus to be successful.

Here's hoping I have the timing down.

With my Prism in place and hopefully mirrored correctly, I shoved my hands into the loose soil and through the weakened weave. I gripped the bottom edge of the spell-crafted fence, and when magic didn't slice my fingers off, I let out the breath I hadn't realized I was holding. The power pulsed against my shield and carried a definite weight. Wiggling my fingers, I adjusted my grip then dared a look at Zev. "Ready?"

Catching his nod, I set my feet, tightened my hold, and slowly began lifting the weakened section. I needed enough room for Zev and me to get through. As I pulled it up, I slipped my magic under the magical line, mirroring the ground to fool the magic into thinking it was still connected. It was like lifting weighted metal curtains, and the heft of it threatened to crush me. I tried not to grunt with effort as I got enough room to angle my squat so I could use my shoulders and back to brace the curtain's edge as I stretched my hands and magic wide, creating a four-foot gap.

"Now," I hissed, feeling the strain in every muscle.

Zev slithered through, then it was my turn. I dove forward, feeling the scrape of magic slide down my back as I landed on hands and knees. A hand curled around my arm and dragged me to my feet. Zev gave Locke a silent hand signal. On the other side of the invisible fence, Locke disappeared into the darkness. He would stay back, keep an eye on the patrols, and ensure our exit remained clear. Zev's grip stayed on my arm as he led us deeper into Trask's property and away from our breach point.

Once inside Trask's security, we simply had to avoid detection. A warning ache in my head reminded me to let my other sight go, as the drain of keeping it open would become too much. We sprinted to the small incline at the back of the toy barn just as two distinct clicks sounded in my ear. Zev and I dropped, lying flat on the ground. The night chorus of insects faded away as gravel crunched softly underfoot.

My skin crawled. Lying out in the open, dependent on a charm-powered spell and with no weapon in hand, was not my idea of a good position. I started to inch my hand down toward my thigh, where I'd stashed the only weapon Zev had let me bring, a folding tactical knife. His steel grip on my wrist stopped me. We froze, listening to the footsteps getting closer.

Just when I knew we were screwed, a soft squawk of a radio sounded. "Rill, need you to check section eight, rear."

"Copy" came the soft response, then thankfully, the footsteps moved away from us.

We waited until the quiet sounds of crickets resumed before we were up and moving again. For once, luck was on our side. Bales of hay were stacked along the back of the toy barn, giving us cover as Zev signaled Evan that we were in position.

With Zev behind me, I crouched and peeked around the bales and saw that, yep, there was definitely a rear entrance for cars, along with a metal door protected by a bright security light.

A pulse of power came from behind me, and only because I knew what to expect did I see the dark shape drop out of the sky toward the security light over the door. Talons hit the light's metal casing with a dull thunk and a wincingly loud metallic screech. The light shook and flickered but didn't break. The black winged shape made another pass, and this time, when the talons shoved the light against the wall, it dimmed and fell dark.

One more silent sweep, followed by a shrill eep and a successful avian cry, then the hawk was taking its late-night filed mouse snack off to be savored. The hawk was just clearing the roof when there was a rush of air and a thin-faced man stepped out of the darkness, a wispy orb of magic held at the ready between his hands.

CHAPTER EIGHTEEN

THE AIR MAGE PEERED AROUND, spread his hands, and dropped them to his sides, palms forward, spilling the wispy magic into searching tendrils. Frozen, I could only stare in horrified fascination as that magic steadily crept forward.

Zev's hand brushed the top of my head, and his magic poured into the cloaking spell, shifting it from irritating to a stinging cloak of nettles. Despite the discomfort, I didn't dare move for fear of giving away our position. I had to trust that whatever Zev was doing would keep us invisible to the ribbons of magic inching closer and closer. It licked around the bales and curled inches from my feet.

My muscles locked, and Zev's fingers dug into my shoulders in unnecessary warning. I held my breath as the questing magic tested the air. Seconds stretched by while that eerily alive strand held my horrified gaze. Finally, it pulled back, and only when it retracted around the bale did I dare to release a noiseless, shaky breath.

The air mage did a circuit of the area, slowly gliding along the back of the toy barn and out in the shadow-strewn area behind it. He approached the hay bales. Behind me, Zev's presence coiled with predatory patience. Still, neither of us moved. I dropped my eyes to the ground and clenched my teeth as the air mage got disconcertingly close. When he stopped, he was so close, it wouldn't take much to touch him. I stared at the scuffed toes of his shoes and prayed Zev's magic would hold.

Finally, those shoes turned and walked away. Only then did I lift my gaze to watch him move under the broken security light. He looked up and studied the fixture. Finally, he spoke, in a low voice. "Looks like some animal nailed the light. Put in a request for a replacement." If there was a response, I didn't catch it, but the air mage took one last long look around then turned and disappeared into the shadows.

Relief left me shaky, but it wasn't until Zev's magic receded to a barely there level and his grip disappeared that I even dared to straighten up from my crouch. Once upright, I looked at Zev, who gave a short shake of his head and lifted his hand in a staying motion. We waited for what felt like forever for Evan's all-clear click to come through.

While we waited, my adrenaline-laced relief was replaced by cautious excitement. If they were watching the toy barn this closely, it meant they were hiding something or someone.

Finally, Evan's click sounded. Zev and I wasted no time hustling to the back door. He kept watch while I used my other sight to double-check for any magical wards. Unlike Lena's depth of spell knowledge, mine was solid enough to be dangerous but not enough to identify the specific nuances. It looked like a pretty straightforward protective lock spell.

Good enough.

I shared a look with Zev and motioned to where the runes lay. "Lock spell," I mouthed.

He stepped in close and raised his brow.

Reading the silent "You got this?" I nodded, shifted my magic into mirror position, and gripped the knob. Magic snapped and bit at my hand, but I twisted my wrist and broke the lines binding the spell.

A sharp pain zipped from temple to temple, and I froze in place, waiting to see if anything else would happen, say, like a fire alarm going off somewhere to indicate our presence or the air mage popping up again. When everything stayed quiet, I looked at Zev, who motioned me out of the way. I stepped back, giving him room to crouch in front of the door. I rubbed my temple to ease the receding ache as he made quick work of the lock with a thin lock pick set then tucked his tools away, grabbed the knob, twisted, and pushed the door open a couple of inches.

Something brushed my ankle, making me jump. I looked down as a field mouse scampered over my foot, through the opening, and disappeared inside. At my startled jerk, Zev looked at me, his eyes holding an unearthly blue glow. I guessed the mouse was our advance scout. Zev turned toward the dark interior, leaving me to make sure no one snuck up on us. The seconds ticked by before Zev straightened and then touched his earpiece, letting Evan know we were going in.

He disappeared into the thick shadows inside the barn. I stopped just inside the door, carefully closed it behind me, then waited for my eyes to adjust. The darkness wasn't as thick as I'd expected. Small lights lined the bottom of the walls, providing just enough illumination to see where we were going. I took in the space, noting that my guess about the repair pit was correct. Zev was a moving shadow slipping along the edges of the space, probably trying to find the same thing I was, an access to the basement below.

I pulled out my necklace and activated the pendant. It flared to life, and unlike earlier, there was no way to miss the heat searing my palm. Elation crowded out anxiety at the unmistakable response. I gave a soft hiss to gain Zev's attention. His dark form stilled, and his magic-lit eyes, eerie in his shadow-covered face, turned to me. I lifted the fist holding the stone, and he nodded in understanding. We didn't have the luxury of playing the hot-and-cold game, so I studied the garage's layout.

There were two ways to access a repair pit. Either the floor was set on hydraulics that rose and fell, lowering the mechanic to the necessary level, or it was an actual pit with a short set of steps or ladder leading down. Either way, there would still need to be basement access, if not for hydraulics, then for all the necessary power lines for lights and tools.

I hoped for steps versus a drop floor, because a drop floor meant noise. My position was at the end of the toy barn, and there were no obvious trap doors or tucked-away utility rooms in view. Over to my left was the repair pit, and off to the side sat tool chests and benches. The far corner was dark, too dark to make out what was over there, but the wall by Zev contained the closed door to the showroom.

My gaze went to the dark corner. I skirted the pit, feeling the stone in my necklace heat with every step. Zev met me near the corner. Sure enough, a door hid the shadows.

I reached for the knob, only to stop before I touched the metal. I licked my dry lips and brought my other sight forward. A mix of orange and gold runes interwoven with red flared to life on the door.

Yeah, they're definitely hiding something.

"What is it?" Zev asked in a low voice as he came up beside me.

"A shit ton of runes," I murmured without looking away as I released the stone. It settled against my shirt, the heat of it seeping through the cloth barrier.

Zev called his magic and raised his hands a few inches above the door. The uncomfortable press of power against my skin turned into a sharp sting. The air in front of us shimmered with a blue flame, and an icy-white burst hit the door, sparking the runes into brilliant life. I remembered him doing the same thing when we rescued Lena from a double-layered occlusion spell. Unlike the complex layers of that spell, this was a single layer, but the runes were interwoven. "What is it?" I asked.

"Daisy-chained obstruction spell with a warning trip switch."

Reading his grim tone, I said, "Let me guess. It'll take too long to unravel."

"Is that sarcasm?"

"*Moi*? Sarcastic? Never." I turned back to the revealed runes and studied how they were linked. Just like the name suggested, the runes were connected at one point on sigil, so the best way to unravel the spell would be unloosing the last set rune to unravel the rest. We just needed to identify it. I studied the collection of flaming lines until I found the one that held a deeper edge of red where the rune doubled back. It sat near the center, but that trip switch... "Can you disable the warning?"

He studied the sigils. "I can, but you'll need to keep the rest off of me."

That I could do. "Deal." I flexed my Prism, thickening the protection, then stretched it to cover Zev until the mirrored magic cocooned us both. "Just don't step away without telling me, or we'll both pay for it."

He worked fast. His blue-tinted power slipped around the interlocked rune for "warn" and curled around the orange lines until the blue and yellow and red blurred into an earthy dirt brown. The dusty color held steady for a heartbeat, then veins of arctic blue crawled through it, crumbling the lines of the rune until they flaked away. When all that was left was a ghostly afterimage of the runes, he grunted, "Now."

I pressed my palm against the sigil in the center then with a flex of will sent a burst of my magic into it. The silent explosion shoved me back a step, and the broken magic ping-ponged around my skull, leaving a throbbing beat. I reached for Zev, and he caught my wrist, anchoring me as I blinked the white spots out of my vision. When the pounding eased and my vision cleared, I caught the last flicker of orange and gold as the final rune shattered.

Zev shifted his grip. "You good?"

"Yeah." I cleared the rasp from my voice. "Yeah, we're good. The door's clear."

Taking me at my word, Zev let me go. "Let me take lead."

"Be my guest." Since we had no idea if anyone waited for us below, I was more than willing to let him go first. He was much better than my folding knife and probably much more accurate.

Zev tugged me behind him as he positioned with his back to the door, grabbed the knob, and slowly swung the door open. When no one rushed us, he pushed the door wide until it rested against the wall.

From my limited vantage point behind him, all I could see was what appeared to be a utility closet. A small glowing orb flicked to life and hovered over Zev's palm, providing enough illumination to determine that the shadowed shapes were nothing more threatening than shelves and cleaning supplies.

Disappointment filled my mouth, but Zev moved forward. "What are you doing?" I whispered, following him. "There's nothing in there."

He shot me a look. "You sure about that?"

I covered the pendant at my neck and opened my mouth to answer, only to stop when the heat of the stone seared my fingers. My eyes widened as I met Zev's gaze. "She's got to be close."

The space was tight with both of us in it, but he moved over to the shelf then dropped to a crouch, bringing his light down toward the floor. He grunted then looked up along the shelf and the wall it rested against. He leaned forward, slipped his hand behind the shelf, palm toward the wall, and skimmed the surface as he rose. "Yeah, there you are," he muttered. He did something, and a click sounded in the small room. He turned, raised his brows in mocking amusement, and pulled the shelf out, revealing a hidden opening. "Abra-cadabra."

"Show-off."

His grin was firefly fast, then he went back to the opening, his head cocking as his expression returned to his steely best. With no warning, the light next to him flickered out. I blinked my vision clear only to see his shadow bend as he leaned in, his head and shoulders disappearing into the inky blackness. He pulled back and warned, "There's stairs. Watch your head." Then his shadow merged with the others and disappeared.

Mentally grumbling about fumbling around in the dark, I tugged the utility door shut despite knowing it was like closing the barn door after the horses were out since the trashed obstruction spell would be a glaring clue, but still... I carefully made my way to the opening.

I used my foot to find the first step and reached around until my hand landed on cool, round metal I prayed was a railing. I followed the stairs down, and when I got to the bottom it was definitely cooler than the space upstairs. The air carried a hint of oil, dust, and metal, and I realized there was a faint amber light coming from somewhere. It was just enough to make out Zev's darker shape as he moved through an open space filled with what appeared to be various machinery that was most likely the repair pit's hydraulics.

Uncomfortable with the disconcerting shadows, I decided to take a peek with my other sight. Zev lit up in shocking blue. Something flickered off to my right, but from where I stood, it was hard to make out. Strangely, those were the only two signs of power I could spot. I saw nothing that was strong enough to explain the intensity of heat coming from the pendant.

Weird.

Zev's low-toned "Clear" sounded before I could mention my concern about the seeming lack of magical security. Then his pet glow light snapped back to life.

"Dammit, Zev," I hissed in a harsh whisper as I lifted a hand to block the unexpected brightness, my vision shifting under the glare. When I dropped my hand, Zev, magic flashlight in hand, was moving to the back right corner with the unidentifiable traces of power.

I crossed the rough cement floor. When I got closer, I realized that a wire cage the size of a holding cell was set into the far corner. Zev stood in front of it, staring at something I couldn't see. His stillness made me uneasy, and my steps slowed. I didn't want to, but I had to ask, "What is it?"

He didn't say anything as I came up beside him. My gaze went to the back of the cage, where a figure lay unmoving on a camping cot near the far wall. I lost my unease and rushed the wire mesh only to have Zev block my way with an outstretched arm. "Don't touch the wires."

I dug my fingers into his arm and rocked to my toes, leaning forward. "Sabella!" I called out, my voice low but urgent. The figure on the cot didn't move. I tried again a little louder. "Sabella." Still nothing. I looked at Zev and stated the obvious. "Something's wrong."

"I know." He shook off my grip and brushed his hand just above the thick wire mesh, taking care not to touch the metal. "Check for any wards," he ordered.

I let my sight shift, waiting for the cage to light up. It didn't, but Sabella sure as hell did. I sucked in a sharp breath. "Nothing on the cage, but Sabella's wrapped up in something."

He muttered a soft curse then tapped his earpiece. "Fields, I've got an electrified cage here. Need a bypass."

Okay, field operations are not my forte. I had all but forgotten Evan and Lena.

"Give me a minute." Evan's voice was rock steady.

Zev and I waited, him much more patiently than me. Silently, I counted the seconds as a minute turned into a minute and a half and headed toward longer when, all of a sudden, a tense quiet fell. Only then did I realize that a nearly imperceptible hum had existed from the active electricity coursing through the wire mesh, which was clearly how Zev knew the cage was armed. There was a soft beep followed by a snick.

"Interrupted the signal," Evan said. "You've got maybe three minutes to get in and get out before the system overrides."

Zev yanked open the door, and we rushed in. I got to Sabella first and crouched next to her. Studying the convoluted weave of runes and sigils that made up the hex holding her didn't tell me much. But the layered complexity of it was worrisome. Underneath the layers of power, Sabella appeared to be sleeping, her face pale and drawn. "Shit, shit, shit."

It wasn't until Zev snapped, "What?" that I realized I was chanting out loud.

To combat the urge to rip through the spells barehanded, I curled my hands into fists. "Whatever hex they've laid, it's nothing I've ever seen." I looked at him and tried not to panic. "Don't ask me to break it."

His expression remained coldly clinical. "You think it'll kill her."

Or my ignorance will. Instead of saying that, I simply nodded.

"Bring her back here," Lena broke in.

I dragged my hands through my hair. "I don't know if we can move her without harming her."

Lena remained calm and asked, "Is the spell attached to anything but her?"

I leaned in, looking closely. "I don't think so. It's like she's mummy wrapped."

"Bring her back," Lena repeated.

"Copy." Zev nudged me out of the way. "I'll carry her. You take lead."

"Wait." I let my other sight fade and stood up. "Just in case, let me shield you."

He appeared to think it over and finally gave a sharp nod.

I didn't waste any time stretching my Prism to encompass him. "We'll have to stay close." Done, I stepped back and gave him room to pick her up. The ache in my head was growing steadily worse, a sign that my Prism was working overtime to offset the pressing magic. Despite that, I couldn't help taking a tighter metaphysical grip and bracing, just in case Zev triggered something by touching her. When he straightened with Sabella in his arms and nothing happened, I let out a shaky breath and asked, "You good?"

He shifted his hold on Sabella, cradling her a little higher against his chest. "Yeah, let's move."

I scrambled up the stairs and out into the utility room then turned to help him maneuver through the opening. Once he was clear, I shoved the shelf back into place and went to the door leading to the garage. I looked over my shoulder. "Turn off your light."

The orb snuffed out, and I turned back, grabbed the knob, took a big breath, slowly opened the door, and slid out. I strained my ears and peered into the shadows. A small squeak sounded to my right. I turned to see Zev's field mouse a few feet in front of me, nose twitching, before it took off. Zev came up behind me. *Okay, guess we're clear.* We headed to the door. I stopped, with my hand on the knob, and touched my earpiece. "Heading out of the barn."

"You've got a sentry moving from the horse barn toward you, so book it," Evan warned.

Heeding his advice, I opened the door and darted across the shadowed lot, retracing our earlier route. Zev stayed close. Even with his arms full of unconscious woman, he made less noise than I did. As we crossed the open yard, my spine itched, but I didn't dare look back or stop.

I had to trust that Zev's cloaking ability would keep us from being spotted as we dashed to the fence where we were to meet up with Locke. The increase in nerve-zapping stings grew as we closed in on the security fence. The soft call of an owl floated along the night, and Zev hissed out a warning breath. I pulled up short to see him shift direction slightly, angling toward the back corner of the property. Trusting him to know what the hell he was doing, I followed.

We went up to the fence, and Locke stepped out of the dense shadows, his gaze sweeping over Zev and his unconscious bundle. "Next pass is in three minutes counting."

As much as I appreciated his warning, I didn't need it to hurry. Setting my teeth because this was going to hurt, I let my vision shift until I could see the magical security fence in all its head-splitting glory. It wasn't the same spot where we came in, but Locke had been busy, digging a shallow dip in the dirt, larger than the one we'd used before. The ends of the security spell weren't as faded, but they were frayed from losing their anchor in the earth.

Good enough.

I crouched in front of Zev, braced for the upcoming pain, shifted my Prism—which felt like handling a huge sheet of unbendable metal—grasped the bottom of the magical net, and shoved up. It lifted but not enough. My muscles screamed in protest, and the ache in my head deepened, but I wanted out of there, and more, I wanted Zev and Sabella safe. So I dug deep, grunted with effort, and forced the net up a few more inches. Finally, there was enough space to squeeze through—I hoped. I bit out, "Now."

Keeping a death grip on the magic, I held it steady while Zev rolled Sabella to Locke, then it was his turn to roll under. Once he was clear, I shuffled and did a series of contortions until all but one leg was on the other side. Then I shoved up the magical net as hard as I could and dove to the side before hitting the ground hard. I hissed as the magic slammed against me, scarping along the back of my shoulder, hip, and along my leg. Even with my shield in place, it felt like I'd left a layer of skin behind. I rolled over, stifled my groan, and got to my feet.

"You okay?" Zev's hand wrapped around my arm, steadying me.

"For now," I admitted. "But don't let go. I'm going to crash soon." The pain in my head was blinding, spiking with each beat of my heart, and without Zev's help, I would be screwed because my vision was pretty much gone. "Sabella?"

"Locke's got her."

The thought of having to expand my Prism threatened to make me cry. "But the hex—"

"He's got it." Zev cut me off. "Drop what you can."

I let my shield retract, uncoiling it from Zev as I took a step. My ankle twisted, throwing me off balance.

Zev cursed, and suddenly, I found myself being picked up. I didn't bother arguing because not only was I all but blind, but the world had taken on a Tilt-A-Whirl vibe. I closed my eyes, buried my face in his neck, and held on, praying I wouldn't get sick. I fought the urge to vomit and pass out, but I lost a bit of time, because the next thing I knew, Zev was pulling a seat belt across me. I blinked blearily into his face and tried to help.

He pushed my hands away. "Just sit still." The seat belt clicked into place, and he held a napkin to my nose. "Can you hold this? Your nose is bleeding."

I got my hand up, and he let go then disappeared as the door next to me closed. I wasn't sure where I was until the sound of a door opening and movement behind me clued me in that I was in the front seat of Locke's Charger. There was more jostling and a couple of muttered comments between Locke and Zev, but I didn't dare turn my head to see what was happening. It wouldn't do for my head to slide off my neck. Then more doors closed and Locke was settling into the driver's seat. The car started, and he said, "Fields, leaving now."

"Copy."

Evan said something else, but his voice faded in and out, and I couldn't catch it. I tried to stay awake, but the debilitating headache and the movement of the car sent me spiraling into a numbing darkness.

CHAPTER NINETEEN

THE RIDE to Emilio's was a blur, and once we came to a stop, my awareness took on a carnival-ride-like atmosphere. My vision was an ugly smear of swimming colors as I stumbled down seemingly endless hallways. Voices vied for preeminence in a deafening cacophony while what felt like multiple people pulled and tugged at me until I wanted to scream. I tried fighting my way free, but it seemed to make things worse. Finally, something coiled around me, stopping my feeble attempts to escape.

Zev's voice pierced the madness in a hard, unyielding demand. "Stop, Rory. Stop fighting."

It took a few moments for my brain to translate his order so I could force my body to be still. Pain washed through me, as if giant fingers were prying open my skull. It got so bad I could barely form the protest, "Hurts."

"Where's the healer?"

I had no idea who Zev was talking to, but the sharp note of worry in his voice cut through my misery. *The hex on Sabella.* "Sabella okay?"

Someone said something I couldn't catch, but Zev's face floated into focus, white lines bracketing his eyes and mouth. "Don't worry about Sabella. I need you to stay awake. Do you hear me?"

I closed my eyes because the darkness was preferable to the dizzying spin of colors.

"Rory!"

"I'm here." My tongue felt thick. "I'm here," I repeated as my back met something solid.

After a rush of movement and sound, Zev was back. "Rory, let go of your Prism. Can you do that for me? Drop your shield?"

Why in the hell would I do that?

"Your brain is bleeding, and the healer can't get past your shield to stop it."

That doesn't sound good. I forced my eyes open and stared blearily into Zev's dark eyes. Something wild lurked in the depths. "'S okay, Zev."

"No, babe, it's not." He got closer until his face blocked out everything else. "Do you trust me?"

Silly question. "Yes."

"Then I need you to release your magic, Rory. Nothing will hurt you, I promise."

"Hurts now."

His lips gained the tiniest of curves. "I know, but if you let go, we can make it better. Okay?"

"Okay." I wasn't sure I got my agreement out because nothing seemed to be working right.

It took an endless moment to remember how to reel in my magic. That was not the easiest thing to do when my instincts insisted the better option was to leave it in place. Spikes of pain kept shorting out my thoughts, interrupting my attempts to keep it together. Something soft brushed across my forehead, followed by a firm press against my temples. Heat seared from each point of contact at my temples and wrapped around the inside of my skull. I let out a pained hiss as the excruciating burn washed through my skull, eating through the unbearable ache until all that was left was a comforting warmth that I wanted to snuggle under and just sleep.

I had no idea how long I floated in that half-aware state, but when the last afterglow drifted away, the blinding ache in my head was gone, and so was the crazy, delusional circus ride. When I opened my eyes, I recognized Emilio's office, where I was lying on the love seat. Zev sat on the floor next to me, his arms braced on his knees and his face drawn with exhaustion.

A dark-haired, silver-templed man sat at my hip, the rolled-up cuffs on his chambray shirt showcasing his deeply tanned olive skin as he pulled his hands away from my head. "Hello there, Ms. Costas." His brown eyes were sharp but kind. "How are you feeling?"

I did an internal check, happy when nothing complained. "I'm not sure yet." I shifted, relieved when my head didn't explode. As much as I wanted to give in to the lingering fatigue, I didn't dare. Not with both Zev and the older man watching me so closely. To combat the urge, I started to push up. The older man moved in to help, and between the two of us, I got in an upright sitting position. "Tired, drained," I added.

He gave me a small smile. "To be expected, especially after a prolonged hyperextension of your talent." He held out his hand. "Dr. Art Garcia at your service."

"Hi." I shook his hand as I tried to piece together what had happened. "Hyperextension?"

"In layman terms, you pushed your power too far for too

long and tore a magical muscle," Dr. Garcia answered, regaining my attention.

I definitely didn't like the sound of that. "How bad, and what does that mean?"

"It's not the end of the world," he soothed, "but it does require that you not use your magic for the next few days, or we'll end up right back here. You and your ability need to rest. You'll have to work your way back to the exertion level you used tonight."

Going magicless for any length of time wasn't really an option. Doubly so with Sabella's current situation and the upcoming council meeting. "And if I have to use my ability?"

The doctor lost his amicable bedside manner and turned serious. "It should be fine for small things. Those, you can probably get away with, but another punishing hit like whatever you just did to yourself? Repeat that performance and your gray matter will end up leaking out of your ears. And that's the best-case scenario. Worst-case, you'll be dead."

Okay, then. I swallowed against a suddenly dry throat. "Got it."

He studied me for a long moment then turned to Zev. "Does she listen like you listen?"

I shared a look with Zev. He covered his small smile by brushing his hand over his mouth and down his goatee before admitting, "Yeah."

With an aggrieved sigh, Dr. Garcia pressed his hands to his thighs and stood up. "Fine, then." He turned and looked at me. "If," he stressed, "you use your magic, the second your head starts to hurt, stop. It's a warning. Heed it. Do you understand me?"

While not the biggest fan of being patronized, I could understand his frustration at having his advice ignored, so I simply nodded.

He turned to Zev, who was getting to his feet. "Now that

she's awake and the bleeding's stopped, I'm going to go check on our other patient." He turned to me and flicked his finger from his forehead in an abbreviated salute. "Ms. Costas. I do hope we don't meet again soon."

I managed a small, apologetic smile. "Me, too, Dr. Garcia."

Zev walked the doctor to the door. I uncurled from the couch, setting my feet on the floor. I was about to stand when Zev was back in front of me, his hand on my shoulders, forcing me to stay down. "What are you doing?"

I batted his hands away. "I'm getting up so we can go see Sabella."

"No, you're going to take it easy for a few more minutes."

"Zev—"

"No," he snapped, his calm demeanor disappearing like smoke. "Sit your ass down, Rory." Taken aback by his temper, I stopped struggling and kept my seat. It didn't seem to soothe Zev, whose anger and worry made his voice sharp. "What the hell were you thinking, risking yourself like that?"

Confused, I ventured, "I was doing what needed to be done so we could get Sabella back."

"No, you were proving a point." He paced in front of me, one hand dragging through his hair, the other fisted at his side. "Being a Prism doesn't make you invincible."

Watching him, it hit me. *Seeing me like that scared him.* And since I wasn't stupid and knew there was a high probability our roles could easily be reversed at any time, I found myself reassuring him instead of taking a chunk out of his misguided but sexy ass. "I know that."

He spun around and threw out an arm. "Do you? You were bleeding from your eyes, nose, and ears, Rory. Then, when we got you to Garcia, he couldn't get through to heal you."

"Of course he couldn't." I ignored the way he stiffened and patiently explained the obvious. "I'm a Prism, Zev."

"Yeah, I know," he shot back sarcastically.

Realizing he wasn't listening, I tried again. "No, you don't know. My magic isn't like yours. Hell, I'm not even sure it reacts the way a typical Prism's would. My magic is instinctive. Whether it's that way naturally or the fact that it's been suppressed for so long makes it that way doesn't matter. When I'm threatened, its automatic response is to protect me. It doesn't differentiate between internal and external threats. I do. If I'm not around to redirect it, it reacts. I was injured, and it did its job. It held all perceived threats at bay."

I shook my head, knowing how strange it sounded, but I needed him to understand that what had happened wasn't a conscious choice on my part. "I'm just starting to figure out the ins and outs of what it really means to be a Prism. What happened tonight was not me trying to show off or whatever it is you think I was doing. I just pushed too hard and too fast. That's all."

For a long moment, he stared at me, emotions I couldn't quite read working behind his eyes. But enough leaked through to leave soft spots around my heart. "Dammit, Rory." He turned and sank down next to me, dropping his head into his hands. "Don't fucking do that again."

I rubbed his back, torn between liking his protective streak and wanting to smack him. I might not reach his badassery level, but I wasn't exactly helpless. Still, I liked what his concern meant. "How about I promise I'll pay closer attention to the warning signs." We sat there for a minute before I guided us out of that prickly little pit. "Where's Sabella?"

"Emilio has Lena working on her in one of the bedrooms." Zev rubbed his face and sat up. "Last I checked, it was slow going, but they were making progress."

I looked around for a clock. "How long was I out of it?"

"About an hour."

"I want to be in there with them."

He studied me. "You think you'll catch something Lena won't?"

I gave an uncomfortable shrug. "Maybe?" When he raised an eyebrow, I bumped his shoulder. "Come on. It's not like either one of us is going to sleep until we know she's safe."

He sighed, stood up, and offered me a hand. I took it, letting him pull me to my feet, then we headed to where my best friend was doing her best to save a woman who knew more about my past than I did.

◆

Zev and I stepped out of Emilio's office and found him, Locke, and Evan all gathered near an open door near a room at the end of the hall. Emilio was pacing. Locke was leaning against the wall next to the doorway, one foot braced against the baseboard, his arms folded over his chest, his eyes half closed. I wondered if he was power napping. On the opposite wall, sitting on the floor and fingers flying over a keyboard, Evan focused on his laptop. A somber pall clogged the hall, and magic swirled through the enclosed space, nipping at me. I shivered and did my best to keep my Prism's reactions in check.

At our approach, Locke turned his head, his gaze dropping to where Zev held my hand before going back up, but other than that look, nothing else indicated his thoughts. Emilio caught sight of us, slowed, and finally stopped near the door as if waiting for us to approach. His normally immaculate appearance was frazzled at the edges, proof that the long day was wearing on him. Evan, being Evan, continued to work on whatever it was that held his attention, but I knew him well enough to know he was aware of our arrival as well.

I waited until we were a loose group gathered around the open door. I peeked in but pulled back at the brush of barely contained pulsating power. The only impression I was able to catch was Lena sitting in the flickering candlelight next to an unmoving figure in the bed. "How is she?" I asked Emilio.

Emilio turned and stared unseeingly at the open door and wrapped a hand around the back of his neck. He shook his head. "Sabella's still unconscious. Ms. Davis said it was a stasis spell."

"A sub-rosa stasis spell," Evan clarified without looking up from his laptop. "According to Lena, the primary hex is keeping Sabella out, but the secondary one is primed to go off if Lena rushes things."

"Details, Evan," I reminded him.

He finally looked up from his laptop, his eyes bloodshot behind the wire frame lenses. "A typical stasis spell is like that fairy tale with the forest princess and the dwarf harem, minus the romantic claptrap of a kiss."

Now was not the time to lecture Evan on the tale of Snow White, even if I agreed about the romantic claptrap part. "Okay, we figured the unconscious part out when she didn't wake up. Has Lena untangled the release command to wake Sabella up?"

"No, because that's tied to the sub-rosa part." Evan rolled his shoulders with an audible pop.

"There's a secondary curse," I said.

"Yep, and it's woven into the stasis spell," he explained. "Whatever is connecting those two spells is a catalyst. A lethal one, in Lena's opinion."

Based on the grim looks all around, and the use of the word "lethal," that was not good news. "Not a combat mage here," I reminded Evan. "Explain what catalyst is."

"Think of it like a kill switch," Zev said.

"More like a trip wire that sets off a domino effect," Evan corrected. "Like that game Operation where if your hand shakes, you set off the warning buzz, but in this case, if your hand shakes, you trigger the catalyst, and it will in turn trigger the secondary hex, which joins forces with the stasis spell, and the whole thing kills Sabella instantly."

Blood rushed out of my head, leaving me light-headed. "Instantly?"

Evan shared a dark look with Zev before coming back to me. "Instantly," he confirmed. "Lena uncovered sigils tied to the catalyst on Sabella's carotid, radial, and femoral arteries." He shared the information as if it explained everything.

It didn't. "I don't understand."

"The sigils are focal points for the catalyst," Locke's unemotional voice cut in. "They're used to ensure control of your target. If your target gets loose or you choose to send them back with a message, whatever hex you've laid will be directed through those specific points. Depending on the message you want sent, a catalyst can either be graphically messy or disturbingly discreet."

Neither option sounded good. "And the one on Sabella?"

"We don't know," Emilio finally said, his voice rough, but I didn't know him well enough to say if it was anger or worry or both.

"Yet," Evan added sharply. "We don't know yet." He shot Emilio a narrow-eyed glare, and the tension in the hall went up a notch. "Lena will figure it out. It will just take time."

"Time is something we're quickly running out of," Emilio shot back.

I wasn't going to get in between Evan and Emilio, nor was I going to park my ass out in the hall. Forgetting that Zev still had my hand, I took a step toward the room.

He pulled me up short. "What are you doing?"

I tugged my hand free. "I'm going in to see if I can help." He opened his mouth as if to argue, but knowing what was coming, I cut him off. "I'll be careful."

His mouth snapped closed, and a muscle in his jaw jumped as he fought his need to push. I waited him out, not willing to back down. It was too important. My private misgivings about Sabella and her connection to my history weren't enough to overshadow my need to help. I couldn't stand aside and not do something. He finally relented with a harsh "Be careful."

I gave him a nod, took a tighter hold on my Prism, ensuring it would behave, and slipped inside the room. As soon as I crossed the threshold, my magic jerked against my metaphysical hold, wanting to curl around me and hold back the power flooding the space. Instead of engaging in a psychic tug of war, I let it out just enough for it to settle in a thin protective layer. Without the distraction of fighting my magic, I focused on what was happening in the room.

Sabella lay like Evan's proverbial forest princess on the bed, pale and unmoving. Lena sat to Sabella's right, perched on the edge of a straight-backed chair someone must have brought in from the kitchen. A thin aura of reddish gold wavered around her. When her eyes came to mine, the same colors danced in their depths. She turned back to her work, and I found an ottoman and dragged it over to the side closest to me and sat.

A couple of minutes ticked by before some of Lena's tension eased and she finally acknowledged me. "You really need to avoid the Carrie look."

Self-consciously, I wiped at my nose, my fingers coming away with rusty marks. "Yeah, blood's not really my color."

That earned a tiny glint of humor that quickly faded. "How bad is it?"

I rubbed my fingers against my pants as I studied the

woman who lay so still between us. "Shouldn't that be my question?"

"Rory." It was a reprimand, pure and simple.

Obviously, Zev wasn't the only one that I'd managed to scare. "I overdid it, and the doctor says not to do it again."

She cocked her head. "Why do I get the impression you aren't going to listen to the doctor's orders?"

"Because you know and love me better than anyone else." When that fell flat, I said quietly, "I can't sit by and do nothing. Not when you and I both know I can help with this."

She searched my face, clearly weighing the pros and cons of my involvement. It was obvious the pros won out when she gave in. "How much did they explain?"

"Double-layer stasis spell linked with an unknown kill switch targeting her pulse points."

Her lips thinned. "That'll work." She set one hand on Sabella's shoulder and placed the other one on her sheet covered hip. "I managed to identify which lines and runes belong to each spell, but I'm having trouble locating where the catalyst is tied in."

"What can I do?"

"I know we talked about it before, but just to be clear, when you look at the magic, you can see it? The way it's laid and how it connects?"

"I can see it, but I don't always know what I'm looking at."

Lena studied Sabella's still form. "Did you get a look when you found her?"

I nodded. "It was like she was wrapped in overlapping layers of magic, kind of like a mummy."

"That was the stasis spell," she murmured more to herself than me. She shot me a look. "Here's what we're going to do. Without killing yourself, can you take a look?"

I gave her another nod.

"Okay, then I need you to describe what you see, but don't touch anything. Just look."

"Got it." I dropped my head, closed my eyes, and lowered the mental wall that allowed me to see magic. I opened my eyes slowly and kept my gaze on my hands, waiting for a warning ache.

My magic, a mix of silver and white, shimmered above my skin like tissue paper. When my skull remained quiet, I slowly lifted my gaze to the bed and then to Sabella. The lines of interconnected power burned in eerie silence, their brightness dimming her features. It didn't look like before. Instead of the previous mummy wrappings, the spells hovered over Sabella's body like a multidimensional quilt. "It's like a 3D quilt of colors and lines."

"Can you identify a top layer and a bottom layer?" Lena asked.

I canted my head. "Yeah, I think so."

"Okay." There was a hint of relief in her voice. "Then the top layer would be the stasis spell, and the bottom would be the sub-rosa spell. Tell me what they look like."

"Right. The stasis spell is primarily green and copper in color. The bottom is either light blue or purple, with white." Something niggled at me. I turned to Lena only to find her wreathed in fiery reds and golds, their colors so intense I dropped my eyes at the first twinge of discomfort. "The bottom colors are similar to what that electro mage used when they ambushed Zev in the garage."

Lena's only reaction was to ask, "Can you see where the two layers connect?"

I studied the undulating magical fabric. It wasn't easy thanks to the fact that the two layers were fluctuating with power. The constant movements made it difficult to unravel what lines were attached to what. Needing a better vantage point, I stood up and slowly inched along the edge of the bed, peering closer at the magical quilt.

When I got to the foot of the bed, I crouched and rested my arms on the footboard. I set my chin on top of my hands so I would be eye level with Sabella and the mattress. As if that was the angle my brain needed, the image clicked into place. "Holy shit."

"What?" Lena's voice was sharp.

"That ouroboros symbol. It's wound between the pulse-point sigils and the spells." The tail-eating snakes writhed in between smoke and shadow as they linked the silvery-blue sigils at Sabella's pulse points to both spells. The air in the room shifted, but I didn't dare look away. Those snakes were damn hard to see, much less follow. If it weren't for the flicker of ice-cold blue that sparked in seemingly random intervals, I would lose sight of them.

"On all the catalysts?"

"If you mean the sigils, yeah." A whisper of an ache woke, and I knew I was pushing my luck. "It's the same symbol used at Sabella's, but it's like it's continually rotating smoke, making it hard to see. The only way to tell is the spark."

"What spark?"

I watched the snake roll, revealing the spark's path. "Every time the spark passes through the sigil, it turns icy blue. Then that same spark zips to the bottom layer and fades." Another warning pulse hit, this one stronger, and I closed my eyes. The afterimage lingered in the darkness behind my closed lids. "I have to stop, Lena," I warned her.

"It's okay."

I opened my eyes to see Lena scribbling something in a notebook. It didn't take her long to flip it around and hold it up. "Did it look like this?"

I moved around the bed and took the notebook from her. Although it was sketched, there was no mistaking the lines from the bottom spell layer, the catalyst sigil, the top layer of the stasis spell, and twisted through it like an infinity loop, the ouroboros. "Yeah, that's it." I handed it back to her, noting the fierce satisfaction on her face. "You recognized it."

"Hell yeah, I do." She set the notebook aside and stood up. "Whoever this was is a devious bastard but not devious enough." She called out, "Evan, I need you!"

CHAPTER TWENTY

I MOVED out of the way as Evan came in, his entire focus aimed at Lena. "What?"

Lena's hands were already moving over Sabella, and her power began to swell, scratching against my shield. "We're dealing with an electro mage. They've set the catalyst to disrupt her heart. I need you to keep it steady and hold off any pulses."

A hand wrapped around my arm, tugging me back. "Come on, Rory. Let's give them the room."

I let Zev drag me to the hallway. He took one look at my face, then his hands were at my shoulders, pressing down. "Sit before you fall down."

I slid down the wall until my ass hit the floor then drew up my legs until I could fold my arms on top of my knees. I used my arms as a makeshift pillow and sat there, head down, eyes closed, listening to what was happening inside the room. Not that Lena and Evan said much, but their power spilled into the hallway. Even through the thin layer of my Prism, Evan's magic left stinging nips behind, while the familiar burn of Lena's power curled around me.

The air shifted, and I looked up to find Zev settling in on the floor next to me. I was still blinking blearily when he curled an arm around my shoulder and gently pulled me in. I laid my head on the shoulder he offered and drifted for a bit, hoping the catnap would be enough to offset the earlier warning signs of an impending headache. Thankfully, it seemed to work because the threatening ache slowly faded into oblivion.

I didn't know how much time passed, but when Zev's body tightened, I shook off my exhausted daze and opened my eyes to see a wan-looking Evan leading a pale and drawn Lena out of the room. Emilio stopped his incessant pacing and stalked toward us. Zev stood up then helped me to do the same as Evan and Lena stepped into the hall. Locke came up on my other side, completing our huddle.

Emilio rocked to a stop. "Well?" His voice cracked on the demand.

"She's sleeping." Lena sounded raspy, as if she'd spent the last few hours screaming her head off. "She should wake up in an hour or so."

Emilio jolted then rushed forward, pausing a moment to squeeze Lena's hand before he disappeared into the room. When Locke slumped against the wall and a shudder passed through Zev, I realized how much tension both men had carried. As for me, relief left me glad for Zev's supporting arm because my legs felt shaky as shit. "Will she be okay?"

Lena shared a small frown with Evan then answered, "I think so, but we won't know for sure until she's up and talking."

"We managed to disarm the catalysts, but there were a couple of close calls," Evan admitted. "Some of the electrical pulses got through before I shut them down. Chances are high she's going to feel like shit for a few days and will need to rest."

"The council meeting is tomorrow," I muttered as an unnecessary reminder.

Locke's muffled snort was ignored, and Zev grimaced, his voice filled with grim resignation. "Knowing Sabella, she'll make sure she's there. If for no other reason than to confront Trask and whoever he's working with, or for, especially after they set her up."

I shared a look with Zev because we both knew Sabella was more old school in the eye-for-an-eye attitude versus the forgive and forget when it came to betrayal. "The bigger issue is getting her to share who it was and why she was meeting them in the first place because she's going to want to handle it on her own."

Zev looked at the room where Emilio had disappeared. "Emilio won't let that stand, especially now that we know Trask is tied up in this mess somehow."

"Not sure Sabella will give a damn about what Emilio wants," I pointed out. "And she's not exactly the ask-permission type."

"Thing is," Evan interrupted, his voice heavy with warning, "she may not be able to tell anyone who it was that she was meeting or what actually happened."

I turned to him. "You said she was okay."

"She is, but without knowing what they threw at her before they trapped her in the spell, and with the potential fallout from being under as long as she was, there's a high probability she may not remember." He flicked a look at Zev. "Especially if her kidnappers had any connections to your ambush team. Which is looking more and more likely, as they like their electro mages and memory spells."

"And that ouroboros symbol," I added. "Using everything we know should make it easier to narrow down our suspects on the hired gun side, right?"

Evan shrugged but didn't answer.

Sometimes, I could brush his comments aside since he was a glass-half-empty type of person, but something in the way he avoided my gaze warned me this time might be different. The grim expressions shared by Lena, Zev, and Locke added weight to Evan's concerns, but I couldn't, wouldn't, accept his grim prognosis. "This is Sabella," I pointed out unnecessarily. "She'll be fine."

It sounded like I was trying to reassure myself about that, but I didn't miss the pitying looks they shared. Instead, I ignored them. Maybe it made me a delusional optimist, but I needed Sabella to be okay because the alternative scared the shit out of me.

Sabella was one of those figures in Arcane society who skirted urban legend territory. She had held her position through decades of infighting and treachery, only to come out stronger and scarier than before. Just whispering her name or tying her to any situation could make even the most powerful person think twice. That was why I was having trouble wrapping my head around the fact that Trask had stashed Sabella in his garage, of all places. It was almost as if he was immune to any perceived threat. Either whoever he was in bed with had some borderline-frightening arrogance, or something or someone bigger and badder was at play.

"Look, we might as well all go get what sleep we can," Lena suggested. "There's nothing else we can do until she's awake, and morning will be here in a couple of hours. We all need the downtime."

No one argued. Murmured good nights were exchanged, and it wasn't long before only Zev and I were left in the hall, while Locke went to take first watch. Unease and worry shivered over me, and I didn't think twice before turning in to Zev's hold. His arm tightened around me. I laid my head against his chest, one arm wrapped around his waist and the other tucked between us with my hand under my chin and listened to the steady beat of his heart.

His hand stroked my back. "You okay?"

I tilted my head back and took in the deep grooves around his eyes and mouth and the lingering worry in the dark depths of his eyes. "I've been better. How about you?"

His lips curved but not with amusement. "Same."

His earlier grimness had lightened, but it was clear he was brooding. Lena was right—we all needed a break. Even if it was only a couple of hours of quiet instead of actual sleep. Too much had happened in too short a time, and we currently had no plays to make, no trail of crumbs to follow. For all intents and purposes, we were at a standstill. I knew if I were left on my own that night, I would do exactly what Zev was doing—brood. So I made a decision and took a risk. "Zev?" I waited until he looked at me. "Come lay down with me?"

The arm at my waist tightened, drawing me closer as he studied my face. He brushed my cheek with his thumb. "That might not be the best idea."

I managed an amused snort. *Sheesh, men.* "I'm not expecting sexy times, you idiot. I just don't want to be alone right now."

My tease earned an actual grin, and he raised an eyebrow in that way I was coming to adore. "Sexy times?"

I rolled my eyes. "Puhleeze, as if that wasn't your first thought."

"First, second, and probably third," he shot back, then his expression gentled. "It's been a hell of a long day."

I stepped back, shifting my hold from his waist to his hand, then led him toward the room I was using. "If I had known on Friday how long our date was going to last"—I kept things easy—"I would've suggested a weekend getaway instead."

He squeezed my hand. "I'll see what I can do next time."

I couldn't help myself. I shot him a quizzical look over my shoulder. "Ooh, confident, are you? I like that in a man."

I grinned when I got a laugh.

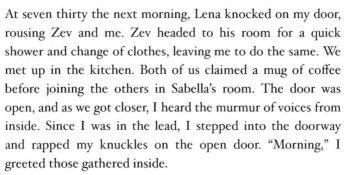

At seven thirty the next morning, Lena knocked on my door, rousing Zev and me. Zev headed to his room for a quick shower and change of clothes, leaving me to do the same. We met up in the kitchen. Both of us claimed a mug of coffee before joining the others in Sabella's room. The door was open, and as we got closer, I heard the murmur of voices from inside. Since I was in the lead, I stepped into the doorway and rapped my knuckles on the open door. "Morning," I greeted those gathered inside.

Over by a chest of drawers, Lena sat on the arm of a chair positioned in the far corner, where Evan juggled a laptop and coffee. Emilio was sitting in another chair pulled up at the far side of Sabella's bed and sipping from a mug, one foot braced on a knee, the picture of casual.

But the tightness in my chest loosened when I saw Sabella, sitting up, blankets neatly tucked over her lap, and a breakfast tray holding a small plate of half-eaten fruit and a cup of steaming tea in front of her. Although pale, she didn't appear any worse for wear. She turned from her conversation with Emilio to give me a smile and hold out her hands. "Rory. Zev. Good morning."

I crossed the room and managed to give her a one-arm hug without spilling my coffee. My throat clogged as I breathed in her familiar scent, a mix of vanilla, sandalwood, and a hint of floral, but I was caught in a storm of contradictions. On the one hand, I was relieved to see her alert and awake, apparently no worse for wear. On the other, all my questions boiled in a stew of frustrated resentment and hurt, threatening to spill forth in bitter accusations despite our audience. I had a brief battle over which one would win, my personal need for answers or my relief that she was still around to give them. Eventually, I ended up murmuring a heartfelt "You scared us." It came out husky, but at least it came out.

I pulled back but stilled when she didn't completely let me go. She held me in place as she searched my face, and whatever she saw dimmed her smile and left a cautious puzzlement. "What's wrong?"

I managed a small return smile but shook my head. "Nothing important." She raised an imperious eyebrow, clearly unconvinced, and I clarified, "Nothing that can't wait until later."

She held on a bit longer then finally nodded and let me go. I got out of the way so Zev could step in. I went to Lena and Evan, noting that last night's lingering cloud of frustration had lightened to determination. Lena was studying Sabella as the older woman spoke in low tones to Zev. Evan was fairly bouncing in his seat, either because of an overdose of caffeine or because he'd finally found something useful. I was hoping we'd caught a break. "Hey, guys."

Lena shifted her attention to me. "Hey, you. So what's up with that?" She lifted her chin in Sabella's direction without taking her sharp gaze from me.

I hastily tried to cover my wince but wasn't sure I succeeded when Lena's eyes narrowed. Sometimes, my bestie was too damn sharp by half. I stuck with what was clearly my theme this morning. "Nothing." Lena opened her mouth, but I cut her off before she could push. "Leave it, Lena."

Her mouth snapped shut and her lips thinned, and in true friend form, she didn't budge. "For now, Rory, but we'll be chatting later."

It was a reprieve, and I took it. "Later," I agreed then turned to Evan. "Tell me you found something."

"Early this morning," he confirmed. "I'm just waiting for the go-ahead to share with the group."

I moved between Lena and the dresser and turned to watch the room. I leaned against the wall and took a sip of coffee. Lowering my mug, I asked, "How long has she been up?"

Lena shrugged. "We came in about twenty minutes ago, and she was already awake and talking to Emilio."

I studied the head of the Cordova Family. His agitation from earlier was gone, and he was back to his coolly aloof head-of-Family best. The only sign that his mask wasn't firmly in place was the involuntary jerk he made when Sabella winced and rubbed her temple after handing Zev her break-fast tray. Emilio covered the slip by turning the move into a polite lean and touched her arm. "Sabella?"

She patted his hand. "I'm fine, Emilio."

His jaw flexed, so he was clearly not convinced, but he eased back in his chair.

Zev, who had set the breakfast tray out in the hall, stood in the doorway, his attention on something or someone down the hall. "Morning," he greeted then stepped back into the room so Locke could follow.

"Morning," the Cordova Hound muttered, rubbing a hand along a scruff-covered jaw as he took in the room's occupants. His gaze landed on Sabella. "Ms. Rossi, nice to see you awake."

"Locke, charming as ever." True affection colored Sabella's voice as she held her hands up to him.

Locke accepted her offering, taking those hands in his for a moment before letting them go. Sabella looked at Zev and waved at the door. Following her unspoken direction, he closed it then moved to stand in front of it, calmly sipping his coffee. It was a silent but obvious message that no one was leaving unless Sabella let them. I covered my smirk with my mug and prepared to get down to business.

Sure enough, Sabella's spine straightened, and her expression shifted from doting matriarch to ruthless general. Despite the fact she was sitting in bed, there was no doubt of who was in charge. "Since we're all here, shall we get started?"

"Why don't we start with who you were meeting at your house?" Zev got right to it.

Her answer was equally blunt. "Dale Peterson."

Zev frowned. "Who is Dale Peterson?"

The answer came from Evan. "A Guild Scout."

"Why are you working with a Guild spy?" That question belonged to Emilio, and from the tightness in both his face and voice, he wasn't happy with Sabella.

Not in the least chastised by his disapproval, Sabella gave him a cold response. "Because the Guild has no stake in the Delphi project."

"And doesn't give two shits about Family or council politics," I added, feeling my way through Sabella's logic.

She gave me a proud smile. "Exactly." She turned to Emilio. "Here's what we know. Someone, either on the council or with direct access to a council member, wants to expose the Delphi project to the public."

"Someone want to share what exactly is the Delphi project?" Lena's question reminded me that not everyone in this room knew about the experimental serum that could either boost or strip a mage's power.

Emilio shared a look with Sabella, but it was Zev's gruff "They're already involved" that seemed to tip the scales. Emilio shifted in his chair until he pinned Evan and Lena with a threatening stare. "What is shared in this room does not go beyond the door. Understood?"

In a blink, Evan shifted from mild-mannered computer

geek to Lena's guard dog and scarily high-level electro mage. "Threats don't inspire confidence."

"Fields," Zev said, gaining Evan's attention. "This information is dangerously volatile, and considering the current situation, it has already claimed a number of lives. Be sure you want to know."

Evan looked at Lena, who turned to me. "Rory?"

"It's bad," I confirmed. "Like blow-your-worldview-to-smithereens bad." Because the fact that there was a way to strip a mage of their magic could send the Arcane society spinning into chaos.

Lena and Evan shared a look, then Lena said, "Tell us."

So Zev did, laying out what we knew of the Delphi serum and its long-reaching ramifications on Arcane society. He started with its origin in Lara Kaspar's research and the fact that it had been developed against the council's decree. That led to an explanation of how both the Trask Family and the Clarke Family had sunk most of their Family's finances into the illegal research that cost numerous lives, innocent and not so innocent, and left both Families hovering on the brink of financial ruin.

Zev went into detail about how the serum could either boost a mage's power to an unpredictable level or strip it away completely. He even laid out how the serum could be weaponized, potentially narrowing or widening the currently fragile divide between the magical and nonmagical classes. That was something the council was desperate to keep buried because no one wanted to see Arcane society fracture and turn into a free-for-all. When he was done, Lena was pale, and Evan looked grim.

"Now that we're all on the same page"—Sabella's voice was quiet but resolute—"we need to figure out who on the council Stephen Trask is working with. Dale called me because he said he found something, but when I got there..."

She frowned and gave a small shake of her head. "I never saw Dale. I got to the house, went inside, and that's all I remember." I caught the tremor in her hand as she smoothed an invisible wrinkle in the blankets.

"So we need to find Dale," Locke said.

"Considering the scene we walked into, I think finding him alive is a long shot," Zev said. "We'd be better off tying the kidnappers to Trask."

"That won't be hard." Evan's comment caught everyone's attention. "I finally untangled a financial trail between Trask and our possible mercenaries."

Emilio lost his casual pose and leaned forward. "When?"

"This morning." He got up and, with laptop in hand, skirted Emilio and got closer to Sabella. He angled his laptop so she could see it. "Recognize him? Top center?"

Sabella took the laptop, brought it closer, and studied the image. "Yes." She pointed at the screen. "And this one." She angled the laptop so Evan and Emilio could see the screen. "This one was inside the house, the first one was in my office, and I think"—she frowned and rubbed her forehead—"later, in a car, maybe? I'm not sure, but they're both familiar." She handed the laptop back. "Who are they?"

"I don't have names, but I do have handles." Evan took his laptop to his chair. "Snake and Charge." His lips curled in disgust, and he looked over the rim of his glasses. "Not the most creative names. They're a mercenary team that tends to take on high-risk, high-paying jobs. Typically, they run the show, but they've been known to hire out if the assignment requires it." His fingers flew, then he was turning the screen toward me. "Recognize any of these faces?"

Zev came over as I studied the six faces filling the screen. I pointed at the stoic-looking female in the top right. "Her. She was the one hiding by the stairwell. She was an illusion mage."

"That would be the one going by Chimera," Evan said.

Zev pointed at the top left image of a heavy-brow male with a square chin and then a female in the bottom row. "Him and her."

I peered closer at the male, recognition slow in coming. A flash of those mean eyes bulging in a red face hit me. "The asshole who tried to scalp me."

"The casting mage," Zev agreed.

"That would be Bull," Evan confirmed.

I couldn't stop my derisive snort at that particular handle. Zev asked Emilio, "Don't they have the bodies in the morgue? Maybe they can get us some ID's."

Emilio was texting on his phone. "I'll see if Mari can get us names."

"This female." I pointed at the one in the bottom row. "She was the electro mage you faced off with."

"Yeah," Zev said.

"That's Stryker," Evan confirmed. "A midlevel electro mage, but there are whispers she may also have a secondary Mystic ability."

"She had a minor illusion talent." Zev's voice was tight. "It didn't play nice."

I went back to the photos. "Him." I tilted the laptop toward Zev and pointed at the younger guy on the bottom row, center. "This is the one your scorpions ate."

Lena's head jerked at that, but it was clear Evan had the photo layout memorized. "That would be Storm. His partner of choice is... was Stryker."

"Seriously? What they'd do, pick their names from a video game?" muttered Locke.

Even though I agreed with him, I was studying the faces on the screen. "Storm, the one on the bottom left, and the one on the top center could be brothers."

"Wouldn't surprise me," Evan said. "That one on top

center is Snake. The one on the bottom left is Charge. They brought in Storm on quite a few jobs that I was able to trace."

Holy shit, Evan found our entire strike team. "Impressive." I handed back his laptop.

Color seeped under his cheeks as he took his computer. "All of these mercenaries lurk in the dark web, but to hire all of them for an operation like this would cost serious bank." He talked and typed simultaneously. "Zev, you indicated Trask was all but broke, which begs the question, where did he get the money to pay them?"

"Someone is providing financing," Emilio said.

"Most likely," Evan confirmed, "which means they could be setting Trask up to take the fall, and he will." He stopped typing and looked up. "Because whoever arranged this not only managed to lay a believable trail to Trask but to bury their footprints and, in some places, managed to erase them altogether. If they weren't such scumbags, I'd be thoroughly impressed and happy to simply admire their work."

"But since they are scum and you've got a reputation to protect," I prompted, "that wasn't an option."

"No, it wasn't," Evan admitted, well-earned arrogance echoing in his voice. "So doing what I do, I reconstructed their trail. Between the team that took on Zev and Rory, there was also the one lying in wait for Sabella. Two high-priced mercenary teams are harder to hide than one."

"It also means access to deep pockets," Lena said.

"Who on the council fits that criteria?" I asked, not wanting to keep spinning in circles.

"There are two names that come to mind," Sabella said. "Jude Novak and Victor Reid."

Locke considered Emilio and Sabella. "So how do we figure out which one it is?"

"We go to the council and ask," Sabella said.

CHAPTER TWENTY-ONE

I CAREFULLY WADED into the silence following Sabella's pronouncement and pointed out the obvious. "Um, yeah, not sure that's going to work. The minute we walk in with Sabella, not only will Trask know he's in trouble, but so will whoever's backing him."

"That's exactly why it should work." Emilio stood up and started to pace, not that there was much room, but he made it work, going from the foot of Sabella's bed to the top and back.

Sabella watched him. "What are you thinking?"

Emilio stopped pacing to explain. "Not only will our main suspect be a captive audience, but if we use what we have so far on Trask, the documented link between him and the first mercenary team, the possible connection to the second mercenary team, the fact Sabella was being held on his property, plus the expected testimony on his screwups with the Delphi project, it won't take much to back him into a corner. I just need to get Mari up to speed on what we've found."

Evan cleared his throat. "Is the council as keen on legalities as the court system? Because if so, my searches may not hold up."

Surprisingly, it was Sabella who said, "Maribel is as good at her job as you are at yours, so the information will stand."

"Do you really think Trask will expose the traitor to cover his ass?" Locke interrupted, his skepticism echoing mine.

"Stephen may be quick to claim successes," Emilio said, "but he's even quicker to deny any responsibilities when it comes to failures. If he knows he's going down, he'll make sure to drag along whoever is tied to him."

I wasn't so sure about that, but before I could say anything, Zev pointed out, "You're forgetting Imogen. She's not going to let Stephen get cornered."

And that's a whole nother can of worms. "Are you sure she's on his side?"

Zev frowned. "What do you mean?"

I shrugged. "You and Emilio mentioned there might be a power struggle happening between her and Trask. If that's true, how likely is it that she's not working for him?" It sounded like some paranoid conspiracy theory, but what if it wasn't?

"She's Trask's Arbiter," Emilio said with cool arrogance. "You don't get to that position if the Family's head has any doubts about your loyalty."

"Not to mention the penalty for betraying a Family is death," Zev added.

That was the penalty for treason, too, but that didn't seem to be stopping whoever was behind the mess.

Lena cut into the rising tension. "If we think Trask is being set up, who's to say Imogen hasn't been made a better offer?" She didn't flinch as Emilio and Zev turned their attention to her. "Families are not immune to betrayal." Her smile was tight, and her voice held an edge of bitter lessons learned. "Everyone has a price, even an Arbiter."

A weighty silence filled the room, only to be broken by Sabella calmly saying, "She has a point." When Emilio turned to her, his expression ominous, Sabella held up her hand. "Emilio, your situation is not the same as Stephen's. You know this. Lena's concerns are valid. Ones we should consider. If we're wrong"—she gave a delicate shrug—"we're wrong and no harm done." She shot Lena a look. "If she's right, best we be prepared."

Lena dropped her gaze, and since we were discussing possible concerns, I decided to add mine. "I hate to rain on your parade, but it may not be so easy to get Trask to break. First, our traitor is smart and patient, something they've proven with Theo Mahon's death. They might be willing to let Trask swing and take him out later." That earned me the combined attention of Emilio, Zev, Sabella, and even Locke. Doing my best not to squirm, I spoke to Sabella. "If we go in and accuse Trask in front of the council, all he has to do is deny everything or provide a plausible explanation on the financial ties. What's to stop him from turning this into a he-said-we-said situation? Considering how many times he's already been screwed over by ex-employees and researchers, it won't be hard to sell the it's-not-me defense. Unless we have a way to prove he's lying, it's just a matter of who's more convincing to the council."

True amusement lightened the thin lines of stress in her face as she dropped her bomb. "Maribel is a truth seeker."

Well, damn. A truth seeker was almost as rare as a Prism, and for obvious reasons, they didn't advertise their abilities either. No one wanted to be around someone who could compel the truth whenever they wanted. I was still processing the ramifications of Maribel's ability when I asked Zev, "Why didn't we sic her on him from the get-go?"

"Because like yours," Emilio answered, "her ability is easily abused by others, so she keeps it quiet." He flicked a look at Sabella. "Her ability is not public knowledge, and she doesn't like to use it."

"Will she do this for us?" Zev asked.

Emilio rubbed the back of his neck. "All I can do is lay everything out and explain what's at stake. It's her choice to risk revealing her ability in front of the council."

She gets a choice? I really wanted to ignore the snarky voice in my head, but it wasn't happening. "It's no different than what you're asking of me," I pointed out, not understanding his reluctance.

He glared at me. "It's not the same."

"Isn't it?" I tried to remind myself that Emilio cared about Mari and considered her family. It was there in the little touches he couldn't hide when they were together, so his protectiveness was understandable. But how risky was it, really, for her? Being a truth seeker wasn't in-your-face magic. It was subtler than that.

Next to me, Zev shifted but stayed quiet, something I appreciated because it hit me just how much Emilio's double standard bothered me. "If I told you I didn't want to testify in front of the council, would you let me walk away?"

He looked away in silent admission.

My smile was small and tight. "Yeah, I didn't think so." I shook my head. "I'm not thrilled about outing myself as a Prism in front of some of the most powerful people in Arcane society, so I get why she'd be reluctant to act, but is she really risking anything?"

He looked at me. "What do you mean?"

"Correct me if I'm wrong, but can't she use her ability in such a way that it won't be obvious she's compelling Trask?" When Emilio gave me a puzzled frown, I clarified. "I mean, she is a lawyer, so I'm sure she knows how to coerce a confession without revealing magic is involved." Unless someone on the council could see magic the way I could, who would even know if she used it? And because his dismissal of my dilemma stung, I couldn't help adding, "If her ability is anything like mine, she probably uses it more than you realize." Yeah, it was bitchy, but honestly, that man needed to clue in that power came in many different forms. I knew my jab had found its mark when his shoulders stiffened, and his eyes narrowed.

Before he could return the favor, Sabella clapped her hands to gain everyone's attention. "All right, then. We have a plan. Emilio, you go meet up with Maribel. Get her caught up on what tomorrow holds and see if she can get us the names for the bodies in the morgue." She looked at Zev and Locke. "You two need to see if you can find out what happened to Dale." A cold darkness swam through her eyes and disappeared. "I would like to have answers for his wife." She turned to Lena and Evan. "You two continue your hunt on the dark web. The more information you get, the better for us."

Evan nodded, and Lena looked amused.

Then it was my turn. "Rory, I need you to stay."

I dipped my chin in acknowledgment and waited while everyone cleared out. I pulled my phone out of my pocket then had to make a quick grab for the photo that came out with it. I held it for a second then tucked it back in my front pocket, fiddling with the stiff edge as my mind raced. Lena gave me a questioning look that I answered with a shrug, then she and Evan headed out first. Emilio brushed a kiss along Sabella's cheek. I thumbed my phone's screen to find everything quiet before shoving it in my pocket, my other hand still on the damning photo. Even Emilio's dark look as he stalked by me and out the door barely registered. Zev took his place at Sabella's side, gave her a hug, and came over to stand in front of me.

"You okay?" he asked in a low voice while Locke chatted with Sabella.

"I think so," I admitted. I pulled out the photo and held it between us.

He looked at it then at me. "You going to talk to her?"

A rushing noise filled my head as anxiety battered me. I swallowed hard and made my decision. "Yeah."

"Good." He wrapped a hand around my neck, tugged me in, and pressed a kiss to my forehead.

I closed my eyes, breathed him in, and let his confidence bolster mine.

He let me go and eased back. "Find me when you're done."

Taking a deep breath, I nodded and dropped my hand to my side, partially concealing what I held.

He left, and my attention went to the woman sitting in the bed like a queen on her throne. She studied me, the benevolent matriarch slowly fading under an unreadable mask as we stared at each other, the silence broken by the door closing behind Zev.

"Something's wrong," she said. "What is it?"

Instead of answering, I walked over, snagged the chair Emilio had used, and dragged it closer to the bed. I avoided her gaze and sat down, holding the photo for a moment before reluctantly offering it to her.

Her gaze dropped to the image, and she stiffened. I was surprised to see her hand shake as she took the photo like it was a snake poised to strike, and in a way, it was. She set it down on her blanket-covered lap and brushed a finger along the battered edges. A wistful smile broke her impenetrable mask, and an aged sadness settled around her. "Where did you find it?"

"In your office," I answered. "Which is a bit of a mess." When she shot me a puzzled frown, I explained, "It was trashed, but this was tucked behind another picture in a broken frame."

She managed an absent nod, but her gaze went right back to the picture as if she couldn't help herself. "I had forgotten it was there." She drew in a deep breath and covered the photo with her hand, protecting it. When her eyes met mine, they carried a steely resolve. "Ask."

A thousand and one questions spun in my head, making it hard to pin down the most important, because they were all important. *Where the hell am I supposed to start?* "You knew my mom."

"And your father," she confirmed without a hint of apology.

"How?"

That got me a pained smile and an unexpected start. "I had a sister, Juliana."

Her admission reminded me of the entry I'd found in the leather-bound book at Emilio's. "She was your twin, wasn't she?"

Sabella shot me a sharp look. "She was, yes," she admitted warily. "How do you know that?"

"I found a book on Arcane Families in Emilio's library. Out of curiosity, I looked up yours and a few others." Realizing how that might sound, I rushed to explain, "I didn't recognize the symbol linking her to you, so I had to use the key provided. You don't talk about her." *Or your family, really, now that I think about it.* Granted, she'd shared snippets about her kids but never anything truly meaningful.

Her eyebrows did that imperious drift toward her hairline, but instead of commenting, she resumed her tale. "No, I don't. We were quite close, and losing a twin..." She didn't finish and probably couldn't considering the weight of emotion in her voice. She looked at the photo in her lap and was silent for a long moment.

I waited, unwilling to interrupt.

Finally, she regained her composure and looked at me, her

chin tilted defiantly. "To answer your question, I need to start at the beginning."

When she said nothing else, I said cautiously, "Okay."

The edge of mulishness faded as she talked. "My Family, the Giordanos, were always in the spotlight, especially as my father was quite vocal in his opinion regarding the Families' responsibilities to Arcane society as a whole. How much do you know about the history of the original Families?"

"Just what they taught in school," I said. "There were twenty-seven Families that originated in and around Europe, and after the carnage of the witch trials, the Mystic Accords were drawn up, and some of them migrated to America. They forged agreements with the First Nations and created First Nation lands and Mystic States. For a while, everyone managed to get along, but then in the late 1800s, everyone got pissed at everyone else, and a civil war broke out. Eventually, the dust settled, and three ruling powers emerged, the First Nations, the Arcane Council, and the US Government to represent the Traditionalists."

Wry amusement lightened the shadows in her eyes. "Simplified but accurate." Her amusement faded. "For generations, the Families believed their status put them above the government's laws, especially the Traditionalists, as that populace held little to no magic. My father didn't share the elitist view of most of Arcane society that magic equaled right and might. Strangely, it was that belief that landed him on the initial council, but it was an uncomfortable fit for both. However, he hoped to be the voice of change and encouraged others to reach outside our society and work with both the Traditionalists and the First Nations to benefit all."

An admirable trait but unfortunately a bit unrealistic considering there were those in Arcane society who had no tolerance for anyone outside their privileged bubble and no intention of ever changing their stance. The best anyone could hope for was for the majority's need for peace to outweigh the desire of the few for power and avoid outright conflict.

I didn't interrupt Sabella's story to share my thoughts.

"Growing up," she said, "I was unaware of just how uneasy he was with his position. He and my mother were very good at protecting Julie and me from the threats aimed in our Family's direction. Juliana and I had each other, our schooling, and a casual group of social friends. It wasn't until we were older that we realized exactly what kind of pressure our father and by extension our Family was under."

Her hands fisted on the blanket, her knuckles turning white. Her voice tightened. "We were just out of high school when our father was called out of the country on council business, and for once, our mother stayed behind with us. Our graduation was coming up, and she was in the midst of party planning. He left his hotel room for a meeting and never came back. His body was found three days later."

Watching how tightly she held herself, I was pretty sure I knew the answer but still asked, "Was it murder?"

She met my gaze, an icy ruthlessness turning her hazel eyes diamond hard, revealing the woman who led a formidable Family. "Yes. It was then Jules and I began to understand exactly what our Family's position entailed. My father's death was a blow my mother never really recovered from. She didn't fall apart, because that wasn't an option. Before his death, those who knew her always spoke of her compassion for others and her innate grace. Afterward, that compassion disappeared, replaced by an unbendable will forged in vengeance. Especially once she took over my father's position on the council. She wielded her power with a cold, unforgiving ruthlessness until everyone involved in my father's death had paid."

Honestly? I couldn't blame Sabella's mother. If the man I

loved had been killed—and I pictured Zev's face—I would go out of my way and then some to ensure payback. "I assume that's the beginning of the Giordanos' fearsome reputation?"

"Yes, it was," she admitted with a hint of pride. "One Jules and I purposely cultivated long after my mother had passed. Our approach to dealing with the other Families and their conflicts differed. I preferred a more subtle approach, whereas Jules was more unapologetic in her engagement. We were expected to take our mother's seat on the council, but neither of us wanted what it entailed, something we made crystal clear."

Imagining just how much that must have pissed off the establishment, I couldn't help snickering. "I'm sure that didn't go over well."

"No," she agreed with a small curve of her lips, "it didn't. Especially as we were not exactly diplomatic in our refusal. We made our share of enemies, some of whom linger to this day. If we weren't who we were, as close as we were, I have no doubt our Family would have shattered under the constant strain, but Jules and I were too close for others to get between us."

Her small smile faded, and she picked up the photo, her voice quieter. "Luckily for both of us, our husbands were extraordinary men, and the four of us had each other's backs. Eventually, things on the political front went from a boil to a simmer, so we decided it was safe enough to start our own families. I had my oldest and one on the way when Jules and Oscar had their daughter, Alessandra. For a while, we could breathe easy, but as always, that peace didn't last."

"Because?"

"Because the Families are not keen on change and rarely satisfied with the status quo. That dissatisfaction is what is behind the constant misunderstandings and rumors, and that caustic mix exacerbates the rivalries to a dangerous degree.

One of those rivalries cost Jules and Oscar their lives and left Alessandra an orphan at nineteen." She held the photo out, offering it to me. "This was taken about a year after their deaths, right after Alessandra met Cristian Castiano. They were married about six months later."

I studied the picture of the smiling young man and equally happy young woman as a haunting sorrow and whispery ache crawled through me.

"Two years after that, I held Lessa's baby in my arms for the first time." The poignancy in Sabella's voice made my eyes burn.

Lessa. Hearing my mother's more familiar nickname, the one I grew up knowing, hurt. "They changed their names." My voice was rough.

Sabella leaned forward and squeezed my knee, waiting until I looked at her before she said, "They did, just before you were born. Cristian and Alessandra Castiano became Chris and Lisa Costas."

I swallowed an aged grief. "Why?"

She let me go and sighed. "Because they were being targeted, just like Jules and Oscar." She sat back, her hands laced together, but I couldn't miss the dark satisfaction lurking deep in her eyes. "I could go into the political and Family reasons, but they are no longer relevant as they no longer exist."

And the reason why is sitting in front of me. I found the thought unexpectedly comforting even as I put the missing pieces of my life into place, but it was a struggle. "Are those reasons why you never came for me?"

"They were. Leaving you where you were was the safer option."

"Was it?" I looked at her and wasn't quite able to hide the bite of accusation in my voice. "Or did it just make it easier for you?"

She winced but lifted her chin to cover it. "Perhaps both," she admitted, earning my grudging respect at her brutal honesty. "When Cristian was killed, your mom disappeared, taking you with her. She covered her tracks well because rumors flew that both of you had been killed. I spent the first year you both were missing hunting down the ones responsible for Cristian's death. Then I turned my attention to the rumors."

"That mom and I were dead?" My voice was curt, but my emotions were all over the place and so mixed up it was hard to pin them down.

Sabella nodded.

A flare of anger erupted at her arrogance. "Did you stop to think that your poking around might have put us in more danger?"

A flash of regret was there and gone, but Sabella didn't back down. "I had no intention of bringing Alessandra Castiano back to life, but I wanted to make sure Lisa Costas and her daughter were safe. To do that, I made sure the rumors stayed intact."

Twisted up inside, I couldn't stop my snarky "How?"

Her eyes narrowed, and she snapped, "Stupid questions are beneath you, Rory."

"Fine." I grudgingly relented but found I could be equally stubborn. *Must be a family trait.* "You killed anyone who said differently. Then what?"

"Threats can be eliminated in more than one way," she chided with pitiless practicality. "Something you'll want to remember for the future." Before I could tell her what I thought of her assumptions about my future, she continued, "By the time I was able to retrace Lessa's steps, I was too late. She had been dead in truth for two years, and you were in the system. I left you there, believing it was the safest option for you while I took care of those who targeted Lessa. When I was done, you were considering joining the Guild, so I decided to remain in the background and did my best to watch over you."

I thought of Sabella's friendly relationship with the Arcane Guild director, the same relationship that had landed me the job that jump-started my contracting career. "You're the reason the Guild took me on." It wasn't really a question.

"Yes," she admitted unapologetically. "I felt it was the best way for you to grow into who you were."

I clawed my way out of the flood of emotions the storm of the past had created and tried to mirror her pragmatism. "Did you know what I was?"

"Not at first," she said, shifting in the bed. "Your parents never talked about your magic, but I wondered."

"And you didn't push to find out?"

"Why would I? It was your parents' choice to share, and since most children manifest their magic around five, they could easily dodge the question. Knowing what I know now, I'm not surprised they didn't say anything. There was enough blood in the family waters without tempting more sharks with your ability."

And there it was, confirmation of why I wanted nothing to do with the Arcane Families. The never-ending vendettas. "Which Family were they running from? My father's? Yours? How many Families were after them?" When she didn't answer, my hold on my anger slipped. "How many people do I need to be looking over my shoulder for when our relationship becomes public knowledge?"

"None. I told you, I eliminated those hunting your parents."

Frustration and hurt gelled with sarcasm. "Did you eliminate the entire Family line?" When she calmly held my gaze, a slow creep of horror rose at what her silence implied. "You wiped out an entire Family?"

A decidedly cold mask slipped over her face. "That's not important. What does matter is it's now safe for you to take your place in our Family."

"Not important?" I repeated, stunned. I stared at the callous woman in front of me and wondered how I could have been so blind to her nature. She sat there, calm as could be, no remorse for basically exterminating entire Families, and for what? Power? Vengeance? Pride?

"Are you sure it's safe for me to go public with our connection?" Not that I wanted to, but I didn't think it was going to be my choice. Bitterness rose because there was no way to escape the inevitable. My entire life had been maneuvered to this point, leaving me no choice but to reveal who I was, what I was, and whose blood swam in my veins. "If you missed one or you pissed off someone connected to them, the cycle will continue, except now, thanks to your actions, I'm the new target." I sounded as bitter as I felt. "God, what a mess."

For the first time, Sabella's composure cracked, and temper broke through. She leaned forward, her voice a razor-edged whip. "Would you rather I let them get away with killing your parents?"

"No, of course not." My denial was a harsh, gut reaction because I had zero regret that the ones who'd killed my parents were no longer among the living, even if I knew how dangerous that thinking could be. "But where does it stop, Sabella? Even you can't wipe them all out, not without serious ramifications. And these can't be the only enemies you've got on your ass."

She crossed her arms over her chest and eyed me with speculation. "You sound as if you care."

"Damn you, of course I care." Unable to sit still, I got up and started to pace. "I cared about you even before I knew who you were." It sucked because hiding behind all the chaotic emotions was the unsettling truth—not only did I understand her logic, but part of me was proud to be connected to her, to call her family. I stopped at the foot of her bed, gripped the footboard tight, and glared at her. "You think I could stand aside if you were killed?"

"I should be insulted that you write me off a little too easily, Rory." She sounded amused, which further infuriated me. "But it's nice to know you wouldn't let my death go unanswered."

I hung my head and focused on taking a couple of deep breaths so I wouldn't scream. When I was sure I could talk without losing it, I looked up and said, "No, I wouldn't, and that's exactly why I fought so hard not to be part of your world." I peeled my fingers from the footboard, flexing them to get my blood circulating, while I managed a deceptively calm tone. "It's a lethal hamster wheel that just keeps spinning until someone stops breathing. That's not the life I wanted."

"But it is the one you willingly stepped into," she said softly.

It was a point I couldn't argue, and because I couldn't, I switched gears. "I saw you, Sabella, caught in that damn spell. The fact you're here and alive is a fucking miracle, and you know it. Your arrogance is just as deadly as these vendettas."

She sighed. "Rory, darling, death is inevitable for everyone. Even me, but I haven't gotten to where I am through compassion and mercy. Those traits don't play well in our world, a fact you would do well to accept."

I opened my mouth with some half-hearted bullshit denial, but she wasn't done.

"Whether you decide to publicly acknowledge our family connection or not, you're now a known factor in Arcane society, especially if you're considering any kind of future with Zev. It is up to you on how you want to be perceived. Will you be a threat others will hesitate to trigger or a tool to be used?"

My spine went ramrod straight, my hands fisted at my side, and I lifted my chin. "I won't be anyone's tool, Sabella, not even yours."

Something scarily close to pride washed over her face. "That's what I'm counting on."

CHAPTER TWENTY-TWO

Zev found me a couple of hours later, hiding in Emilio's library, brooding. Without saying a word, he came over to the chair I was in and picked me up. I gave a small squeak of surprise and threw my arms around his shoulders so I wouldn't end up on the floor. "Hey!"

He ignored my startled protest and sat down with me on his lap. Once settled, he asked, "What happened?"

I liked the feel of his arms around me, and some of my tension leaked away. I settled back with my head on his shoulder and one hand against his chest. Under my palm, the steady beat of his heart was comforting. I recited my conversation with Sabella. When I was done, I was grateful to find my chaotic emotions had subsided, as if sharing had drained some of the emotional storm away. Unfortunately, I was still treading water, out of my depth on what to do about the recent revelations.

Zev stroked a comforting hand up and down my shoulder as we sat in contemplative silence, then he broke it by asking, "So what happens now?"

It was a good question, and I'd spent the last couple of

hours trying to pin down the answer. "I don't know." I absently plucked at his T-shirt. "You warned me."

His chest rose and fell, and his breath ruffled my hair as he rubbed his chin over the top of my head. "Yeah, I did."

When he didn't say anything more, I lifted my head and pushed back so I could see his face. We were only a few years apart in age, but it was the hard-earned knowledge in his eyes that made him seem older, harder. He knew better than I what it meant to be integrally tied to an Arcane Family. Since he was an Arbiter, his job was twofold, to be his Family's shield and to dispense justice, or vengeance, as needed. There were no easy choices in his world, and it was a world I'd willingly walked into because I wanted him. All of him. Not just pieces.

But if I was honest, at least with myself, my choice wasn't just about Zev. Deeper, darker reasons lay underneath my decision, proof that I was Sabella's family in more ways than one. First was retribution, my need to see the ones who'd stolen everything from me paid and paid dearly. Suspicions had haunted me and fueled my cynical view of the Arcane Families, but I'd never had anything solid to use. Finding out my suspicions were valid and that Sabella had already settled that bill didn't ease the burn but just shifted the unpaid emotional debt. Her question echoed in my head. *"Will you be a threat others will hesitate to trigger or a tool to be used?"*

And that was my second reason. When it came down to it, my choice was easy. I was no one's tool.

"Hey." A brush of warmth against my cheek and along my jaw pulled me out of my thoughts. Zev watched me with a puzzled frown. "What's going on in your head?"

"Tomorrow's meeting with the council." I dropped the hand pressed against his chest. "How worried should I be?"

"About what?"

I tucked my hair behind my ear. "Any of it. My ability, my connection to Sabella."

His gaze sharpened then drifted over my face as his hand settled on my hip. "Truthfully? There's no way you're leaving there without revealing you're a Prism."

Yeah, that's what I figured. A growing knot of unease was setting up shop in my gut, but I powered through. "And the family thing?"

He didn't answer right away but took his time thinking it over. "I don't know, but if it was me, I'd brace."

I grimaced. Nice to know I wasn't just being paranoid.

"Does it really bother you that much to be linked to Sabella?" he asked.

"What?" It took me a second to process his question and the fact he'd misinterpreted my expression. "Oh, no, that's not it." Because my biggest concern was how to go from hiding in the shadows to fearlessly striding into the spotlight in such a way that the circling sharks would think twice before bloodying the water.

"Then what is bothering you?"

There was an underlying note in his voice that struck me. Perhaps I wasn't the only one looking for my place, a disconcerting insight he'd pointed out to me recently. Since he was right, it had been hard to argue, but maybe Zev was looking for the same thing. That sense of family, of connection, the kind that came with ties you didn't want to lose. Just because he was raised alongside Emilio and was the Cordova Family Arbiter, that couldn't fully account for the lack of his own personal ties to the something or someone that belonged only to him, someone to call family. Which might explain his unflinching loyalty to Emilio.

Sabella, by giving me my history, had managed to strengthen those familial ties into a constricting knot. The nature of them was something that Zev would totally understand since he was quite at home in the arena of Family politics and intrigue. "It's inheriting her enemies," I admitted. "I appreciate knowing the how and why behind my parents' deaths, but all that drama tied behind it? I don't want to be Sabella's weakness." *Or yours.*

"Then don't be." His response was unflinchingly honest.

I choked back a derisive snort. "I don't think it's that easy."

"Of course it isn't." His words carried a harsh bite. "Start out expecting to have your ass handed to you on a regular basis. That way, you won't be disappointed."

Stung by his callousness, I stiffened, and heavy sarcasm layered every word. "Gee, thanks for your support." *Asshole.* I managed not to say that last part out loud.

His fingers dug into my hips, holding me in place, eliminating escape. "The only way you prove you're not something to be exploited or broken is to get up and, no matter how futile it appears, strike back smarter and harder than before. Strength is much more than the simple application of muscle to a problem."

I searched his face, noting the forbidding glint that turned his chocolate-brown eyes into a storm-ridden darkness lit by sparks of unrelenting determination. "So you're basically telling me to go full throttle."

His lips curved into a fierce grin. "That's one way to put it."

I raised my brows. "There's another?"

"Yeah." His grin turned wicked. "Time to go balls to the wall, babe."

CHAPTER TWENTY-THREE

THE NEXT MORNING, I brought Emilio's Maybach to a stop outside the gates of what appeared to be a very posh, very private country club. An armed man stepped out of the security booth, and I lowered my window as he approached. When the window was down, he bent so he could see inside the car. "Welcome to Ponderosa Estate."

Next to me, Zev leaned over from the passenger seat and lowered his sunglasses. "Cordova Family. We're here for the ten o'clock session."

"Yes, sir, you're expected. Your party is waiting in the Caballero room." He stepped back and lifted his hand. At his signal, the gate began to roll back.

Zev resettled in his seat while I waited for the gate to clear then pulled through. I braced for the warding magic he had warned protected the grounds. As the Maybach's tires rolled across the metal grate, the brush of magic rippled over my skin, the disconcerting sensation akin to walking through thick spiderwebs. The hair on my arms stood at attention, but I suppressed my reactive shudder. The weighty power of protective magic wasn't unexpected considering this was the preferred meeting place for the magically elite.

Once we were past the gate, the drive led us straight to the jewel of Ponderosa Estate. The stunning piece of architecture mixed brick and stucco with the familiar lines of Frank Lloyd Wright, all while blending in with the surrounding Sonoran landscape. Off to the side was space for parking, and we were not the first to arrive. A handful of other high-end vehicles, including a couple of equally pricy customized electric ones, had already claimed their spots.

"Looks like Mari beat us here," Emilio said from the back seat. "That's her Volvo."

Spotting a Volvo S60, a sexy red number, I pulled the Maybach into one of the nearby empty spaces and shut it down. Quiet reigned for a moment. I didn't know about anyone else, but I wasn't quite ready to brave the lion's den.

"Zev, have you heard from Locke?" The question came from Sabella, and despite her outwardly calm and collected demeanor, a thread of tension filled her voice.

He pulled out his phone, thumbed the screen, and checked for new messages. "Nothing yet." He twisted in his seat so he could see her. "He wanted to follow up with a potential lead and said he would let me know if anything came of it."

Although Locke was continuing the hunt for Dale Peterson, the Guild Scout who'd called Sabella back to her house the day of her abduction, no one was holding out much hope that he was still alive. But like most Hounds, Locke wasn't one to give up a hunt until it was finished, one way or the other. Not to mention, there was a faint hope that maybe Locke would get lucky and find us something other than circumstantial evidence.

Like, say, Dale's body with a handwritten confession from Stephen? Nerves brought out my inner snark, apparently.

An incoming message pinged on multiple phones. Since mine was silenced, that left the other three to check their devices. A sharp inhale from Sabella was echoed by a muttered curse from Emilio. But it was Zev's frown that had me asking, "Now what?"

Zev looked up from his phone, his eyes a turbulent storm and his face grim. "Leander Clarke had a stroke last night. He's in critical condition."

Shock bounced through me, leaving me speechless. Leander was one of those testifying in today's meeting. His stroke was just the latest in a string of shitty luck for the Clarke Family. If it wasn't so karmic, I would almost pity them. Leander Clarke was the head of the Clarke Family, the same Family behind the now-defunct research lab LanTech. Much like Stephen, Leander had made some decidedly poor choices, starting with hiring a retrieval team to kidnap Emilio's nephew and heir in an effort to gain the foundational data that the Delphi serum was based on. But that bad decision led to other, even worse, decisions, such as ignoring the council's edict and employing a psychopathic researcher whose loyalty belonged to some mysterious entity. All of it coalesced into the financial fallout that had left the Clarke Family portfolio teetering on the edge of ruin and to the tragic death of their Arbiter, Bryan Croft.

"So what happens next?" When everyone turned to look at me with varying degrees of question, I amended, "Will the council delay the meeting since Leander isn't able to make it?"

Sabella's soft laugh carried true amusement. "Oh, we're not getting out of this that easily, Rory. The council will move forward and deal with Leander later."

Right, okay. So no last-minute postponement of the inevitable. "Then I guess we better get this show on the road."

With that, we all got out and headed to the heavy

wooden doors. Zev held them open as we passed through. My skin prickled, not just from the artificially cooled air that carried a hint of sage and spice but from the low-level onslaught of active magic. My Prism tightened around me and took the discomforting edge off. I shifted my shoulders and waited for Zev. Together, we followed Emilio and Sabella.

We turned down a hall and found Maribel waiting for us outside a set of closed double doors. "Emilio, Sabella." She came forward, a briefcase in hand. "Did you get the message about Leander?"

I ignored their hushed exchange as three figures approached from the other end of the hall. I touched Zev's wrist in warning, but he'd already spotted them too. I didn't need to see the arrogant set of the rigidly straight shoulders or the near permanent scowl on the oldest of the three to recognize Stephen Trask. To his right was an overly slick corporate type with a smarmy smile that made me think the man was Trask's legal representation. To Stephen's left, a tall, sophisticated brunette with unusually light eyes, and all the warmth of an ice cube, glided with the lethal grace of a stalking cat—Imogen Frost, Trask Family Arbiter and Zev's ex-girlfriend.

As the trio drew closer, Stephen's gaze zeroed in on Sabella, but his scowl was quickly replaced by an aloof mask. Imogen wasn't quite adept at hiding her reaction, or she just didn't give a damn. I was betting on the second.

Something flickered in her eyes before her attention went straight to Zev then dropped to where my fingers lay on his wrist. Her gaze lifted, her red lips thinned, and her eyes narrowed with jealousy. Despite the urge to stick out my tongue, I refrained and held her stare. But my maturity went only so far. I slid my fingers over the back of Zev's hand until our fingers tangled. When his fingers curled with mine, I didn't miss the hint of red seeping under her cheeks. She really did bring out the brat in me.

Stephen stopped a few feet away, haughty arrogance in every line. "Sabella, always a pleasure."

"Stephen." Sabella inclined her head as regally as any queen.

He turned to Emilio, his voice cooling by several degrees. "Cordova."

"Trask." Emilio's greeting was patently empty.

Mari, Zev, and I remained silent, riding out the introductory power plays. Even as an observer, I couldn't miss the underlying tension. Stephen's lawyer broke it first, his voice filled with forced joviality. "Well, we should go in."

Emilio reached for the closest door, pulled it open, then inclined his head, indicating Stephen and his party should go first. Stephen made a derisive snort but strode inside, leaving Imogen and the slimeball to follow. They disappeared into the room, taking much of the tension with them. Emilio shot a look at Mari, who answered with a slight negative shake of her head. I wasn't sure what his silent question was but figured it had something to do with Mari's truth-seeking abilities.

Sabella didn't suffer from the same lack of translation. She patted Emilio's arm. "It's early yet. Don't worry." Then she swept inside, and we all trailed along.

Once we were in the room, the press of active magic deepened, adding to the urge to dig at my itchy skin. I didn't need to use my other sight to know that this room was ringed in even more wards, the air heavy with them. In reaction to the increased threat of power, my Prism shifted, adding another layer between the uncomfortable rasp and me.

To fight the urge to rub my arms, I studied the immense room and its occupants as I crossed the tiled floor. Instead of the expected corporate-boardroom type atmosphere, it was like walking into someone's massively oversized living room. The far side of the room held thick glass doors that led to a gorgeous courtyard. Inside, couches decorated with the occasional throw and pillows were paired with plush chairs positioned throughout, most collected in conversational areas.

The only indicator of the day's meeting was in the five leather executive chairs matched with side tables and positioned at the head of the room. They were filled with what I assumed was the Arcane Council. The two women and three men exchanged greetings with Stephen as the Trask party settled into the chairs to the council's right. Sabella led us to a seating group on the left. I listened as she exchanged air kisses and handclasps with the council members, memorizing names and faces.

Christina was a tall, Rubenesque woman in her late thirties or early forties with raven-black hair and dark eyes that missed nothing. She stood out among the others in her tailored maroon boot-cut pants and matching Mandarin-collared blouse embellished with gold metallic touches. She was clearly a woman comfortable making a lasting impression.

Next to her and almost disappearing into her shadow—which was strange considering the power he held as an Arcane Council member—was a decidedly average-looking man Sabella greeted as Jude, making him one of our possible backers.

Next to him was our second potential backer, Victor Reid, the stout wiry-haired councilman who looked to be the oldest of the group. Despite his frame, his voice was deep and carried easily through the room.

At his side was an older woman, Olivia, whose demeanor echoed Sabella's, quietly composed and gracious. Her blond hair held streaks of white, and she wore her pale-green skirt suit and red-soled heels as comfortably as I would wear a T-shirt and jeans.

Then there was the last, most unexpected member, Mateo Medina. Him, I recognized. His face had been splashed all over the tabloids, as he was one of the Arcane's most notorious bachelors. He did the whole tall, dark, and dangerous thing well, but his "dangerous" wasn't like Zev's. It was colder, more ruthless. Anyone who put a hand up to pet him would come back with a bloody stub.

Eventually, greetings and small talk died down, and everyone settled into their seats. I spent the first hour trying not to fidget as I listened to the council question Stephen, Sabella, and Emilio on the events leading up to the Delphi investigation. As the minutes ticked by and nothing notable happened, my tension leeched away, and my attention drifted. Even the jitters I'd woken up with had faded. It made me wonder if I shouldn't have rethought my decision to forego my typical coffee intake this morning. A few trips down the hall would've helped keep me alert. Caught up in my musings, I almost missed it when things shifted.

"Sabella, do you believe that Stephen Trask and Leander Clarke willingly chose to disobey the council in regards to the Delphi project?" There was no accusation or drama to Olivia's quietly posed question. It was a bit disconcerting considering that she'd remained mostly silent and simply listened.

"I do," Sabella answered with the same unruffled calm. "In fact, I believe that Stephen's unhealthy, single-minded obsession with this project is behind quite a few of his decisions, including those that led to the most recent developments."

Victor leaned forward, a frown furrowing his craggy face. "By recent developments, you mean your claims of being abducted?"

She raised an imperious eyebrow. "It's not a claim. It's a

fact. I was ambushed in my home on Sunday, abducted, and held against my will."

"And you believe Stephen is behind your attack?"

Her chin notched higher. "Well, considering I was retrieved from his home, yes, I firmly believe Stephen is behind that attack and other recent troubling events."

"That's a baseless accusation," snapped Stephen's lawyer.

"That is what we're here to find out." Jude coldly shut him down, and for a moment, the power behind the meek mask slipped out. He turned his attention to Emilio. "The statement we received from your lawyer indicates you sent a team out to retrieve Sabella. Correct?"

"Yes." Emilio kept his attention on the council, completely ignoring the spate of hissed whispers coming from Stephen's side of the room. "They located Sabella in a warded cage in the basement of Trask's garage."

More hissed whispers came from Stephen's side of the room, and when I made the mistake of looking, I got caught by the murderous rage in Stephen's glare aimed our way. The lawyer was whispering frantically in his ear. I broke away from Stephen only to clash with Imogen's icy regard as she stared at both Zev and me. Something in her gaze left me uneasy, but there was nothing to do about it. I turned away, swallowing my anxiety.

Christina shifted in her chair, crossed her legs, and tapped her nails against her chair's armrest. "Sabella, you stated, 'other recent troubling events.' Would you care to elaborate?"

"That is why we're here." Sabella's relaxed pose didn't change as she gave the councilwoman a small smile. "I believe my abduction is a direct result of my inquiries into the circumstances surrounding the death of Mr. Mahon."

Jude shifted in his seat, tugging at his collar. "We all agree those circumstances raise serious concerns."

"Yes, well, it's not every day a council prisoner dies while in custody," Olivia murmured dryly, earning a variety of looks. It was interesting to see the range. Christina's small smile was amused, her eyes sharp. Mateo's expression was coolly detached but watchful. Victor's agitated frown carried an edge, while Jude managed an air of puzzlement.

"It's under investigation," Victor shot back.

"I'm well aware of that, Victor," Olivia said. "Regardless of the investigation's results, I think we can all agree that Mr. Mahon's death is very much tied to the Delphi mess. If Sabella feels her abduction is part of that, I see no reason to doubt her."

"Neither do I," Jude agreed then turned to Sabella. "Does that mean you believe Stephen is the mastermind, for lack of a better term, behind both your kidnapping and the recent death of the council prisoner?"

On Emilio's far side, Mari shifted in her seat but stayed silent. I couldn't tell if her reaction was from a lawyer perspective or a truth seeker one. Either way, this was not like any hearing I'd ever witnessed. No stern judges, no lawyers arguing semantics, and even more telling, no jury of one's peers. Instead, it was more like a deceptively benign corporate board meeting. Yet the room fairly crackled with underlying disquiet. Probably because when this particular board agreed on a termination, it was more likely to be on a lethally permanent basis.

Sabella's light laugh carried no amusement and regained my attention. "Mastermind might be reaching, Jude, but yes, I have no doubt he's involved."

"That is such bullshit!" The outburst came from Stephen, who leapt to his feet, trembling in clearly outraged fury. His slick-looking legal counsel grabbed his arm and hissed a warning.

Next to me, Zev tensed. I looked over to see both Emilio

and Mari watching Stephen intently. Then my attention was recaptured by Stephen's theatrics.

"No." He shook off the restraining hand of his lawyer. "I will not stand here and let the two of them"—he swept a hand toward Emilio and Sabella—"turn me into a villain."

"Enough!" Victor's command whipped through the room and lashed at the gathered occupants. "Stephen, you will sit down and refrain from interrupting the testimony, or I will ensure your obedience." The threat that reverberated under the coldly uttered words left no room for misinterpretation.

Red-faced, Stephen stared daggers at Victor as tension sang through the large space. I held my breath and braced as Stephen's belligerent position—hands curled into fists at his side, his body coiled to attack, his face twisted with fury— didn't change. His jaw was clenched, and a muscle visibly worked as he struggled with the justifiable reprimand.

At his side and in direct contrast to his unmitigated fury, a frostily composed Imogen simply curled her hand around one of Stephen's wrists. At first, he appeared not to notice, then a shiver shuddered through him as a faint pulse of active magic brushed against me. He turned and frowned at her. She gave a small headshake, a warning that Stephen finally heeded. Stiffly, he straightened and reclaimed his seat, his jaw set in mulish discontent.

Victor continued to glare at him before turning to Emilio. "Your claim also stated that you can link Stephen to the attack on your Arbiter and Ms. Costas, correct?"

"Yes, sir," Maribel confirmed before Emilio could, then she pulled out a sheaf of papers. "My firm hired an independent investigator to track down the financial transactions between the identified mercenaries who attacked Mr. Aslanov and Ms. Costas. These same assailants were also connected with Mrs. Rossi's abduction. The firm was able to trace the myriad of transactions back to financial accounts belonging to Stephen Trask."

When Victor made a motion for the papers, Mari got up, crossed the space between the council and us, then handed over a set of papers. She returned to her seat, pulled out another set of papers from her briefcase, and handed them to Trask's lawyer. Before the ruffled slimeball could look at them, Stephen yanked them out of his hands and flipped through them.

Over the next few minutes, Maribel, with occasional input from Emilio, laid out what Evan had uncovered, tying Snake's little gang of hard-asses to the Trask Family portfolio. As they did, the council members passed the papers among themselves.

Trying not to be obvious about it, I watched Stephen as the questions grew more pointed and Mari made her case. Slowly but surely, she forced him into a corner, and minor cracks appeared in Stephen's arrogance. Temper was replaced by wariness, tightening his shoulders and turning his spine rigid. In contrast, Imogen's icy demeanor never cracked.

"This is ridiculous," Stephen spat, his movements jerky as he tossed the papers at his lawyer. "I'm being set up." He glared at Emilio and Sabella. "They're setting me up."

Emilio's relaxed position didn't change. "I have no reason to set you up, Trask."

"Don't you?" he shot back. "You're still pissed about your nephew. You weren't satisfied with ruining my lab. You want to bury all my research. And Sabella." He stopped and shook his head. "Sabella's got her own agenda, and God only knows why she has it out for me. Maybe the two of you are working together to take me down."

"I don't need Emilio to do that, Stephen," Sabella chided gently.

"Don't you?" He raked our group with a furious glare and

stopped on me. He stilled, and his voice lost its angry edge only to be replaced by a studied calculation. "No, maybe you don't, but it wouldn't stop you from putting your pawn into play. A pawn who could easily be overlooked and ignored as they set me up."

Refusing to look away first, I held his burning gaze and braced as the weight of the room's attention shifted to me. My brain spun, trying to figure out his avenue of attack.

"What are you implying, Stephen?" Mateo asked in a lazy drawl.

Stephen straightened his spine as he turned and addressed the council. "What do we really know about Sabella's pet Transporter? I find it strange that a mere nobody is somehow integrally involved in not only apprehending Mahon and the information he stole but also managed to get herself assigned as Sabella's proxy in a high-level, confidential Family matter with the Delphi project."

Since he had the council's attention, he visibly regathered his composure. "Maybe the one you should be looking at isn't me but Ms. Costas. We all understand how valuable the Delphi serum is. There are various factions who will go to any lengths to obtain it. Including positioning an unknown to worm their way into getting her hands on it."

"Excuse me?" The question shot out before I could think twice. *But come on. Is he serious?* My furious question was drowned out by the outraged voices of Emilio, Sabella, and Mari. While I waited for their protests to die down, I looked at the council and found more than one member giving me serious side-eye.

Well, shit, looks like Zev was right.

My secrets were poised to be exposed in all their messy glory. Yet instead of being scared shitless about admitting who and what I was to a room filled with what was arguably

Arcane society's most powerful players, I was strangely calm and clearheaded.

It wasn't that I was being naively arrogant. Sometime in the last couple of days, I'd realized something. My choice about being part of the Arcane elite was made months ago, when I tried to keep a little boy from becoming a pawn in a game that he didn't even know about.

Every decision since had simply moved me deeper across the board until I was just as tangled as any of the others in play, and the only way out was through, which meant uncovering the real threat. And somewhere along the way, while I was navigating the maze of deceptions and intrigue, I had gone from solo player to team player. Proof of that was in those around me.

Maribel arguing tenaciously in my defense, Emilio ensuring that both the council and Stephen knew the Cordovas stood behind me, and Sabella, unruffled and unbending, a woman who knew the importance of playing the long game and who'd withstood the sacrifices needed to achieve it. But the most solid proof of how much my life had changed sat at my side, his support unwavering—Zev.

I felt him nearly vibrating with the need to tear Stephen apart, but he was holding strong, letting me fight my own battles. He had crashed into my life, knocking it and all my expectations, including a few I wasn't aware of, off course, but the roads he sent me down had been exciting, scary, and sometimes, painful as hell, but no matter how bumpy it got, he stuck with me. Sometimes taking the wheel and others riding bitch, but right now, it was my turn to drive.

Full throttle, balls to the wall.

"Enough!" Victor boomed, quieting all the voices.

But Stephen, caught up in his impending triumph at turning the tide, wasn't done. "If you're not a pawn, Ms. Costas, then I have to wonder what it is you have on our illustrious Mrs. Rossi. Whatever it is must be damning. Otherwise, why would she involve a Transporter"—he sneered the title as his gaze burned with contempt and malicious glee—"who has no proven investigative skills, no combat mage training, no skills outside of driving a car, with highly confidential Family business?"

Asshole. Offended pride and righteous indignation ignited an ice-cold fury.

Before I could respond, Sabella spoke up, her voice hard enough to shatter bone. "My reasons are my own, Stephen. I don't owe them to you."

"No, you don't," he agreed with blatantly false politeness, "but you do owe them to the council."

"I will admit to wondering about her role as well." Mateo's admission broke the rising tension between Sabella and Stephen and gained everyone's attention. The councilman looked at Sabella, mild curiosity on his face. When Sabella gave him a questioning look, he offered a small shrug. "You aren't one to do something without reason, Sabella."

I caught a flash of triumph on Stephen's face before he went back to his curled-lip best. The bastard thought he had Sabella cornered.

Well, fuck that.

"I have no need to lie for anyone." I held Stephen's hateful gaze even as I addressed the council, disdain coating every word. "First, I'm a highly respected premier Transporter, a position earned, not given. Second, the Guild doesn't hire incompetent people, and our training is unmatched, something you, Mr. Trask, would do well to learn. Third, I am not Sabella's pet anything. I'm her niece."

CHAPTER TWENTY-FOUR

FOR A MOMENT, Stephen's hostility was wiped away by shock, but I wasn't quite done slapping his ass down, and I knew my smile was all kinds of nasty. "Well, great-niece if you want to be technical about it."

Next to me, Zev's dark chuckle competed with the gasps and murmurs swirling around the room as Stephen swallowed hard and shot a worried glance at the council members and another one to Imogen. The female Arbiter was strangely still as she stared at me.

I looked away and caught Emilio's shock as he looked from Sabella to Mari, who gave him a barely there nod before he reclaimed his expressionless mask. Sabella, being Sabella, simply smiled at me, a hint of pride and satisfaction swirling in her eyes.

Interestingly enough, it was Jude who regained control of the room, and once it quieted down, he turned to Sabella. "Is this true?"

She gave him a slightly puzzled look. "As she so aptly stated, she has no reason to lie, and neither do I."

"Sabella," Victor said, a conciliatory note in his voice.

"We've known each other for years, and this is the first I've even heard of a possible niece."

Sabella lost all traces of her geniality, and in its place rose the formidable matriarch of the Giordano Family. "I am not required to make personal business public. Not even to you."

"This is —"

"Not our business, Victor," Olivia interrupted, her beautiful contralto voice undercutting the boom of Victor's impending argument. When the older council member frowned at her, she added, "We need to remain focused on the issues at hand. Let's get back to the charges against Stephen and the implications of his alleged actions."

A silent stare down ensued, but my attention was diverted by a soft beep from Zev's phone. I turned to see him reading his screen, his body going stiff.

"What?" I whispered.

He angled the phone so I could see it. Locke had sent a text and a photo.

I grabbed his wrist, bringing the phone closer. "Oh my God."

Locke found Dale Peterson.

Our exchange caught everyone's attention. "Something you'd like to share?" Mateo asked.

Instead of answering, Zev handed the phone to Emilio. The head of the Cordova Family stared at the phone, and Mari leaned over to see as well. Her face paled, but her voice was rock steady when she answered, "We found Dale Peterson."

I caught Stephen's jerk, but I wasn't the only one. Mari was watching him closely.

Mateo frowned. "Dale Peterson? The Guild Scout Sabella hired?"

Mari turned to the council. "Yes."

"Your expression tells me he won't be in to testify,"

Christina said, tapping her red nails against her chair's armrest.

"It would be difficult, unless you have a necromancer on call," Emilio said, handing the phone to Zev.

"How did he die?" Victor's question was a short punch.

"Cursed," Zev said. "According to our Hound and the Key he's working with, Peterson's body carried the same signature as used by the paid hit man identified as Snake."

Everyone's attention shifted to Stephen, then Jude looked at Zev. "Where was he found?"

"In a dumpster outside the Cotton Center," Zev answered. "Which happens to be listed under the Trask corporate portfolio."

The smarmy lawyer rushed to fill the weighted pause. "That particular building houses multiple offices. Anyone could have dumped the body there. Unless you have proof that puts Mr. Trask there, you're still working with circumstantial evidence."

"Do you have something more concrete, Mr. Aslanov?" Olivia asked.

"We do," he answered. "We were able to recover video surveillance that shows a car registered to Trask pulling behind the building."

Stephen shot to his feet, shock snaking through his sneering facade. "I don't know what you're playing at Aslanov, but it wasn't me."

Next to Emilio, Mari straightened, but I was distracted by the thickening shadows crawling along the edges of the room and drifting closer. A strange whispering rustled in my ears while a spike in power woke the room's wards and left me grappling with my Prism. Dread coiled through me, and I went to grab Zev's wrist in a vain attempt to warn him, but it hurt to move. The warding and my Prism fought for dominance, leaving me pummeled in the middle.

Stephen's gaze skittered over the council, an edge of panic crawling in his eyes, and landed on Imogen, who quickly looked away from the group. "I was... we were—" He stared at her then the council, his face paling. He turned back to Imogen, fury in every line as he took a step forward, fists clenched, his body gaining a smoky-gray aura. "You—"

Magic erupted, searing through the room's wards before spilling into the room, igniting chaos.

My Prism snapped into place with breath-stealing suddenness as strange whispers rose in a frenzied ear-piercing wail while unnatural shadows coalesced and rushed Imogen. She shot to her feet, and power ripped from both her and Stephen, almost in unison. The Trask lawyer scrambled out of his chair and slipped on the spreading ice that slicked across the tile. He crawled away from the fight.

A circle of power flared to life, trying to contain the spill of magic whipping between Stephen and Imogen. Silvery streaks of Imogen's elemental ice met the ashy smoke of Stephen's whatever the hell it was he commanded. His nightmarish shadows circled Imogen, darting in to test her defense, but she managed to hold them at bay. For now.

Eerie shrieks filled the air, drowning out everything else. Zev grabbed my arm and pointed at Sabella, Emilio, and Mari before joining Mateo and Olivia as they circled Stephen and Imogen. I took my place in front of Emilio, Sabella, and Mari, only then realizing that the ice was creeping closer.

Something about it didn't feel right. I set my feet and reached for my magic. Like relaxing a muscle, I let my Prism stretch out until it encompassed those behind me. The spreading ice stopped inches from my toes, the ice-cold burn there but bearable.

A pained grunt yanked my attention back to the duel. Blood dripped from a thin cut in Stephen's cheek, mixing with the mist coating his skin. Thin, painful slices marred his flesh, some deeper than others, and blood stained his shredded clothes. But it was the pure black of his eyes that left my hindbrain jittery.

As disturbing as his appearance was, Imogen's was just as drastic. She looked even worse off. Her clothes hung on her gaunt frame, the skin of her face barely held the bones in check, and dark circles were ringing the unearthly glow of her eyes. Her skin was nearly glowing it was so white.

Although my Prism managed to keep the worst of the battling magics at bay, the unceasing pressure was relentless. It was like being buried under a pile of rocks, one painful boulder at a time. I sensed movement in the room, but between the smothering power and the deafening shrieks of Stephen's haunts, all I could do was hold my position, keep those behind me safe, and let the others handle Stephen and Imogen.

A flicker of blue broke through the silvery incandescence of Imogen's magic and morphed into Zev's familiar figure. Behind Stephen, another figure, lined in blood red, emerged from the shadows to mimic Zev's position. A third form moved up, this one emanating a golden glow that nudged the gathered shadows aside to reveal a serenely composed Olivia. At some unseen signal, Mateo and Zev's magic curled around Stephen and Imogen in near-perfect synchronicity, locking around the combatants like magical restraints while Olivia's magic slid in between, trapping both Stephen and Imogen in cages.

The additional wave of magic slammed against me, and I shuddered. A hand gripped my shoulder, and the suffocating pressure pulled back. I turned to find Sabella watching me with concern. "Are you okay?"

I managed a rough "Yeah." The shadows in front of us disintegrated, and the unearthly wails began to fade. My answer wasn't a lie because whatever it was that Mateo, Zev, and Olivia were doing had the power flooding the room receding enough for me to regain my footing.

"Stephen Trask. Imogen Frost." Olivia addressed the two bound mages, her voice carrying through the room. "You have violated the conciliatory rules of the council. Would you like to explain yourselves?" It wasn't a request.

Stephen glared at Imogen, who was watching Olivia. His voice was rough with rage. "Despite the evidence, I had nothing to do with Sabella's kidnapping. Nothing to do with the Scout's death. I'm being framed."

"Yes, so you made clear earlier. That still doesn't explain this." She waved a hand at the two of them.

"Except I bet I can prove exactly who's setting me up." He tore his gaze from Imogen to glare at Zev. "The video your Hound recovered, the car that was registered, was it a silver BMW?"

Zev, his magic still curled around him, nodded once.

Stephen's grin was more a baring of teeth. "I know exactly who was driving that car this morning."

"You bastard," Imogen hissed. "I was doing what you told me."

Stephen struggled against the blood-red bindings, nearly crazed in his fury. "You bitch! I didn't tell you anything!"

"You know we can easily clear this up." Sabella's calm comment cut through the drama playing out.

Olivia turned to her. "I'm all ears."

"We simply need to ask the right question." Sabella turned to a pale Mari. "Mari, would you mind?"

The dark-haired lawyer straightened her spine and moved. I pulled my shield back, letting her go as she walked around Olivia to stand near Zev. "Not at all."

"Sabella, *donna bella*," Mateo drawled. "Questions will not help clarify things. These two are bound and determined to play out the whole he-said-she-said situation to its bitter end."

"It will if they are questioned by a truth seeker," she said.

Stephen's smile was far from nice, but Imogen stiffened, her gaze skittering over the gathered council members ranged behind Olivia before bouncing back. That one look set the hair on the back of my neck on end, and before the primal warning rose to a screaming pitch, I was moving, even knowing I was too far away to stop what was coming. "Zev, Mari!"

Desperation being the mother of invention, I grabbed my magic and flung it like a cloak around the two of them then snapped it closed just as two streams of magic, one silver, one a poisonous green, slammed into my Prism with ferocious force. The combined impact sent me crashing to my knees with a pained grunt as agony speared through my skull. Even as a lethally bitter chill sank into my bones, fire seared my nerve endings with agonizing intensity, and my muscles seized.

Unable to move, unable to breathe, I shoved everything I had into thickening the shield, determined to keep whatever the hell Imogen threw away from Mari and, more importantly, Zev. My Prism bucked in my metaphoric hold as red and white streaks tore through my vision, leaving it in tatters, and a metallic taste coated my tongue.

My magic continued to fight even as my grip slipped in horrifying slow increments. As darkness began to win, someone screamed, and voices rose in an indecipherable roar. Suddenly, the lethal paralysis holding me in its brutal grip disappeared. I sucked in air and choked as my lungs tried to remember how to work. The edging darkness pulled back, leaving my vision wavy. Someone leaned over me, and I tried to bat them away, but my muscles had been replaced with water.

"Rory, take a breath. Rory, can you hear me?"

I recognized Mari's voice and did my best to follow her instructions. Something slid under my diaphragm and lifted, arcing my spine and easing the last bit of pressure on my chest. I dragged in air then let it out in a shaky breath. Luckily, my vision also leveled out so I could use Mari's eyes as a focal point.

"Good. Again," she encouraged with a small smile that was cut short by a wince. I noticed her lip was split and a bruise was coming up along her jaw.

By the fourth time through, my lungs caught on and got with the program.

The bracing arm under my diaphragm slid away, leaving me lying flat on my back and blinking up into Zev's concerned face. "You good?"

"Need... minute," it came out raspy, but at least it came out.

He looked at something behind Mari, something I couldn't see from my prone position between him and her. When he turned to me, the predator who lived within crawled through his eyes, and it was beyond pissed. "You scared the shit out of me."

"Out... of me... too," I admitted. A couple of more deep breaths and I could ask, "What happened?"

His gaze flicked up to whatever was happening and came back to me. "No time to explain. Can you get up?"

I took inventory. My Prism was still intact, but every inch of me ached, my head pounded, and my chest felt like it had been ripped open and was being held together with duct tape, but otherwise, I was alive. "If you help me up, I should be okay."

Mari and Zev each gripped an arm and carefully pulled me up. We had to do it in increments because when I sat up, my head spun so badly I almost passed out. I breathed the dizziness away and finally made it to my feet.

"You got her?" Zev asked Mari.

Mari shifted her hold, curling an arm around my waist as I looped my arm over her shoulder. "Got her. Go."

Zev waited a second to make sure the two of us didn't collapse before stepping back. "Rory, go ahead and drop it."

Confused, I asked, "Drop it?"

He waved a hand, and I realized the three of us were enclosed in a thick version of my Prism, so dense it was like looking through layered, faceted glass. Somehow, I had managed to keep my shield up through the entire ordeal. It also explained why my skull felt like it was about to split in two. I released the death grip my subconscious had on my magic. The shield wavered then thinned into nothing. The pressure on my head stepped back, and the relief was enough to make me whimper. Mari's arm tightened, and I whispered, "I'm good."

Zev strode forward, and I finally took in the council room. My mouth fell open. *Holy shit.* It looked as if a tornado had torn through it. The tile floor was buckled in places, some of the chairs had been reduced to rubble, and cracks snaked through the wall of glass on the far side.

In front of us, Emilio was helping a disheveled Christina to her feet while Victor wiped at the blood dripping down his face. I caught sight of the sprawled body of Trask's lawyer off to the side, and I wasn't sure if he was dead or unconscious.

Zev stopped near Mateo, who was crouched over something I couldn't see because Zev's back blocked my view. "Is she—?"

"Dead." Mateo's answer came out harshly. He pushed to his feet, his gaze moving beyond Zev and straight to me. His magic remained as a lingering, disconcerting red glow in his eyes. He turned to Zev. "I have questions."

"Don't we all." Zev looked up, and his shoulders went rigid.

Mateo pivoted, looking at whatever had caught Zev's attention. "It seems Sabella's about to get us some answers."

Curious, I shuffled forward, forcing Mari to move with me. Together, we came up on Zev's other side, and I got my first look at the rest of the room. I barely clocked the pale-purple glow from my left, where Olivia worked over a prone Stephen, or Imogen's lifeless body sprawled at Mateo's feet.

Instead, my attention was utterly caught by Sabella. She stood apart from the chaos, her magic rippling around her in a terrifyingly beautiful cloak of amber and gold. She was the legendary matriarch of the Giordano clan and the reason others tiptoed around her. Held in midair and wrapped in ribboned flames of the same color was Jude Novak. Despite his bindings, Jude still fought, tendrils of poisonous green trying to strangle the amber gold of Sabella's magic. Power pulsed, and the resulting wave left me weaving on my feet. Amber gold shattered green, and Jude's mouth opened in a silent scream.

"Sabella, we need him able to talk," Emilio warned as he pulled one of the intact chairs over for Christina to sit.

"I'm aware, dear." Her voice was an unsettling mix of cold and maternal. She sketched a rune in the air, where it hung for the briefest moment before winking out. Then she turned and walked over to join the rest of us, Jude trailing along like a whipped dog on a leash. She caught sight of me and frowned. Behind her, Jude's whimper was abruptly cut off. "Are you okay, Rory?"

I swallowed a mix of hysteria and trepidation. "I will be."

A familiar warmth seeped in, softening the edge of awe-inspiring power. "Good." Her gaze swept over the scene, a flash of sorrow that was there and gone when she spotted

Imogen's body. "Foolish girl," she murmured, then her gaze shifted to Mateo. "Can she be moved?"

He looked at the body. "I would suggest waiting until a Key has cleared the body."

Sabella dipped her head in agreement then surveyed the rest of the room's occupants. "Olivia, how's Stephen?"

Olivia was in a closed knee squat, her hands moving in a pattern above Stephen. "I can hold him for a bit, but I'll need a healer soon." She rose gracefully, brushing her glowing hands over her skirt.

"I'll call one in." Victor dug a phone out of his pocket.

"Thank you," Sabella said.

"And a Key," Mateo reminded him as his gaze moved over the rest of the room.

Victor nodded and, with the phone at his ear, strode a few feet away to get reinforcements. Mateo found whatever it was he was looking for and walked away, leaving Mari, Zev, and me standing over Imogen. With no one in my way, I got my first unhampered view of her crumpled on the floor, almost as if she'd dropped where she stood. A faint silvery shimmer emanated from her skin, like light dancing over a sheen of glass or—horror crept through me—crystallized ice.

I sucked in a sharp breath and grabbed Zev's arm. "Is that—?"

The sharp shake of his head cut me off but confirmed my suspicion about why Sabella was concerned over moving Imogen's body. Zev's warning coincided with the return of Mateo, who carried a throw that he laid over Imogen. Under my hand, the tight muscles in Zev's arm eased, and the reality of Imogen's death finally penetrated my numbed stupor. *Am I sorry she's dead? Yes? Maybe?* I wasn't sure what I was feeling, but it wasn't grief.

She'd deliberately targeted Zev and Mari, which all but screamed guilt for whatever part she'd played in this mess, so

I wasn't too broken up about it. But at one time, she had been important to the man at my side. My grip shifted, sliding down to cover his fist, offering what comfort I could. He slowly unclenched his hand and wove his fingers through mine.

"While we're waiting," Sabella said into the weighty quiet, "let's hear what Jude has to share." She looked at Emilio, Zev, and Mateo. "Boys, if you would, let's gather some chairs for us, please."

The three men did as requested, clearing a space and arranging the surviving chairs near where Christina was seated. While it meant Olivia moved away from Stephen, it offered an illusion of privacy for Imogen's body. Sabella crossed the room, dragging Jude behind her. There was something unsettling about her dignified passage through the wrecked room and the casual way she negligently controlled Jude's writhing form.

Christina watched Sabella and, in a bland tone at odds with the simmering anger in her eyes, asked, "Would you like to use a containment circle?"

When Sabella agreed, Christina got up stiffly and moved to the empty spot the men had cleared. "Zev, could you bring me a chair, please?"

Zev dragged over a chair, the leather ripped and torn, placed it where Christina indicated, and stepped back. Sabella brought Jude over, then an invisible hand all but shoved him into the chair. The amber ties of her magic looped over him, binding him in place. Sabella and Zev stepped back as Christina, with a soft word followed by a sharp spike of power, ignited a complex containment circle. "That should hold him."

"The healer should be here in fifteen, Olivia," Victor said, pocketing his phone.

"Thank you." Sabella looked at the remaining council

members. "Normally, I'd defer to your authority, but in this situation, I hope you'll indulge me?"

As polite as her question was, the steel beneath it made it clear it wasn't really a question. Still, all four members inclined their heads in silent agreement.

"Good, then let's get started, shall we?"

CHAPTER TWENTY-FIVE

ONCE EVERYONE TOOK A SEAT, it didn't take Sabella long to get the whole twisted story from Jude. Watching her interrogate the clearly unrepentant councilman under the approving eyes of the remaining council was an eye-opening lesson in the innate casual ruthlessness at the core of the Arcane elite.

There was no empathy, no compassion for Jude to appeal to, not that he tried. He appeared to deliberately goad Sabella into doing her worst, and she obliged, her magic slipping under his skin and running through his veins in visible amber fire, extinguishing the flare-ups of poisonous green. I gave him credit. He put up a good fight, but it didn't last long. Finally, he broke, spilling the whole ugly story.

I wasn't expecting him to start where he did, with Emilio's dead ex-sister-in-law, Dr. Lara Kaspar. It seemed after Emilio's brother, Alan, divorced her ass, Lara was quick to discover she didn't like living on a budget. In an effort to regain the financial security she'd enjoyed as the wife of the heir to the Cordova Family, she decided to explore her options. First up was taking out her ex-husband before he could fully change his will. Unbeknownst to her, Alan had moved quicker than expected and named Jeremy sole heir, removing Lara from his will completely. By the time she made that discovery, it was too late, and Alan was already dead in what was publicly declared a tragic accident.

To add to Lara's trouble, she now owed money for the completed hit, money she didn't have and couldn't earn as a researcher for Stephen Trask's Origin labs and his Delphi serum project. So she decided to sell her research to her employer's competitor, LanTech. But while she was fishing for potential income, she caught Jude's attention and, by extension, that of his unnamed partners. They made her a better offer. Avaricious soul that she was, Lara decided to collect double the paychecks and sell the research to both LanTech and Jude.

When Lara's double cross came to light, she'd paid the ultimate price with her life. However, her research was left incomplete, and upon her death, her intellectual property went to her son, Jeremy, who at ten became Emilio's ward and heir to the Cordova Family. In an effort to reclaim Lara's research, Jude's group kidnapped Jeremy before Stephen and Leander's hirelings could, all three factions intending to exchange Jeremy for the research. That was where I entered the story, as the unwitting contracted driver for Jude's Mr. Jones, and initially crossed paths with Zev.

For the next six months, Emilio's retribution for the failed kidnapping bankrupted LanTech and brought Origin to its knees. With no recourse left, LanTech began to liquidate its assets and lay off its employees. One of them was a financial manager named Keith Thatcher. Furious at losing his job, he stole encrypted files from the LanTech servers in the hopes of making money off the information. He didn't realize that buried in those files was the research for the Delphi project.

Enter Keith's ex-wife's then-fiancé, Theodore Mahon. Theo was Madeline's junior by about twenty-plus years, and while Madeline was a savvy businesswoman who'd made a name for herself among the Arcane elite, when it came to personal relationships, she fell short. Jude maneuvered Theo to captivate Madeline's attention so Theo could use Keith's security access at LanTech. It was a long game that worked until Keith discovered someone had cursed him with an Acarpous Hex. He reached out to the Guild to hire a Key to reverse the limp-dick curse, which was how Lena had gotten dragged into the mess.

When she showed up for their appointment, she stumbled into a confrontation between Keith and Theo that ended with Keith dead and Theo, an illusion mage, wearing Keith's face and now in possession of the stolen encrypted drive. Theo kidnapped Lena and tortured her to force her to break the encryption hex on the drive. Thankfully, Zev and I tracked her down and got her out. While I stuck with Lena, Zev hunted down Theo and dragged his ass back to the council.

It was during Theo's hearing that the three-way battle for Lara's research erupted in front of the Arcane Council. Emilio won that battle, and Jeremy retained control. However, Leander and Stephen were forced to admit to the council what the Delphi project encompassed—the ability to turn up or turn off a mage's magic. That did not go over well, and the council ordered the project shuttered.

Stephen and Leander didn't listen, and when their research teams began dying, they believed the Cordova Family was behind the deaths. Stephen believed it was Emilio, but Leander had it right when he stated there was another group with more to gain if the serum became a reality. The Cabal. Most believed the group was an urban myth. Yet as I listened to Jude talk, a fervent light in his bloodshot eyes, I realized it was all too real. There really was a rogue group of shadowy, power-hungry, monied mages and scientists intent on replacing the existing Arcane society with their own, purer version.

They wanted the Delphi serum and managed to recruit Neil Pasternak from LanTech and Dr. Kerri Michaels from Origin to complete the project and deliver a working serum. While everyone's attention was on that investigation, Jude was busy planning how to keep Theo's mouth shut while he waited for Neil and Kerri to deliver the serum.

But they never got a chance.

"I thought all our work was lost," Jude admitted, his tone sullen. He pinned me with a seething gaze. "Then Frost mentioned her suspicions about you being injected, and I realized if she was right, there was still a chance. We just need your blood." His lips twisted with cruel amusement. "It didn't take much to convince Frost to work with me. She didn't like you"—he turned to Zev—"or you either."

"And Trask?" The question came from Mateo as he studied Jude with a clinical coolness.

"He's a fool," spat Jude. "Unable to see beyond his pride and ego to understand the fastest way to lose loyalty is to throw it away. It was easy enough to match the zeros to her conscience for betraying that ass. With her position, it was simple to set up Trask as the one behind the attacks." He glared at Sabella. "She balked at taking you out. Her mistake."

"Now it's yours," Sabella said, his animosity not making a dent in her composure. She turned to the council. "I think that's enough for now."

"Not quite," Mateo said. "I have a few more questions."

Sabella arched a brow. "For Jude?"

"No." His gaze slid to me. "For you."

I swallowed hard under that penetrating gaze, and despite the persistent ache in my head, managed a steady "About?"

Without looking away, he answered, "About what happened here."

Next to me, Zev stiffened, and I couldn't help shooting Sabella a panicked glance. Resignation filled her face. I looked at the other council members only to find them watching me with varying degrees of speculation. My stomach knotted.

Will you be a threat others hesitate to trigger or a tool to be used?

Sabella's question echoed in my head. Taking a deep breath, I gave in to the inevitable. "I'll be happy to answer them, but"—my gaze moved past Mateo to Jude—"not in front of him."

No way would I reveal what I was in front of a man intent on betraying everything and everyone, regardless of the cost. If he knew I was a Prism, he would take the first chance he got to share it with the Cabal. Between my connection to Sabella and my magic, my future held enough threats. I didn't want to add more.

"He's no threat now," Christina scoffed.

I lifted my chin, refusing to wince when the ache in my head deepened at the movement. "So long as he's breathing, he's a threat."

"I concur." The comment came from Olivia. She waved a hand, and magic swept past me, the warm gold a calm contrast to Sabella's amber. It wrapped around Jude, who went limp, eyes closed, held upright only by Sabella's bindings. I turned to Olivia to find her studying me, a tiny spark of humor lurking in her eyes. "Will that suffice?"

Since I had no clue what Olivia's ability was, I turned to the one person who would, Sabella. She gave me a small smile. "He's under until Olivia brings him back around."

I turned to Olivia. "Thank you."

She inclined her head.

I straightened my spine and faced Mateo. "Ask your questions."

He went straight to the heart of it all. "You were moving toward Imogen before Jude threw his curse."

"Not Imogen," I admitted. "Zev and Mari."

"To protect them from Jude?" That question actually came from Emilio.

"And Imogen," Sabella added quietly.

"You deflected a combined attack from Jude and Imogen?" Christina asked.

My "Yes" was followed by Victor's muttered, "She should be dead."

"But she's not." Sabella's answer was lost under Christina's lethally sharp inquiry. "How? Jude is one of the most powerful toxin mages alive, Imogen was a combat-trained ice mage, and you're..." She waved her hand as if searching for a word. "A Transporter."

Their barrage of questions intensified the ache in my head, but before I could answer, Victor cut in. "Jude mentioned you were injected with the serum, but here you are, apparently no worse for wear."

I opened my mouth, but before I could say anything, Mateo jumped in. "And you killed Imogen by turning her curse on her."

Magic snapped around me, too fast to identify, and my reaction was pure instinct. My Prism slapped it back, and Christina jerked away with a pained hiss, a welt twining up her arm. She shook it, and her eyes narrowed as she studied me. "You're a dual mage."

It took a lot, but I held her gaze, straightened my shoulders, and lifted my chin. "I'm a Prism."

And just like that, I took my spot on the Arcane stage.

◆

Once the shock passed, the Council grilled me for what felt like forever. I was pretty sure they would have kept me longer if the healer and Key hadn't shown up to take away Stephen and Imogen. Olivia followed along. Then it was Jude's turn to be dragged away by a pair of grim faces I never wanted to meet in a dark alley. As soon as he disappeared, so did the unrelenting pressure of magic from Sabella, the containment circle, and whatever else was floating around. As the magical threat faded, my Prism eased down, and the near-debilitating ache in my head began to retreat as well.

I had moved to a couch to curl up in a corner and close my eyes for just a moment while people moved around the room. Zev stayed close. I could feel him hovering nearby like a protective cloud. He wasn't the only one. Mari sat at the couch's other end, quietly talking with Emilio, who was perched on the couch's arm. Sabella was talking with the council, but I was beyond exhausted.

"Rory."

I forced my eyes open to find Zev crouched in front of me. "I am not answering any other questions."

"You don't have to," he said. "Sabella's handling them for now."

"Good."

"You won't be able to avoid them forever." He stood up and offered me a hand.

I took it. "Not planning on it." I uncurled from the couch and, with his help, got to my feet and slowly stretched, testing my head. The dull ache remained, but it was a hell of a lot better than before. "You have any aspirin?"

He frowned. "Dr. Garcia's going to be pissed."

"I'll be fine." I hoped.

Zev grunted, pulled out his phone, and sent off a text.

I tried to read it but failed. "Who'd you text?"

"Dr. Garcia," he said unrepentantly. "He'll meet us at Emilio's."

Arguing with him was pointless, so I let it go. We stood shoulder to shoulder, watching Sabella talk to the three remaining council members. "Think they'll convince her to join?"

Zev snorted. "I doubt it. Sabella likes to go her own way. If she's stuck on the council, she can't play her games."

A couple of looks were aimed my way, especially from Mateo and Christina, but whatever they were discussing didn't bring them over, which worked for me. "What's going to happen to Jude now?"

"They'll bring in an interrogator and get names." We watched as Sabella made her way to us.

"And the Cabal?" I kept my voice low.

Zev shrugged. "Until we have actionable information, not much we can do."

I sighed and leaned a little more against him, knowing he could take my weight. "You think we can finish our date from Friday?"

His arm went around my waist and pulled me in close. His chuckle was soft. "You sure you want to tempt fate like that? The last time was kind of a cluster."

I rested my head against his shoulder. "Fourth time's the charm, right?"

"Something like that." I felt him brush a kiss against the top of my head and caught Sabella's knowing smile. "You ready, babe?"

I turned to look at him. "For?"

He stared down, his eyes warm, his gaze rock solid. "What comes next."

"And what's that?"

His grin was all kind of wicked. "A hell of a ride."

EPILOGUE

DAYS LATER

ZEV and I managed to finally get a romantic weekend away. No kidnapping, no mercenary hit men, no cock-blocking roommates or interfering family drama. Just him, me, his Harley, and an open road. He even let me take the wheel a few times.

It was pure magic.

When we got back, a package was waiting for me from the Arcane Council. Zev and Lena sat at the counter as I opened it to discover a thick set of papers. While watched by my best friend and the man who was determined to ride things out at my side, I started reading through the pages. It didn't take long for the words to sink in. Stunned, I looked up. "The council wants me to be their contracted Transporter."

"Let me see those," Zev said.

I handed the papers over.

"What are you going to do?" Lena asked, watching me carefully as Zev started reading.

I shook my head. "I don't know."

"You'd be a fool to turn them down." Her voice was strangely empty.

"Maybe more of a fool not to," I muttered.

Something in her face eased. "You going to discuss this with Sabella?"

In the days after the council disaster, Sabella and I had had a chance to talk while I drove her to innumerable meetings. Our relationship was shifting from employer-employee to a cautious trial of aunt and niece. I still wasn't quite sure how I felt about everything, and my ability to trust her motives was still shaky, but so far, she hadn't balked at answering any of my questions. Our relationship remained within the confines of the council, but I knew that wouldn't last much longer. Eventually, it would get out, and then I would have to deal with whatever came my way. But I'd see where things took us. "No, this is my career, my decision."

"It seems pretty straightforward," Zev said. "But I'd ask Mari to look it over."

"I can't keep trading on Emilio's favor," I pointed out. It was part of an ongoing discussion between us. How I didn't want to become too reliant on the Cordova influence, or Sabella's, for that matter. Whatever lay in wait, I needed to be my own power, and with Zev as a sounding board, I was figuring out how to work those critical alliances.

His lips twitched. "So don't. Your business will still need legal representation, and I'm sure Mari would consider taking you on as a client."

The idea of having a lawyer on call intrigued me, especially if it meant no more cleaning bills due to slime-spitting frogs or tap dancing around council inquiries. I mentally calculated what my operating budget could handle. "I'll call her."

Lena snagged the pile of papers and dragged them over,

scanning them as she asked, "Wonder why the council needs a Transporter?"

"They don't," Zev said. "But once her relation to Sabella and her ability leaks, everyone's going to be watching to see what she does and who she answers to. It will determine how they deal with her."

And that was the other thing Zev and I had been discussing, my options on steering clear of Sabella's baggage, because there was no way I was ready for that. I'd taken the first step when I told Sabella I would be keeping my name and not formally tying myself to the Giordano Family. Unlike my aunt, I wasn't convinced she'd eliminated all the threats that hunted down my parents, nor was I in a hurry to find out. I needed my own road with the Arcane elite. I looked at the contract, my mind turning over the offer.

Lena gave a delicate, derisive snort. "No matter what she decides, they'll come at her. Half of them will be worried about pissing off Sabella—"

"And Emilio," Zev added.

"And Emilio," she conceded. "But the other half will want to see what she can do."

"But how likely are they to come at me if I work for the council?"

She blinked and set the papers down. "You're actually considering this."

"I am."

She looked at me, worry lines furrowing her brow. "Girl, are you sure? It's a nasty-ass pit of vipers out there."

I couldn't stop my short laugh. "Yeah, I know, but the council is the closest thing we have to a neutral party. I need time to figure out how to be a Prism and to establish connections for the future. If working for them gives me a chance to do both, then why not?"

"Because it's the Arcane Council," she stated. "And anything involving the council will be dangerous."

"She can handle it," Zev chimed in, his vote of confidence earning a smile from me. "Besides, the first time someone tries something, I'm pretty sure they won't know what hit them."

Lena sighed, and wry amusement replaced her frown. "Fine, but just remember to call me before you get ass deep in shit because I'm not ruining any of my good shoes for you. No matter how much I love you."

"Deal." It was an easy promise to make because I wasn't alone anymore. Hell, maybe I never was, but right here, right now, I knew not only would Lena be there, but so would Zev, and it was a humbling realization. No matter what the road ahead held in store, I was ready.

"Balls to the wall, baby," I murmured, returning Zev's laugh with a fierce smile.

◆

- You have arrived at your final stop! Thank you for riding along with Rory and Zev. Plans for future Arcane adventures are under construction. Until then -

◆

If you need a detour and you like fast-paced, suspense-filled, dark urban fantasy and paranormal romance, then step into the world of the Kyn where the supernatural walks alongside humans, their existence kept secret behind the thinnest views with **SHADOW'S EDGE.**

Slip into the shadows with your copy available in Kindle Unlimited.

————— ◆ —————

Curious about the Kyn? Then don't miss out on exclusive short stories & new release information by subscribing to Jami's newsletter at:
https://www.subscribepage.com/Jami-Subscription-Books

Do you want to share your exciting discovery of a new read? Then leave a review!

Or you're welcome to swing by and visit Jami's website at:
http://jamigray.com

————— ◆ —————

If you're interested in a detour, turn the page and explore Jami's other series.

————— ◆ —————

KYN KRONICLES SERIES

Urban Fantasy/Paranormal Romance Series

Welcome to a world where the supernatural walks alongside humans, their existence kept secret behind the thinnest of veils. Now modern man's scientific curiosity is determined to rip that curtain aside, revealing the nightmares in the shadows.

**Binge the series today at
www.amazon.com/dp/B07MDWGTRT!**

◆

SHADOW'S EDGE

Raine's spent a lifetime hunting monsters, but can she stop her prey from exposing the supernatural community one bloody corpse at a time?

SHADOW'S SOUL

When a simple assignment turns into a nightmare, can Raine and Gavin unravel old vendettas before they both pay the ultimate price?

SHADOW'S MOON

Compromise isn't in Warrick's vocabulary and Xander won't abandon the hunt. As the line between instinct and intellect blurs, will they survive the fallout?

SHADOW'S CURSE

When the queen of chaos locks horns with death's justice, Natasha and Darius set a dangerous game in motion, leading two predators into a lethal dance of secrets.

SHADOW'S DREAM

Tala can't forget the past. Cheveyo can't change it. As the dreams they shared linger, can they escape the encroaching nightmare before it's too late?

Stay tuned for the final installment arriving late 2021

PSY - IV TEAMS BOOKS

Welcome to a world where facing danger requires the unique skill set of the men and women of Jami Gray's PSY-IV Teams. As sparks, and bullets fly, love, action, and adventure will target these unique couples as they race through each breath-stealing operation.

Binge the series today at
https://www.amazon.com/dp/B07D4H14DR

◆

HUNTED BY THE PAST

Cyn & Kayden

To escape a killer from their past, can a reluctant psychic trust the man who walked away?

TOUCHED BY FATE

Risia & Tag

A seer's secrets become her only bargaining chip in a high-stakes game of lies and loyalty determining her fate.

MARKED BY OBSESSION

Meli & Wolf

A woman in hiding. A telepath who sees deeper than her scars. Can they forge a bond stronger than the obsession stalking them before time runs out?

FRACTURED BY DECEIT

Megan & Bishop

After a brutal attack by a telepath, Megan turns to Bishop for help, but how does he keep her safe when she's threat?

LINKED BY DECEPTION

Jinx & Rabbit

Forced to play intimate criminal partners, will Rabbit & Jinx risk turning illusion to truth as they race to untangle a web of conspiracies and lies?

FATE'S VULTURES BOOKS

Post-apocalyptic Romantic Suspense Series

Known as The Collapse, the ravaged aftermath of Mother Nature's fury colliding with man's merciless need for survival has left civilization teetering on the brink of disintegration. Decades beyond the first brutal years, there are those who believe there is a possible future worth fighting for, worth dying for. Betrayed but not broken, they hold to their code, one considered outdated and useless. Loyalty to each other, shields for those without, warriors born and bred.

Ride along with FATE'S VULTURES and binge the series today at www.amazon.com/dp/B07PHM191J

◆

LYING IN RUINS

Charity & Ruin

On a shared mission of vengeance, who will tear them apart first—their suspicions or their enemies?

BEG FOR MERCY

Mercy & Havoc

Will an assassin and a mercenary find their balance on the thin line of loyalty, or will it snap under the weight of their wary hearts?

CAUGHT IN THE AFTERMATH

Vex & Math

Caught between a looming conflict and the fallout of a brutal betrayal, will they survive vengeance's aftermath?

FEAR THE REAPER

Lilith & Reaper

To ensure a future for those they've sworn to protect, two adversaries must navigate a minefield of past betrayals and broken promises to defeat a common enemy, before it all goes to hell.

This complete series is available wherever books are sold!

ARCANE TRANSPORTER BOOKS

Urban Fantasy Series

Binge this complete urban fantasy series thrill-ride today!

Need to ensure you delivery, magical or otherwise, makes it to its destination? For guaranteed delivery, hire the best in the west, Rory Costas, Arcane Transporter. (Independent contractor - not responsible for damage incurred in transit.)

Check out this series at
https://www.amazon.com/dp/B088FCSVKB

◆

GRAVE CARGO

When a questionable, but lucrative delivery job takes an unexpected turn, will Rory survive the collision or crash and burn?

RISKY GOODS

A dead mage, a missing friend, and an unpredictable alliance merge into a volatile package sending Rory careening through the Arcane elite's deadly secrets.

LETHAL CONTENTS

A failed assassination, a kidnapped ally, and a treasonous scheme pit Rory and Zev against a devious enemy determined to watch Arcane society crash and burn.

ABOUT THE AUTHOR

"Taking a refreshing approach to fantasy magic, this fast-paced, economical thriller is told from a highly likable perspective." —Red Adept Editing

 Jami Gray is the coffee addicted, music junkie, Queen Nerd of her personal Geek Squad, Alpha Mom of the Fur Minxes, who writes to soothe the voices crammed in her head. You don't want to miss out on her multiple series that combines magical intrigue and fearless romance into one wild ride -- Arcane Transporter, Kyn Kronicles, PSY-IV Teams, or Fate's Vultures.

Printed in Great Britain
by Amazon

83504000R00180